The Red Earth of Alabama

by

Michiro Naito

authorHOUSE™

1663 LIBERTY DRIVE, SUITE 200
BLOOMINGTON, INDIANA 47403
(800) 839-8640
WWW.AUTHORHOUSE.COM

First published by AuthorHouse 12/21/04

ISBN: 1-4208-1559-8 (e)
ISBN: 1-4208-1560-1 (sc)
ISBN: 1-4208-1561-X (dj)

Library of Congress Control Number: 2004099263

Printed in the United States of America
Bloomington, Indiana

This book is printed on acid-free paper.

Chapter 1

1

The day was hot and unpleasant. Just as well Koji Suda had nothing to do. He sat idly in his Tokyo apartment-office, as he always did when he had no work. At least he had managed to haul himself out of bed that morning, only to bury himself in the sofa in front of the Panasonic. For the past two hours, Suda's activities had been limited to going to the bathroom and fixing a bowl of corn flakes for a late breakfast. He felt no need to get out of his pajamas, much less take a shower or give himself a decent shave, since he had no plans for venturing outside or meeting anyone anywhere.

Summer in Tokyo could get awfully muggy. How Suda's father had done without an air conditioner remained a mystery. But then again, he was an unmistakable member of the entire previous generation of Japanese men who had staunchly believed that coping silently with life's hardships was a virtue. Needless to say, Suda did not belong to that fraternity. When he witnessed turnip-colored mildew extending its grubby tentacles along his bedroom walls like an alien invader from a 50's horror flick, Suda didn't think twice about installing the air conditioning unit.

Suda's father had died the previous summer and left him his only wealth—a modest two-bedroom condominium apartment in midtown Tokyo. Working as a night watchman in a local department store after retirement, Suda's father had led a lonely life, especially since his wife had died ten years earlier. He had been a private investigator in his younger days, a pretty good one from what Suda had heard, but that was not the main reason why Suda had decided to become a private eye himself.

Suda had a "good" job up until some five years before. Most anyone in Japan would turn blue with envy if they heard the name of the company Suda had worked for. Having gone to college in the U.S., Suda's credentials and fluency in English enabled him to muscle his way into one of the most prestigious companies in Japan.

There was one problem, however. It was not that Suda wasn't a hard worker. To the contrary, Suda prided himself on being a good corporate soldier. Seven in the morning to eight at night was a norm. Often, he had had to stay in the office until midnight, placing overseas calls, preparing presentations, or constructing macros for his spreadsheets. He had taken pride in what he was doing. He had taken pride in doing his job better than anyone else in the field. The problem for Suda was his co-workers. Perhaps Suda was too naïve. He should have realized that there were those who advanced in corporate culture with no apparent ability other than the ability to play political games. Suda did not particularly think he was a purist, but when he discovered that his inept co-workers were being promoted for political reasons, he had more than he could take. So he had decided to call it quits. Just like that.

Did he regret it? Perhaps a little. He missed the steady income. Being a private investigator gave him a lot of free time, which he had appreciated initially, but he had never thought he would be so free that he would often have to worry about when he was going to receive the next paycheck. Suda did not think he was a lousy detective though. He thought he was pretty damn good at what he did, in fact. But as in most businesses, scale counted in his business also. People were generally conservative and preferred to use larger better-known detective agencies. The only thing that was going for Suda was the price. He came cheap.

Boredom was another bug that kept on eating him. He could only watch so much television per day, but getting rid of boredom in other ways, unless he was an expert pachinko player or a dedicated net surfer, could be very expensive in the city of Tokyo. So there he sat, curled up in the comfort of his living room, just wasting time watching a noon TV talk show.

On that day, however, the TV set didn't have to work much longer. Suda's skirmish with boredom ended abruptly with the peculiar sound of the electronic door chime, which he had also inherited along with the condo.

"Who the hell?" Suda eased off the sofa.

Not many people came to visit Suda at his place with or without prior notice, especially since he had broken up with his girlfriend. Certainly he was not expecting anyone. In any case, whoever at the door was a much-welcomed guest. Anything to break the monotony.

"Maybe an attractive woman?" mused Suda with a half-smile, as he languidly padded across the room to the door, pulling up his pajama bottoms.

The chime lilted again.

"Yeah, I can hear you."

When Suda opened the door, momentarily he thought he had a vision. There was a beautiful young woman, her slender body bathed in the flooding rays of a dazzling August sun. Her posture was firm and erect, and her mysterious coffee-colored eyes were cast strongly and upwardly at Suda's unshaven face. Impeccably clad in white two-piece summer suit, sans a drop of sweat in the heat of summer, she looked as though she had just descended from heaven.

"Hello," was the only word that came out of his mouth, as he clumsily blocked the doorway in his crumpled pajamas, hand still clutching the TV remote.

"My name is Miho Suzuki," she said hesitantly, in an almost inaudible voice, eyes holding his inquisitive gaze.

The way she introduced herself was nothing extraordinary. When she bowed slightly, her long lustrous raven-black hair cascaded over her shoulders. Suda judged her age to be between twenty-five and thirty. Married, as the wedding band on her delicate finger attested. At first he thought she was a saleslady who went door to door selling cosmetics or insurance policies, but her expression suggested otherwise. There was something desperate and serious about her. She was a potential client, Suda thought, although he seldom received a client this way. He usually got a phone call first, and he usually met his client outside.

"I'm here to ask for the service of Mr. Koji Suda." She confirmed Suda's suspicion voluntarily.

"Oh, I'm Koji Suda." He almost winced at the eagerness he heard in his own voice.

Undoubtedly, to have met her in his pajamas and with an unshaven face was embarrassing, not to mention the channel changer in his hand. How much more professional could he have appeared? So much for the first impression. Suda politely asked her to wait outside and quickly shaved off his stubbles and put on his business shirt. By the time he added a silk tie and the summer suit, tripping as he stepped hurriedly into his pants, he regretted that he had not made himself take a shower when he had gotten up, but there was no time for that now.

In spite of his fear that his potential client might have left, when he reopened the door after some ten minutes, she was still there, her expression unchanged and resolute.

"Please come in," Suda offered, smiling awkwardly.

A two-bedroom condo in midtown Tokyo might sound lavish to outsiders, but the truth was that it was barely big enough for Suda living alone, and he was not particularly being picky, either. Nevertheless, Suda considered himself fortunate to have a place to live free of debt, considering the overcrowded and still, after all the talk of a major recession and deflation in Japan, overpriced Tokyo housing market.

Suda led the woman to one of the bedrooms, which he had converted to a makeshift office. An antique solid-oak desk, which he had also inherited, sat in need of a good polish facing a bow window against the far wall, and a black leather swivel chair was pulled up snug against it. To the left of the desk was a filing cabinet and over-sized bookshelves stuffed with dictionaries and other reference books. On this side of the desk, there was a small chamois leather sofa, with an imitation-oak coffee table in front. However he had organized it, the room had come out looking cluttered simply because of its sub-standard size, so Suda had given up on rearranging it long before.

"How about a drink?" Suda asked the woman.

She had reticently proceeded to the center of his office, apprehension etched on her face.

"May I have a glass of water, please?" she turned and requested, lowering her head ever so slightly.

Her voice was high-pitched but not at all bothersome. Urbane was probably the best word to describe her if sexual connotations were to be avoided. With a glass of iced water in her hand, Miho Suzuki situated herself on the sofa somewhat tentatively. Suda sat behind his desk, facing her, his head filled with expectations. Unjustified expectations, Suda realized himself, but attractive women were rare among his clients. Perhaps it was her expensive perfume. He couldn't help wondering about her life, her home, and her husband.

Suda was not a bad-looking man, or at least he didn't think he was. Perhaps not as tall and slender as many Japanese women would want their men to be, but on the whole he still attracted some attention from young women when he walked down the streets of Tokyo. Looks alone, however, wouldn't keep women around you. He had learned that lesson the hard way when his girlfriend had broken up with him five years earlier. When he quit the "good job," along went the steady income, prestige, and the girlfriend. Suda had not been so innocent as to think that money and prestige were not important in life, but up until then, he had never experienced this simple fact of life so forcefully and personally.

Miho took a good swallow and set aside the glass of iced water on the coffee table. Then with her big brown eyes staring up into Suda's face, she said, "I am here about my husband."

So this is another one of those cases where a distressed wife wants her husband checked out, Suda thought. She suspects that her husband might be cheating on her, Suda conjectured as he leaned back in his chair, leveling his eyes at her.

"I went to Kokusai Detective Agency, and they suggested that I should come see you."

"Oh, I see…"

Those bastards at Kokusai Detective Agency again! Suda clenched his teeth. Kokusai Detective Agency was the largest investigative agency in Tokyo if not in Japan, and its name was venerated throughout the nation. Whenever there was a need for professional investigation, people's first choice was Kokusai. The problem with Kokusai, however, was that they didn't like what was commonly called a "small customer case." A missing person case was the perfect example of a small customer case.

Small customer cases were often very time-consuming and required enormous manpower while producing a relatively small profit for the company. Dealing strictly with corporate customers would be much more efficient and profitable, but for the sake of public relations, the agency couldn't simply say "No" to every small customer. So they took on simple small customer cases such as a background check for employment or marriage and "distributed" more complicated cases to other smaller agencies in the form of a "suggestion" or "recommendation" to the client.

Suda had taken on several of those "distributed" cases in the past, many of which involved foreigners in one way or another. The cases that involved foreigners were often referred to as the "blue-eye cases" and were also shunned by the men in Kokusai. After five years in business, Suda had come to be known by some insiders in Kokusai Detective Agency as the one who could handle "blue-eye cases" because of his fluency in

English. Suda appreciated the business, but he didn't like the way Kokusai delegated their business to him as if he were one of their subsidiaries.

"My husband is missing," revealed Miho grimly, leaning her slender body toward Suda. "I want you to find him. I'm here to ask for your help."

Suda valued what he could read in his client's face and body language just as much as the spoken words. Miho Suzuki's intense eyes and tightly clutched hands eloquently expressed her sentiment. Her sincerity was genuine as far as Suda could discern.

"We've lived in America for a year," she continued, her voice quivering with emotion. "Just when we started to feel comfortable there, he disappeared."

I'll be a son of a bitch, Suda said to himself. This is no ordinary "blue-eye case." America is filled with blue eyes!

2

Birmingham, Alabama. Suda felt giddy as he stepped out of the posh airport building. Not only was he blinded by the late afternoon sun, but also the wave of stifling heat came blasting its way onto Suda's face as if he had just opened the door to a furnace. Getting here from Tokyo was an unpleasant experience as well, taking a good whole day, changing planes and going through immigration and customs in Dallas, another summer hell spot. Suda hardly slept in the planes, either. For one thing, he hated to fly; for another, a ghastly baby with an unreasonably big head wailed steadily in front of Suda's seat on the flight from Tokyo. More than once, he wished desperately that he had had a parachute.

Birmingham International Airport was just like any other modern regional airports, with newsstands and fast-food restaurants lined up along the corridor that connected the gates to the outside. There were those who got warmly hugged and kissed by the loved ones as they walked out, and there were those, like Suda, who had no one to greet them. Birmingham was the largest city in the state of Alabama, so Suda was told, but judging from the size of the airport, the city probably could accommodate no more than half a million residents. This was not the end of the trip, however. Now he had to pick up a rental car and drive for an hour to the city of his final destination, which lay about fifty miles southeast.

As he hovered over the rental car counter, waiting for the credit card approval, Suda felt anything but enthusiasm for this case. Having to nose around in a foreign land would be troublesome enough, let alone some country town, but the real quarrel was the one he was having with himself. He was getting underpaid, in his opinion, and it was nobody's fault but his own. For a difficult case like this, he knew he should have asked for more money, a premium, so to speak, but looking at his client's beautiful face torn with anguish, he just couldn't increase the fee. Perhaps that was the price a man had to pay for his chivalry.

The area encompassing the three states, Mississippi, Alabama, and Georgia, in the southeastern portion of the continental U.S. was customarily referred to as the "Deep South," often conjuring up the images of slavery, racism, and the Civil War. In the 1960's, the Deep South became the boiling pot of the civil rights movement, and Alabama, in particular, acquired international notoriety when Dr. Martin Luther King, Jr. led the famous protest march from then a little-known town called Selma to Montgomery, the state capital. Much had changed since then, and much had not. The Deep South was still known as the bastion of social conservatism, a majority of its people consistently voting Republican since Reagan took office in 1980.

This was Suda's first visit to the Deep South, and he had to confess that his image of the South was skewed by what he had seen in movies or what he had learned in history books. Once on the road and out of the bustling highway traffic through strings of shopping centers and restaurants, Alabama pleasantly surprised Suda with its luscious abundance of raw natural beauty.

Along Highway 280, which stretched southeastward from Birmingham on to the Georgia State border, a sweeping panorama of unbroken forests reached the horizon and beyond like a thick wet carpet. A thousand shades of green were so rich and profound that one might only associate them with the tropics. Every so often local townships came and went, leaving fleeting impressions of what the Old South must have been like, with paint-peeled mansions from the bygone era, churches with white steeples, and hand-written roadside signs advertising the sale of boiled peanuts. Sometimes Suda caught a glimpse of a farm fenced in by five-strand barbwire where cows idly grazed in the sun. Other times he saw gentle hills swallowed by an almost chaotic mixture of plant life, perhaps indicating the heavy dosage of rain its soil regularly received. The mishmash of thick vegetation looked familiar to Suda. In fact, except for the red earth, it was reminiscent of rural Japan.

Moeling was the name of the city where Miho and her husband, Kentaro Suzuki, had lived for the past year, up until a month before, the time of his disappearance. It was a small city by any measure, with the population less than 20,000. Kentaro had come to this city as part of a team dispatched by the powerful Japanese electronic concern, Zatech, in order to establish a factory here. Such moves by Japanese corporations had become a common occurrence these days. For Japanese corporations, the fear of protectionism had always been one of the major causes of such moves. Japanese industrialists and politicians had always been keenly aware of the protectionist sentiment in the U.S. against foreign goods. The establishment of protective walls in the U.S. would have meant a death sentence to most export-dependent Japanese companies and ultimately to Japan itself. For their survival, Japanese corporations had no alternative but to strategically move their factories abroad, particularly to the U.S.

Many U.S. states, on the other hand, especially those states that had largely been left behind in the great economic expansion in the last decade of the 20th Century, welcomed the presence of foreign companies and factories. More factories meant more jobs, and more jobs meant prosperity for the citizens and higher tax revenue for the states.

Kentaro Suzuki was a corporate soldier sent by Zatech to set up a remote post in this foreign land. He was sent here to study such issues as the social climate, quality of labor, availability of transportation and a possible distribution network, and local taxation laws, all of which were matters of life and death for a company. With his immediate supervisor, Iwao Takeda, and his co-worker, Masao Sato, Kentaro was also to discuss and close the deal on the potential factory site, to supervise the construction of the factory and the selection of local personnel including factory workers, and to handle other tasks related to opening a factory in the city of Moeling.

According to Miho, her husband's disappearance was almost coincidental with the closing of the negotiations on the factory site with the city and state officials.

"Only a few days before they closed the deal, he disappeared," she bleakly apprised Suda in his Tokyo office.

"But they closed the deal anyway?"

"Yes, of course. They couldn't let something like this interfere with business. The president of Zatech flew all the way in from Japan to sign the papers."

"Do you think your husband's disappearance had anything to do with the negotiations?"

"I don't know. But I know there're some local people who are against this whole thing. My husband used to tell me about some phone threats he received."

The answer came as somewhat of a surprise for Suda. He, probably along with many Japanese citizens, was under the impression that the animosity and distrust against Japan, so violently exhibited in the 1980's, were all but eradicated from the U.S. The disappearance of Kentaro was reported to the local police immediately. But Miho did not trust the local police.

"It's a small town police force. I don't know if they are serious about searching for my husband." She sighed helplessly and took a sip from the glass of iced water.

In fact, Kentaro had been missing for more than a month, but the local police had yet to produce any hint of his whereabouts.

"I also contacted the Japanese embassy. I thought they might be able to help me. But they said the embassy was a diplomatic agency, not a police organization, and the only possible help they could offer was to pressure the local government and police through their contact with Washington," said Miho.

Those who got into some sort of trouble in a foreign land could probably attest to the fact that the embassies were pretty much useless when it came to helping private citizens. For the Japanese embassy, Kentaro Suzuki was just one of tens of thousands of Japanese citizens who resided in the U.S. Whether they would or even could put much effort in pressuring Washington or the local police for a missing private citizen was doubtful. Of course, if the request had directly come from Zatech, it might have been a different story since the Japanese government and industries still kept generally close and friendly relations. The problem was that for some reason the Zatech headquarters in Tokyo had not been very enthusiastic about resolving the current case.

"I thought the company would really pressure the local officials to search for my husband, but I don't think they are doing that. You know they have already sent another man, Mr. Yoshikawa, not to help look for Kentaro, but to fill the vacancy left by him. As far as Zatech is concerned, my husband is just as good as dead." Miho raised her voice, looking as though she was about to break into tears.

The company owned the house Miho and her husband had resided in. A month after Kentaro's disappearance, the company requested that Miho move out so the new guy, Yoshikawa, and his family could move in. Miho wanted to stay on until she found out something about her missing husband, but both her family and the Suzukis insisted on her returning to Japan. For them, America was a dangerous place to live for a young woman without her husband.

"What about Mr. Takeda and Mr. Sato? How are they reacting to all this?" Suda inquired.

"They are too busy with their own lives. Sure they're sorry for me, and I think they're worried about my husband, too. But, you know, the company comes first. They can't help it." Miho let out a guarded laugh as though she was trying to hide the true feelings she held inside her. Naturally, she was feeling betrayed.

It was Miho's parents who suggested that she use a private investigator to look for their son-in-law. Miho was not willing to deal with the local Alabama detective agencies because she could not bring herself to think some American would be serious about finding a missing Japanese businessman. Kentaro's parents and his two brothers agreed. That was how Suda ended up in the planes. That was how Suda ended up in the Deep South.

3

The facts surrounding the disappearance of Kentaro Suzuki, as they were articulated by Miho, were as follows:

Kentaro had left his house at one in the afternoon on Sunday, July 13th. He was driving his car, a late-model silver Mercury Sable, to Atlanta that day for the meetings with lawyers on the following Monday. Since the meetings were scheduled from early morning on, Kentaro was going to spend the night in Atlanta.

"The city of Moeling has no commercial airport. So we had to drive pretty much wherever we went," Miho explained to Suda.

She didn't hear from him that day, which worried her a little because whenever Kentaro had gone on a trip before, he had usually called her at night. Kentaro carried a cell phone with him, but Miho, as a rule, did not call her husband while he was on a business trip unless there was an emergency. Kentaro generally disliked being disturbed with personal matters while he was tending his business duties. But on Monday, Kentaro's boss, Takeda, received a phone call from Kentaro, who reported that the meetings had gone well. Miho did not receive a phone call from her husband, however.

Kentaro was supposed to come back the next day, Tuesday, July 15. He did not. Not only did he not come back, he probably never went to Atlanta. When Takeda called the lawyers in Atlanta on Tuesday afternoon to thank them, he was told Kentaro had never showed up. In fact, Kentaro had called them on that Monday morning to cancel all the meetings. The hotel in Atlanta where Kentaro's reservation had been made told the same story—the room had never been occupied by Kentaro. Miho tried to reach her husband on his cell phone countless times after that day. Needless to say, the phone was never answered.

Two possibilities flashed in Suda's head. One was that Kentaro had decided to run away voluntarily for some unknown reason. The fact that his car was missing along with him seemed to support this hypothesis. The other was that Kentaro, after being abducted by someone, had been forced to make those phone calls. The first possibility was unthinkable for Miho.

"Kentaro was a good husband and a good company man. He loved his work. He loved me very much. He would never have run away like that, abandoning me or his job," she asserted with conviction.

The tears in Miho's eyes appeared to tell the truth. Suda had no reason to doubt Miho's words. But the latter possibility left too many questions unanswered. Why would anyone abduct Kentaro? Suda thought of some local thugs kidnapping Kentaro for money, but there had been no ransom request after his disappearance. If some anti-Japanese group had killed Kentaro, why did they have to hide his body? Had they killed him by mistake and decided to hide his body? Why had Zatech not received any statement about Kentaro's disappearance from such a group? Why would anyone have gone to the trouble of forcing Kentaro to make the phone calls? Why did he not call Miho?

The arrangement was that Suda was going to stay in a local motel, and no one was to know Suda was a private investigator. He would introduce himself as Miho's brother who came to look for his sister's missing husband. Since Kentaro was a tall slender man and didn't look anything like Suda, he could not pretend to be his brother by any stretch of the imagination. Such an arrangement was necessary for two reasons. First, the Zatech Corporation would not have tolerated some private eye running around in a town where they were about to open a new factory. Public relations were a major concern for any Japanese companies trying to open a new factory or facility on American soil. They did not want even a hint of scandal connected to their organization. Suda suspected this was the reason why the company was so reluctant to help look for Kentaro. They would like to keep this thing as quiet as possible. The second reason was a more obvious one. As anyone would, Suda suspected foul play in the disappearance of Kentaro, and if anyone found out Suda's true profession, he or she would most likely clam up. If Suda were to be Miho's brother, on the other hand, people would likely be more cooperative out of sympathy.

Early in the evening, Suda checked into a local motel, a single-story stucco structure surrounded by towering pine trees. The motel was situated adjacent to a gas station, at the corner of a major intersection in town, but the room was surprisingly quiet once the outside door was closed. Despite being exhausted, Suda wanted to make a quick go 'round in the town to get a better idea of the geography. He purchased an area map at the motel counter and, after flushing down a cheeseburger and fries with Budweiser in the motel restaurant, decided to go on a small excursion in his rented Camry.

At a glance, the city of Moeling looked like just another sleepy small town in America. A weed-choked railroad track used solely for freight trains ran from east to west, dividing the town in half. Supermarkets with vast parking lots sat in the middle of the city, vying for the patronage of the city's residents. The old downtown area appeared deserted and lonesome with the shop doors closed, as the swank shopping malls along the highway attracted the bulk of the customers. A gigantic textile company with its factory and office complex sprawled over several acres of gently rolling hills and well-manicured land. And there were pine forests. Wherever he went, Suda smelled the air moist and warm perfumed with the pungent scent of pine resin.

The house where Miho and Kentaro had lived stood quietly in one of the prime residential sections of the city, only a few minutes away from the motel by car. Gracefully nestled in the woods, the single-story brick house was one of the classiest in the neighborhood. Painted in milky white, with a small limestone fountain in the front yard and a graveled circular driveway, the house somehow reminded Suda of Miho herself. The lawn was well watered, and the garden of flowerbeds and evergreens was immaculately tended. Suda could see the light coming from inside the house through sheer lace curtains. The Yoshikawas, the replacement family for Miho and Kentaro, must have been having dinner. A picture of Miho and Kentaro having dinner together inside the house flickered in Suda's head at that moment. A loving couple with so much to look forward to. What had happened to him?

According to Miho, Zatech's company policy was to force their Japanese workers in foreign countries to live apart from each other. Apparently, Zatech believed Japanese living together in one area like some isolationist group would make a bad impression on local residents.

"But we ended up getting together all the time anyway," Miho reflected, smiling sadly. Suda remembered the charming dimples on her cheeks when she smiled.

A "family atmosphere" had always been one of the selling points of Japanese companies. Economists and business analysts had used to say that it was one of the strong points of Corporate Japan. Oddly enough, though, after some ten years of recession in the country, they now advocated that "family atmosphere" was one of the weak points of Japanese companies.

The Zatech office, a small boxy concrete building on about a half-acre site surrounded by a group of pine trees, sat in the central location of the city not too far from Suda's motel. The outlet store of the textile company, the Bartlet Corporation, was just across the street. No one could miss its modern architecture with a huge company logo painted vividly in red and blue. The Bartlet Corporation hired a large chunk of the city. Not only the people in Moeling, but also the people from nearby Dadeville, Goodwater, and Alexander City came to work for the company. When Zatech would open its factory here, manufacturing state-of-the-art DVD players and LCD Digital TVs, it was going to be the second largest employer in Moeling.

As he drove by the Zatech office, Suda saw lights and workers at the desks inside. It was nine o'clock at night. Just like in Tokyo, the Japanese were still working.

4

Suda paid a visit to the Zatech office in the afternoon, the day after his arrival in Moeling. Intentionally, he did not make an appointment beforehand. He wanted to see the reactions of Kentaro's co-workers when he announced the purpose of his visit.

Suda's first impression of the office was that it was an amazingly small office for a company the size of Zatech. Aside from Takeda's separate office in the corner of the room, there were five desks in total, all with computer terminals on top. Bookshelves, file cabinets, a fax machine, a copier, several telephones with answering machines. Just usual office stuff. The word "outpost" came to Suda's mind. An outpost in the enemy territory. The construction of the factory was to begin any day. Suda sensed the kind of tension in the air, which he had not felt since he had quit his job as a businessman.

"I'm Miho's brother. Koji Suda," Suda introduced himself to Kentaro's office mates.

No harm done in using his real name since, according to Miho, nobody at the office knew Miho's maiden name. The atmosphere was not hospitable to Suda by any means, perhaps because it was a busy day, and he was obviously intruding. No one seemed to pay much attention when he announced that the purpose of his stay in the U.S. was to look for the missing man.

Kentaro's boss, Iwao Takeda, looked younger than Suda had imagined—a man in his mid-forties with gold-rimmed eyeglasses and thin lips. He was tall, dark and lean, much like Kentaro, with a lot of black hair. He possessed energetic eyes and gregarious demeanor. He looked like the kind of man who prided himself on being a good company man.

"Yes, we're all very worried about Mr. Suzuki," said Takeda, glancing at the business card Suda had handed him. "But I am optimistic. I'm sure Mr. Suzuki is doing well somewhere. He's a tough fellow."

The way Takeda said it didn't sound sympathetic at all. In fact, it sounded very much perfunctory. Not a very good actor, but perhaps not a dishonest man, either. Suda took a dislike to him in any case although he was careful enough not to show it on his face. Takeda reeked arrogance, much like Suda's former supervisor in his white-collar days.

Masao Sato, Kentaro's colleague, was a nerdish, rather quiet man in his thirties with a complexion like white paper. The man probably never went out in the sun. He didn't say much, and when he spoke, Suda could barely hear him. What a contrast with Takeda. He carried with him a mushy atmosphere—not an ounce of muscle in his body. He reminded Suda of an octopus. Quiet and mushy. He said something to the effect of "I'm sorry about your brother," as he disdainfully peered at Suda's business card. Suda didn't overlook the lurking ego in his face.

The types represented by people like Takeda and Sato were not at all uncommon in Japanese corporate society. Suda had always been puzzled and bothered by those who took on a strange aura of importance, an elitist attitude, simply from the fact that they were working for certain companies.

Although the Japanese corporate culture had considerably changed since the burst of the bubble at the end of 1989, still most Japanese men, for better or worse, went through a dramatic metamorphosis when they entered the ranks of white-collar workers. Often they became obsessed with work and would come to believe that the work they did was more important than that of others. Suda had seen it happen among his old friends, and frankly, he had been repulsed by it.

The newcomer, Yoshikawa, wearing thick "coke bottle" glasses, was the friendliest. He was probably the same age as Takeda or he might even have been a little older. He looked like an old-generation Japanese with buckteeth and an incessant little smile.

"Please let me know if there's anything I can do for you," Yoshikawa offered in a subdued tone.

There were other members of the office. A personal secretary of Takeda's named Lisa Parkins was a tall good-looking blonde with long runner's legs and a baby-smooth tan. Suda judged her age to be in the mid-twenties. In the whole time Suda hung around the office, Lisa did not show a smile even once, probably worried about wrinkles. And there was another administrative assistant who took care of the rest of the team. Her name was Jean Konopinsky. She was also in her mid-twenties, brunette, with an effervescent smile. Petite and quite charming, she talked a lot with a strong regional accent. She said she was engaged to be married.

"As you can see, we need a thousand hands to take care of all that needs to be done. Why don't you come back tonight? I'll take you to a nice restaurant in town."

To Suda's surprise, the invitation came from Takeda.

The police station of the city of Moeling evoked the image of an old Southern mansion that Suda had seen in many movies. The columned two-story white stucco structure was encircled by hedges of azalea and shaded by large oak and magnolia trees, facing the burnt-red brick post office and gray granite town hall in the downtown area of Moeling. Suda would never have thought it was a police station had it not been for a wooden sign conspicuously displayed on the front lawn that read, "Moeling City Police Station."

The traffic downtown was light, pedestrians being sparse and mostly people past their prime. How all these shops survived with so few customers was a puzzle. The sun glared down as mercilessly as the day before, pasting dark shadows of every standing object, including Suda's rented Camry, onto the seared-dry pavement. Stepping out of the comfort of the air-conditioned automobile was a painful experience. A T-shirt and shorts would have been the proper attire on a day like this instead of the suit and tie. Whoever invented conventional business attire had never been to Alabama in the summer.

The police station looked nearly empty inside when Suda walked in as if he were taking refuge from the heat of the sun, wiping sweat off his forehead with the back of his hand. The high-ceilinged interior smelled of old wood and new paint, and was much more spacious than Suda had imagined from outside. A young woman in a police uniform was typing something behind the reception counter. Not a very efficient typist from the sound of it. Several cluttered office desks were lined up in rows with a narrow pathway in the middle leading to another office in the back. To his left, there was a square window on the wood-paneled wall separating the main room from the dispatch room, from which occasionally a dispatcher's voice reached Suda's ears with the rasp of characteristic static in between. The policewoman behind the counter looked up at Suda and looked down again, apparently paying no attention to Suda's presence. Her rich brunette hair was styled to fit under the police cap.

"Hi," said Suda in a neutral tone, walking up to the counter.

The woman stopped typing and looked up again at Suda's face.

"Can I help you?" she casually asked Suda, resting her fingers on the old-fashioned IBM electric typewriter.

"I think so."

She was not being unfriendly, Suda presumed. She was just preoccupied with something. When she came up to the counter, she didn't forget to put a charming smile on her face.

"I'm here to ask about a missing person," said Suda, returning a smile. "A Japanese man disappeared about a month ago..."

"Yes...What do you wanna know?" Her Southern accent implied she was from the area.

"Well, have you found out anything new?"

The woman stared at Suda with reasonable amount of caution in her eyes, slightly tilting her head. Beautiful green eyes, Suda thought.

"May I ask who you are?" She was no longer smiling.

"I'm his wife's brother."

A police badge glittered right above her left breast, and a nametag on the right read "V. Royce."

"Hey, Sergeant!"

As she turned around shouting toward the back of the room, Suda had a flashback to his college days. She reminded him of his girlfriend, Caroline, of long ago. Blonde and blue-eyed, Caroline didn't look anything like this police officer, but she carried the same cheerful and athletic aura. She was strong in character but always on edge. She was a ball of fun, but often drove Suda to the point of mental exhaustion. At the end, Suda broke up with Caroline because he no longer wanted to participate in her life in the fast lane.

"Please wait here. A sergeant will talk to you," said the policewoman shortly and went back behind the typing desk.

The sergeant, who had apparently been sitting in the dispatch room, was a mountain of a man. He ambled out languidly and introduced himself in his gravelly voice as Sergeant John Brown, stretching out his tree-trunk right arm and shaking Suda's hand unenthusiastically. A man in his early fifties, with a Boris Karloff visage and cement-colored teeth, he walked at a leisurely pace without saying a word as he led Suda to the office in the back. The office belonged to the chief of police, Ronald Shugert.

Chief Shugert stood up from behind his large and well-organized mahogany desk and welcomed Suda cordially. He gripped Suda's hand firmly and showed him to a chair, offering a cup of coffee, which Suda politely declined.

"Ron, this man's here about the missing Japanese man," Brown said to Shugert.

Upon discovering the stated purpose of Suda's visit to the city, Shugert did not hide a troubled look on his face.

"We're doing our best, believe me, Mr. Suda," said Chief Shugert apologetically once Brown had left the room, as he half sat and half leaned on his desk with his arms crossed in front. "But as you may know, a missing person is usually very difficult to find. Sometimes it takes years."

Chief Shugert must have been in his late fifties. Getting close to his retirement age, he probably wanted to avoid any trouble if at all possible. With thick black-framed eyeglasses and almost totally white hair on top of a chiseled granite face of pinkish hue, he looked too distinguished to be a police chief in a country town like Moeling. The only thing that could have given away his origin was his thick Southern accent spoken with a deep sonorous voice.

Suda had to be tactful. He was a total stranger and an intruder as far as the police were concerned. He had to somehow draw as much information as possible out of Shugert without getting too pushy. The last thing Suda wanted was to antagonize the local law enforcement. After hearing Shugert's brief explanation on how the investigation had progressed thus far, however, Suda felt he could go a little deeper into the heart of the matter.

"Chief Shugert," Suda said. "What do you think of foul play as a possibility in this case?"

Chief Shugert's face darkened at Suda's question.

"Well, there's a possibility. We're not eliminating any possibilities right now. It's just that we have too many questions unanswered."

"You don't think he just up and left on his own, do you, sir?"

"That's a distinct possibility, too." Chief Shugert grimaced and paused for a moment, rubbing his face with his hand.

"Mr. Suda," he continued hesitantly. "I don't know how to put this delicately, but it seems your brother in law was involved with a woman other than your sister."

The answer caught Suda completely off guard. From what Suda had been told about Kentaro, it was so out of character that the existence of another woman had not entered his mind even once.

"Are you saying that Mr. Suzuki was unfaithful to my sister?"

Suda watched Chief Shugert slowly lift his coffee cup off his desk and take a sip.

"Well, there are some witnesses," said Shugert, creasing his brows. "Mr. Suzuki was seen with a woman other than your sister on more than a couple of occasions."

"Who is this woman?" Suda asked, leaning forward in the chair. Miho certainly had not mentioned anything about such a woman.

"We don't know." Shugert shook his head. "I hope you understand, Mr. Suda. We're not suggesting that Mr. Suzuki's disappearance had anything to do with this woman. It's just one possible lead."

"Who are these witnesses?" Suda pressed. "Maybe he was out with a secretary in his office." Immediately Suda thought of Lisa Parkins and Jean Konopinsky at the Zatech office.

"One of the witnesses works in his office. I think he would have recognized the woman if she had worked in the office with him."

The witness Chief Shugert was referring to turned out to be Kentaro's boss, Takeda. There were other witnesses, as Shugert said. A gas station attendant just outside of the city limits saw a woman sitting in Kentaro's car. A blonde with sunglasses. A motel clerk in Birmingham positively identified Kentaro Suzuki and told the police he spent a night there with a blonde woman. A waitress in a restaurant near the motel saw them together. She had waited on their table.

"Chief Shugert, have you told this to my sister?"

"No, we haven't. We saw no good reason to do that. We didn't want to embarrass Mrs. Suzuki. As I said, this may have nothing to do with his disappearance."

Kentaro Suzuki was a nice looking man, judging from the picture Miho had given to Suda. It would not be surprising if he had been popular among women. But obviously being popular and being unfaithful were two separate issues. A wife's ignorance of her husband's behavior was not an uncommon story in life; nevertheless, perhaps naively, Suda had not anticipated the existence of another woman in this particular case. The impression he had gotten from Miho of Kentaro as an absolutely faithful and good husband was so strong that the new revelation was almost like looking at a painting by Picasso. According to Miho, Kentaro was the last man on earth to have an affair. But, from the way Chief Shugert was talking, it seemed as though Kentaro had run away with the woman.

For Suda, however, that would be more unthinkable than a simple affair. Kentaro was not some aimless part-timers that drifted from job to job. He was an elite by any measure. Would a Japanese man like Kentaro give up his prestigious job and a beautiful wife and, in effect, his family and a life in Japan for some foreign woman that he must have met relatively recently? Giving up his job had been tough enough for Suda. He was sure he couldn't have done it had it meant he had to give up his wife and family and the life in Japan along with his job. But what about Kentaro? Had he snapped and gone off the deep end? Did he not love his wife and his job? Was he not a devoted company man? Perhaps Kentaro was not at all what Suda had thought him to be.

"I understand the Zatech office has received several threatening phone calls in the past year," continued Shugert, reading Suda's troubled expression. "We are looking into that possibility also. You see, Mr. Suda, as a city and as a state, we're dying to have your factory open here. It would bring us jobs and prosperity. But there are those who are dead set against it. This is a very conservative town. People don't like new things very much. People are afraid of new things."

When Suda left the police station, he felt that the maze he had walked into had suddenly become more complex. Although he had never expected this case to be an easy one, Suda's guess had been along the line of a racially or nationally motivated kidnapping. But, as Chief Shugert said, obviously there were many questions yet to be answered. In particular, Suda was dogged by the question of the phone calls. Whether he was kidnapped or ran away on his own, why did Kentaro make those phone calls? What was he trying to achieve? And why did he avoid calling his own wife, Miho?

5

Cooperation from the local police in the investigation would make Suda's job much easier. Shugert was clearly worried about losing the factory. The mayor had probably given him strict instructions as to how to treat a Japanese in town. The power of Japan's economic muscle, though considerably weaker than what it once was, still appeared plenty formidable and certainly manifested itself in a most unexpected place, and Suda was an accidental beneficiary. There was naturally a limit to what the police could disclose to Suda, however. After all, he was just a private citizen and not even a local one. Suda requested the names and addresses of the people who claimed to have witnessed Kentaro with the blonde woman, but Shugert politely declined. Takeda's name seemed to have come out as more or less a slip of his tongue.

Suda went back to the Zatech office at a little after six. Takeda was the only one in the office, still feverishly working at his cluttered desk. Now that Takeda was an important witness, Suda had very good reason to see him.

"I wasn't sure what time you wanted me to come back," Suda apologized.

Takeda seemed much friendlier than he had been earlier in the afternoon. He laughed out loud and said he was just finishing up last-minute work. While Takeda was clearing his desk, Suda took another good look around the office. In an office as small as this, coordinating everyone's work must not be too difficult, but rather, trying to get along with one another must become essential. Having to face someone you hate every day would be simply intolerable.

"O.K. I'm through. I hope you're hungry because I am," Takeda announced merrily, lifting his attaché case off his chair.

Takeda owned a black late-model Cadillac. He said he had wanted a Lexus, but to appease the local people, he had opted for an American car.

"I don't think people nowadays really pay attention to these things, but we can't take the smallest risk. Actually, Cadillac is not as bad as you may think, Mr. Suda," Takeda jokingly said to Suda as he steered the car gently out of the parking lot. "How do you like Chinese food? Or maybe you prefer a steak."

"Anything is fine with me."

Takeda took Suda to a steak house only a few blocks away from the office. It was one of those franchise establishments, with a nondescript standardized facade, but according to Takeda, the best steaks in town were served here. The restaurant was packed, which meant either the food was either great or dirt cheap, but they had no trouble getting seated. Suda noticed but ignored the glances of curiosity at him and Takeda from many of the customers in the restaurant.

"It's sad but this is just about the best restaurant in town," Takeda remarked sarcastically, perusing the menu. "This is a country town after all, but the food is delicious and remarkably cheap."

In fact, the T-bone Suda ordered turned out to be magnificent, and it was, with a baked potato and tossed green salad, probably one-fifth the price he would have had to pay in Tokyo. Suda chose to wait to bring up the subject of Kentaro. He wanted Takeda to be relaxed before getting to serious business. Takeda asked Suda what his job was, as his business card contained no information about his occupation. Suda told him that he was a free-lance writer with a lot of free time. He made up some cock-eyed name of a magazine he was supposed to be working for, and Takeda seemed to have bought the story.

"One thing that concerns us about opening a factory here in the U.S. is the quality of the labor," Takeda confessed as he carried a juicy piece of sirloin to his mouth. "They're not as well educated as the Japanese workers, and unless we keep our eyes on them, they tend to slack off. I know American companies appear to be doing well nowadays. But I think much of it is due to the funny accounting and financial engineering they use. I know there're a handful of excellent entrepreneurs like Bill Gates and Michael Dell, but most Americans don't have much work ethic. They lie and cheat whenever they can. Cheating is engrained in this culture, unfortunately, and it goes all the way from factory workers to new graduates to CEOs. Do you know, Mr. Suda, some people here don't even know how to read and write? I can't imagine using that sort of people in our factory."

This was the same old story Suda had heard from other Japanese managers who had worked in the U.S., but Suda didn't come here to be lectured to about Takeda's management theory. After the second bottle of Budweiser, it was time to change the subject.

"I've been to the police station," Suda informed Takeda.

Takeda looked mildly startled but kept on moving his knife and fork.

"I spoke to Chief Shugert," Suda continued. "He told me about a possible affair my brother-in-law was having with some blonde woman."

Speaking Japanese in a foreign land was convenient. Aside from Suda and Takeda, nobody could understand what was being said.

"Is there any truth to it?" Suda asked, gazing squarely into Takeda's swarthy face.

Takeda dabbed at his mouth with the cloth napkin, and still, there was a moment of hesitation before he began to speak.

"Well, since you came here to look for Mr. Suzuki, I'll tell you everything I know, and I'll tell you what I think has happened to Mr. Suzuki," said Takeda furtively, holding Suda's gaze. Even though he spoke in Japanese, Takeda lowered his voice as he continued.

"I think Mr. Suzuki had a girlfriend. But I don't think that had anything to do with the situation we're in today. I saw him only once with his girlfriend. Mr. Suzuki used to go to Birmingham on occasion, for business, of course. Before we hooked up with the law office in Atlanta, we were planning to get our legal consultation from a law office in Birmingham. Mr. Suzuki was in charge of our financial matters but also acted as a liaison between our legal team in Tokyo and local lawyers here, so I sent him there often...Oh, maybe once a month, but sometimes twice a week."

Suda had just come from Birmingham.

"It's only about eighty kilometers from here to Birmingham," Takeda went on. "You can see it on a map. You can easily get there and back in a day. Atlanta is a little tiresome for a round trip on the same day, especially if you have work to do in the city...Anyway, I think he met this girl in Birmingham."

"You saw him in Birmingham with this woman?"

"Yes," replied Takeda firmly. "I saw him come out of a movie theater with the girl. That day...It was Friday. I like to go to Birmingham on weekends sometimes. I'm from Tokyo. I miss city life."

Takeda was married with two children, but he didn't bring his family with him to the U.S. It was not uncommon for a Japanese businessman to leave his family back in Japan, particularly when the children were of school age. The major concern of Japanese parents who resided in a foreign country was the education of their children. There was a well-publicized understanding in Japan that the quality of pre-college school education in the U.S. was far inferior to that of Japan. Besides, most parents wanted their children to grow up like Japanese, not like Americans.

"That day, Mr. Suzuki drove to Birmingham in the afternoon," Takeda reflected, taking a sip of his beer. "I thought he was planning to come back the same day, but apparently he didn't, because I saw him there. I almost said hello to him, but something told me not to. He got into the car with the girl and left."

The image of Kentaro with some mysterious blonde woman in the car was becoming more of a reality in Suda's mind.

"How do you know he was having an affair with her?" Suda asked.

"I thought it was pretty obvious, from the way they were acting. I believe the police checked the motel he used to stay at and found..."

"Yes, I was told there were some witnesses there, too."

Now there was no doubt. Kentaro Suzuki had been having an affair with a local woman. If the woman could be traced, maybe his whereabouts would follow.

"But for me, it's hard to believe Mr. Suzuki would disappear like this because of that woman," Takeda said with a deep sigh. "He was an excellent company man. He would not abandon his job like that."

Takeda lifted a pack of Marlboros from the inner pocket of his jacket and tugged out a cigarette. Suda watched him light the cigarette with his Cartier lighter and pause as if he were debating whether to go on. Then he extinguished the cigarette forcefully in the glass ashtray on the table and moved his face closer to Suda.

"Please don't go around telling people this, but I have to explain to you what's been going on in this city."

Suda smelled the nicotine on Takeda's breath.

According to Takeda, the city politics of Moeling had long been dominated by one family, the Bartlets, the founders and the principal owners of the Bartlet Corporation. As a major employer of the city, what the Bartlets wanted had gone through without much questioning or complaining for decades. To go against wishes of the Bartlets had long meant ostracism, and naturally many residents secretly resented the Bartlets. But here came Zatech with its enormous capital and political power. For many who had long agonized over the dominance of the Bartlet Corporation, Zatech presented a golden opportunity to break away.

When Zatech announced its move to the U.S., a number of states competed feverishly for its factory site. The factory would hire 1,000 people initially, and an expansion of the facility was already in the planning stage. It would have meant big bucks. Zatech, on the other hand, had its eyes on the South from the very beginning. The climate was mild. The labor was cheap. And the unions had been traditionally weak. Already a number of Japanese companies, most notably Toyota and Honda, had been quite successful in the South.

Among the final four states, Tennessee, Georgia, Alabama, and Mississippi, it was Alabama that finally won the favor of Zatech. And it was the city of Moeling that was awarded the factory site. There were some ugly internal political struggles in the state of Alabama and in the city of Moeling—Takeda didn't go into detail, but it was the Bartlets, fearing the loss of their political influence, that had fought this deal tooth and nail. The city of Moeling was split into two groups. The current mayor was the leader of the pro-Zatech sect. The U.S. congressman from the district led the anti-Zatech band. But the once mighty Bartlet family didn't prevail. Perhaps it was the sign of changing times. The city of Moeling voted by a small margin for the resolution to open its doors to Zatech.

The story didn't end here, however. The Bartlets would not give up their power that easily. Ever since the Zatech office had been set up in the city, the Bartlet Corporation had exploited every single opportunity to fuel anti-Japan sentiment and to overturn the resolution.

"It's not going to happen," said Takeda, leaning against the back of the chair. "The Bartlets have lost most of their power now. The textile industry is a dying industry in this country however they try to revive it. I think most people in the city have disliked the Bartlets for a long time. They just didn't know what to do. In a sense, we're their savior."

Takeda did not doubt most of the threatening phone calls had come from either the Bartlet Corporation or someone in their camp.

"I wouldn't be surprised if Mr. Suzuki's disappearance had something to do with the Bartlets," said Takeda as if he had just tasted something bitter in his mouth.

"What would they gain by kidnapping Mr. Suzuki?"

"I don't know." Takeda shrugged. "Maybe trying to scare us off. Maybe they killed him. You know, Mr. Suda, if a crime is committed here, the only people who have the means to cover it up are the Bartlets.

They've lost a lot of power, but they still command a large voice in this city. I know there are some loyal fanatics out there willing to do anything for the Bartlets."

Suda didn't believe everything that Takeda had told him since Takeda was a Zatech man, and thus his view was bound to be skewed at least somewhat. Nevertheless, Takeda's story had a sobering effect on Suda. If he were to continue investigating Kentaro Suzuki's disappearance, it appeared that sooner or later he would have to lock horns with the Bartlets, the only people who had the means to cover up a crime, according to Takeda. Suda had no intention of risking his life to find Kentaro. He felt sorry for Miho, but not that sorry.

"I wanted to ask you about the phone calls," said Suda as they walked out of the restaurant.

"Phone calls?" Takeda looked at Suda curiously.

"Yes. It's very puzzling to me why Mr. Suzuki made those phone calls before he disappeared. Why did he have to call the lawyers in Atlanta to cancel the meeting? Why did he call you and lie to you that the meetings went well?"

"I thought about that, too. If I had been more perceptive, I might have been able to tell something was wrong, but that was a very busy day," said Takeda apologetically.

As they stood in the parking lot by Takeda's Cadillac, a warm damp wind gently brought in the first sign of rain. The sky was dark without the moon or the stars.

"Do you think someone forced him to make those phone calls?" Suda asked.

"I have no answer for that." Takeda shook his head. "If someone had, the only reason I can think of is that someone didn't want anybody looking for Mr. Suzuki so soon. They needed an extra two days to hide him or something. So they forced him to make those phone calls to gain some extra time. If he had not made the phone call to cancel the meeting, I'm sure I would have heard from the lawyers one way or another on that Monday."

"It's rather odd my sister didn't receive a phone call from Mr. Suzuki if that had been the case," Suda pointed out. "She would be the first one to worry if she didn't hear from him for two days."

"Maybe it was a hidden message from Mr. Suzuki," Takeda speculated. "By not calling his wife, he wanted to let her know something was wrong." And he unlocked the door of his car.

Speculation. All speculation. As they drove back, neither said another word. Not because there was nothing left to discuss, but because there were too many things left to discuss.

"Of course, if I can be any more help, please let me know." Takeda promised full cooperation as they parted that night.

A very productive day over all. But Suda had one more thing to do. He wanted to call Miho, not to mention anything about her husband's blonde girlfriend, but to ask about his behavior in general. Had his behavior pattern changed in recent months? Had she noticed anything unusual about him? Suda had already asked her all this in Japan, but now that a completely new piece was introduced to the puzzle, the questions would be asked with a different focal point in mind. Miho was very cooperative in answering all the questions Suda presented on the phone. Some questions were very private, but she didn't hesitate to answer them. As a result, nothing new came out except one thing. Miho confirmed that Kentaro had spent a night alone in Birmingham on a few occasions.

Suda hardly slept that night.

6

The downpour of torrential rain the night before had left behind spots of water puddles. Heated by the morning sun, the standing water soon turned into thick shimmying mist, the air so heavy and damp that Suda could almost wash his face in it. Only the plant life rejuvenated appeared lively, with thirst at least temporarily quenched. The summer in Alabama could be just as muggy as Tokyo, Suda found out.

Suda had a plateful of fruits for breakfast in the motel restaurant, and that was plenty to sustain him until lunch. He didn't have any plans for the day, since he wouldn't be able to talk to any of the Zatech employees until that evening, but he knew he needed to speak to some of the locals to get a more balanced picture of what had been going on between the Bartlet Corporation and Zatech. Where to start was the question. The most accessible people were the front clerks of the motel. Suda was a paying guest. They would have to answer at least a few questions out of courtesy.

When Suda walked up to the front, a young woman, probably a high school student working her part-time job, was alone behind the counter, engrossed in a phone conversation, apparently with her boyfriend. When she saw Suda, she immediately hung up the phone as if she had been caught at the scene of an assignation.

"Good morning, sir. What can I do for you today?" The girl grinned, looking mildly flustered. The braces on her teeth caught Suda's eye.

"I'm a guest staying at this motel," Suda announced formally. "I was wondering if you could tell me something."

"Yes?" She cocked her flaxen-haired head slightly to one side, intent on what Suda was going to say.

"I saw a huge tract of land all fenced off over there," said Suda, pointing in the general direction of the factory site. "Do you know what's going on?"

"Yes, sir. A new factory's gonna be built," she replied politely.

"A new factory? Whose factory is it?" Suda tried his best to affect ignorance.

"Zatech. A Japanese company. I think they'll be making computers." Her knowledge was not exactly accurate but close enough.

"I see…Yeah, I remember. I read it somewhere. Wasn't there a nasty fight in this town about the Japanese company moving here?"

"Something like that." The girl was not going to say any more.

"Do you know anything about it? I mean what went on?" Suda plowed on.

"I really don't know that much about it…"

Her reply was interrupted by an aged couple walking in to check out of the motel. They looked like typical retirees enjoying a yearly trip. Speckled with a few lighthearted remarks and compliments along the way, a customary exchange between the guest and motel clerk ensued with the returning of the room key, handling of a credit card, and checking and signing of the charge statement. The process seemed to take ages.

"You were saying…" Suda immediately resumed the inquiry once the old couple finally left, on their way to Disney World.

"Oh, yeah…Well, I really don't know much about city politics, so I'm afraid I can't tell you much."

"Who do you think I should talk to?"

"Gee, I don't know." She cocked her head again. "My parents know more than I do, but that won't help much, I guess."

She giggled, amusing herself with her own statement. Suda decided to shift the subject, hiding his displeasure with the answers she had given to him thus far.

"Do you know about a missing Japanese man?" he asked.

"Yes…Has he been found?"

"No, no…I was just wondering if you know anything about him."

"Are you related to him?" Her freckled face lit up with curiosity.

"Not really, but I read about it somewhere."

After what he had heard from Takeda, Suda wanted to be more cautious about revealing the purpose of his stay in this town. If half of the population in the city had been anti-Zatech, disclosing the true intent of his visit could have seriously jeopardized Suda's mission. Of course, the damage had probably already been done. In a small town like Moeling, rumors could spread very fast. Suda wanted to keep the damage to a minimum nevertheless.

"I guess it's kind of famous by now."

She didn't know what to say after that. She just gazed at Suda like he was a man from Mars. This girl was kind of spacey.

"I wonder what happened to the man? Do you know what he looks like?" Suda pushed a little further. From his experience, he knew that often a valuable piece of information could be obtained from the most unlikely sources.

"I've seen his picture on TV, but not in person," she replied blankly.

Suda had already heard from Miho that Kentaro's picture had appeared on the front page of the local newspaper and on the TV news. Although the city of Moeling did not have its own TV station, the residents watched broadcasting from Birmingham and Montgomery, which meant the news of Kentaro's disappearance was received by a relatively large audience. In spite of such efforts by the city and the police, apparently no one had yet to volunteer any trustworthy information as to Kentaro's fate.

When someone wants to have a chat with local folks, a good place to visit is a barbershop. This holds true in Japan as well as in America, provided, of course, you speak the same language. Suda needed a haircut anyway. His hair was getting just long enough to cover his ears and begin to bother his sense of neatness. Suda remembered a barbershop among the row of stores alongside the street that led up to the police station.

The sun was about to peak in its sweeping arc and, along with the drenching humidity that was no doubt tipping the 90 percent mark, fast turning lethal. Suda moved his car languidly along the street, past an office equipment shop, a record-CD shop, a women's clothing store, a flower shop, and a drug store, to the barbershop, his destination. When he parallel-parked the car and cut off the engine, cracking the windows open, his impulse was to jump into a swimming pool and float there with his arms spread, feeling the cold water gently cuddle his entire body. A gorgeous woman would be waiting for him at the poolside, stretched out on a deck chair in her yellow bikini, with aquamarine sunglasses and a golf visor and with a tumbler of tropical drink in her delicate hand. Suda shook his head in self-deprecation as he climbed out of the car. The investigation had just begun.

There were no customers in the barbershop when Suda opened the glass door and received the full benefit of the air conditioner in the room.

"Hi," said Suda, looking at the two men in barber's outfits.

The men were seated side by side, apparently having been engaged in desultory talk, on the scruffy vinyl chairs for waiting customers.

"Hello," one of the men replied, but Suda was not sure which one.

Clearly, they were not certain what to make of the oriental man who had just walked in out of the blue. In fact, they looked a bit startled when they discovered that Suda was a customer. Two white men close to or maybe past their retirement age. One, with silver-rimmed eyeglasses, was tall and wiry. The other, also bespectacled, with white hair and a tattoo of an anchor on each forearm, was shorter and a little on the heavy side. There must have been some mysterious rule about who was going to cut hair first. Without a word, the tall one stood behind Suda's chair.

"Are you from Japan?" The heavy one, a friendly fellow, opened his mouth as soon as the tall one started moving his scissors. Suda was already getting used to the differing Southern accents spoken in these areas.

"Yes, I am," Suda replied.

"I was in Japan for a while," the heavy one continued, his face brightening. "I was stationed there in 1963. Yokota was the name. Do you know the place?"

"Yeah. I'm from Tokyo, so I know where Yokota is."

The tall one joined in, and the conversation took off like a rocket. They must have been awfully bored by themselves before Suda came to the shop. The tall one said he was in Okinawa as a navy man. Suda didn't mind talking about Japan and how much it had changed since the 1960's, but he had to break in at some point and get them to speak about the war between the Bartlets and Zatech.

"I just arrived here the day before yesterday. I'll be working for Zatech. I guess you heard about that, huh?" Suda probed, keeping his head still.

"Yeah, we sure have. That's gonna be a big factory, seems like," the heavy one said, opening his arms as if he were making a historical statement.

"I heard some people didn't want us to move here. Is that true?" Suda pushed on.

"You mean the Bartlets. I can hardly blame them. They ain't gonna be the king of the mountain any more," said the heavy one and meaningfully winked at Suda. "We don't mind y'all being here as long as y'all give us a fair deal. Ain't that right, Louis?"

"That's right. This is a free country," the tall one, Louis, agreed emphatically as he reached for the clipper. Clearly these two belonged to the pro-Zatech group, which made asking questions a little easier.

"Thanks for feeling that way. I was worried for a while. One of our employees has been missing for some time, you know."

"Yeah, I wonder what happened to him?" Louis' voice came from outside Suda's peripheral vision. "Have you heard anything about the man, Fred?"

The heavy one's name was evidently Fred.

"No...That's really too bad, though..." Fred frowned and shook his hoary head in sympathy.

"What was this city like before we moved in?" asked Suda in an offhanded manner, to get at the point of the inquiry. "I heard there was a lot of infighting in city hall."

"Well, we really don't know what went on. Them politicians do anything to get elected. Maybe you can tell us what happened."

The tables were skillfully turned on Suda by Fred, perhaps unwilling to discuss the ugly issue with an outsider.

"I don't know that much myself. I'm just an employee. Those decisions are made way above my head."

The barber's eyes glinted at Suda's evasive answer. He glanced up at Louis, and then at Suda again.

"You know, don't take me wrong," said Fred, with a tight smile. "This is just what I heard. You know those rumors. You can't trust them. But, I heard...Now I'm not saying this myself...But I heard you people paid a lot of money to the Bartlets to shut them up...Now I don't know the truth of this..."

Fred's face turned red as he spoke, wary of Suda's reaction. There was an awkward moment. Suda didn't know how to respond. Louis was silently mixing the shaving cream for Suda. When Fred started to continue, a customer came in, apparently a regular, and the conversation died there on the floor. Neither Louis nor Fred said anything about Zatech or Kentaro afterwards.

The information was valuable if what Fred had said was true. If indeed Zatech had paid a large sum of money to the Bartlet Corporation to silence them, there would have been no reason for them to keep on threatening Zatech much less abduct Kentaro. But there was a huge hole in this scenario. It was the city of Moeling that had wanted Zatech to come here, and Zatech could have gone elsewhere if they had so wished. Why would Zatech then allow themselves to incur unnecessary expense to move to this particular town in the U.S.? Maybe it was the city that paid money to the Bartlets—taxpayers' money to shut the Bartlets up. If the people in the city had found out that their money had been spent to bring a Japanese factory here, they might have been up in arms against it. So someone leaked the rumor—Zatech had paid the money to the Bartlets. In either case, if some under-the-table deal had been struck, the Bartlets had, at least in theory, no reason to abduct Kentaro.

Neither Miho nor Takeda mentioned even a hint of such a deal, however. On the contrary, Miho and Takeda implied the Zatech Corporation was still under attack by the opposing force. It seemed absurd that the Zatech employees had not been informed if such deal had existed anywhere. What was the truth? The sun was still too high to visit the Zatech office. Chief Shugert might be able to shed light on this matter. When he stepped into the car and hauled the door shut, Suda's mind was already in the tidy office of Chief Shugert at the Moeling Police Station.

<h1 style="text-align:center">7</h1>

The police station was deserted again, perhaps a good sign that most officers were out patrolling the streets. Not only did the absence of the charming female officer disappoint Suda to some degree, but also he was told that Shugert had left for the day. The middle-aged police officer was superficially polite in talking to Suda. When he was about to leave the police station, Suda was abruptly stopped by Sergeant Brown, who seemed to have materialized from nowhere.

"You know, I don't know what Chief Shugert told you yesterday, but we want you to leave the investigation to us," Brown grunted as he flopped heavily down on his squeaky swivel chair.

He didn't bat an eye as Suda sat across his desk located next to the dispatcher's room. Suda, sensing certain hostility in Brown's gravelly voice and deep penetrating eyes, didn't know what to make of his blunt request.

"We understand how you're worried about your brother and all that, but we don't want you to get into a mess around here," continued Brown as he tapped on his desk with his thick knobby fingers, glowering uncompromisingly at Suda.

"I have no intention of doing an investigation on your behalf." His voice didn't come out as strongly as he had wished, but Suda managed to regain his countenance and held the big sergeant's baleful glare that suggested lurking temper.

"Well, I think you're asking too many questions, if you ask me," Brown responded coldly.

Brown was like a bear. He was a colossal man. Probably 6'6", weighing some 300 pounds. Aside from his impressive physical size, his silver Smith & Wesson revolver gleamed ever so intimidatingly. All Suda could do was to stand his ground.

"Look, Sergeant, I didn't come here all the way from Japan to do nothing. I have a certain responsibility to my family," said Suda with fire in his voice.

A man like Brown was probably used to chewing people up, but Suda had no intention of cowering before this obvious bully.

"Are you telling me you're gonna keep on nosing around here?" Brown raised his hectoring voice, almost roaring.

It was obviously a calculated move by him to intimidate Suda. Suda did not budge as the tension mounted to an almost intolerable level.

"I'm only telling you I'll do whatever I please within the law. I'm not breaking any laws here," Suda contended fiercely.

"Well, don't come crying to us if you get hurt."

"Are you telling me it's not your duty to protect an innocent citizen?"

Brown was far from being conquered. He sneered wryly and threatened, "I'm warning you, you can get hurt."

Suda was shrinking inside as Sergeant John Brown's thunderous voice resonated around the room, but he managed to keep his cool composure.

"If you'll excuse me, I have to be going."

Suda stood up forcefully, rattling the chair, with his eyes boring into Sergeant Brown's large crooked face. This time, he did not try to stop Suda.

As he shut the heavy wooden door behind him, Suda was thankful he had gotten out of the police station in one piece. As he walked toward his car, letting out a sigh of relief and feeling testy, a police car pulled into the driveway. The door flung open, and a policewoman jumped out. She was the female officer he'd seen the day before. Suda stood there in the driveway, hoping he could have a word with her, but she didn't even glance his way as she strode past him.

John Brown ruined the day for Suda. Not only that, now he knew he was not welcomed by everyone in the police department. Getting his foot into the police station wouldn't be easy next time. Suda had planned to visit the Zatech office that evening, but he was too tired. The confrontation with Brown seemed to have drained all his energy. Besides, he had hardly any sleep the night before, and jet lag was still bothering him. He'd had it for today. It was only four o'clock in the afternoon, but he went back to his room and went to bed feeling dejected.

When Suda woke up, he found himself ravenously hungry. The digital clock at his bedside read 7:55 PM. He dragged himself out of the bed, brushed his teeth, took a quick shower, put on clean underwear and socks, and wore the best clothes he had brought to go out to eat. Suda went back to the same steak house Takeda had invited him to the previous night. The place was pretty much empty, probably because of the time of night. He ordered a 16-oz. New York strip, a baked potato, a green salad, and iced tea to drink. After his day, he needed to replenish his energy. He hated to eat out alone, particularly in a nice restaurant, but inviting Zatech employees for dinner was out of the question, and he didn't know anyone else who might go out with him.

It didn't take him long to finish his dinner. After a good serving of chocolate cheesecake, his full stomach gave him enough peace of mind so that he could look around his surroundings. When he found a familiar face at a table about thirty feet away, he almost flipped. There she was with a couple of girl friends. The policewoman! She had her hair down, and she was not in uniform—she was in blue jeans and a white polo shirt, but there was no doubt—it was her. Suda was not sure whether she had noticed him, but he was sure he wanted to talk to her. If he could make her his friend, he might be able to get access to the police records of the case. That was his motive, he swore. But consciously articulating that motive would never have occurred to him if she had not been an attractive woman.

Suda debated for a while. Those friends of hers were in the way. Much better than a boyfriend, though. As the New York strip and the chocolate cheesecake settled in his stomach, he began to feel more courageous. He stood up and simply walked to the table that had just been cleared by a middle-aged waitress to make room for deserts.

"Hi," said Suda with a broad smile, slightly bending at his waist.

The girl looked startled. Her friends looked horrified.

"Remember me? You're the police officer, aren't you? We met yesterday."

He felt like a fool standing there, hovering over the table. Always the first moment is the most awkward.

"I'm sorry to barge in like this, but I'd like to talk to you." Suda lingered.

Her friends began to giggle, peering at Suda and then at the still startled policewoman. Suda didn't think anything was funny.

"What do you wanna talk to me about?" the police officer said finally. Her response didn't sound very friendly. Apparently, the police officer didn't think anything was funny, either.

"About my brother-in-law."

"I don't know anything about your brother-in-law," she said briskly with her emerald green eyes fixed on Suda's face.

"Please. I won't take too much of your time. I promise."

"I'm busy now. Why don't you come to the station tomorrow?"

"Anytime is fine. But not at the police station."

She was looking at Suda's face with a reasonable amount of suspicion and bewilderment. Suda tried his best to look sincere and friendly—he prayed it would work. She still didn't smile, but said "O.K."

Suda returned to his table and waited, nursing a glass of iced tea, for some fifteen minutes before she stood up and came over with a faint swagger in the tight blue jeans and black western boots.

"We're all going to a bar. If you don't mind talking to me in my car, we can do that," she suggested, still not cracking a smile.

Suda had no argument.

The two friends took one car, and Suda and the policewoman took another, a flame-red 5.0-liter Mustang convertible, leaving Suda's car in the parking lot of the restaurant.

"By the way, I'm Vicky. What's your name?" she asked, taking the wheel. So the "V" in her nametag stood for Vicky.

"I'm Koji."

"What?"

"Koji."

"Koji?"

"Yeah."

Vicky smiled for the first time that night. She was one of those people with perfect teeth and a perfect smile. The way she drove her red ragtop Mustang was a little too rough for Suda's taste, however. Caroline had driven her car like this, too. She had had a lot of speeding tickets.

"What do you wanna ask me about your brother?" Vicky asked with her eyes on the road ahead.

"Actually, I went to the police station today. I had a little trouble with Sergeant Brown," confessed Suda, watching her long white arms stretched to the steering wheel.

"I thought that was you." She chuckled, shooting an amused glance at Suda. "You know, Jenny told me about it. Brown is an asshole. Don't worry about what he said."

"You know what happened?" Suda looked at her quiet profile.

"Yeah, Jenny was there. She's the dispatcher. She was pretty impressed by you for standing up to Brown. Not many people can do that." She turned to Suda and grinned warmly.

"Thanks." Suda's courage had just received a much-needed booster shot. Words of an attractive woman can work miracles.

"But I can't tell you anything about your brother-in-law 'cause I really don't know anything," she said, her eyes back on the road.

"I just want to know your opinion. You are a police officer. I just want to know what you think."

"You don't mind my friends listening in?"

"No."

"Then let's talk when we get there."

The headlights of the Mustang cut through the darkness like a surgical knife as Vicky pressed down the accelerator even further. To Suda's relief, Vicky appeared as though she was truly enjoying the ride with him. A few minutes later, after crossing a short concrete bridge, Suda was on a lakeshore where the bar was perched, next to a marina, with a ten-foot totem pole by the front door advertising the joint. The wooden structure was akin to a log cabin aside from the fact that there was a simple neon sign above the entrance marking its unmistakable function. The parking lot was nearly full, predicating the bar's popularity, but Vicky was able to find a place to squeeze her car in.

"Here we are," she said brightly, peering at Suda.

A balmy breeze from the lake gently carried Vicky's scent to Suda's nose, arousing his senses mildly, as she strutted ahead, leading him to the door of the nightclub. Once inside the solid oak double doors, Suda found himself in a kind of disco with a rotating mirror ball that hung from the ceiling and a roomy parquet dance floor in the center. There was no live band, but the place was packed with young men and women dressed casually and tastefully, some dancing, others chatting and carrying on with drinks in their hands.

"This is one of a kind around here," Vicky shouted through a rhythmic piece by Christina Aguilera, looking back at Suda, her eyes amused.

"Where do they all come from?" Suda shouted back.

"Pretty much from everywhere," Vicky yelled into Suda's ear, twisting her body toward him. He felt her warm breath for the first time. "This is close to the lake, so many of them are vacationing around here. This place is only open in the summertime."

Excitement in Vicky's voice, mixed with the rumble of the intoxicating ambience, pulsed through Suda's body. It was impossible to have a serious conversation with the loud music blasting his ears, but Suda didn't mind. Vicky didn't seem to mind, either. In fact, Suda wondered if she had arranged this purposefully.

"Hi, I'm Cathy."

"I'm Linda."

When they got to a table, Vicky's friends introduced themselves to Suda. Linda was a petite blonde who looked much younger than her age, with her twinkling but intelligent eyes behind her designer eyeglasses. She was a law school student and was visiting her family for the summer. Cathy, a spunky brunette with a husky voice and a freckled face, worked in a local bank. They were high school friends, Vicky said. They all laughed trying to pronounce Suda's name. He bought drinks for the girls and ordered a glass of Michelob for himself. Vicky was moving her body to the beat of Madonna, which was definitely touching Suda's sexual cord.

"Is this where you hang out at night?" Suda asked Vicky, deliberately leaning toward her.

"Only when I have the next day off," she shouted into Suda's ear.

"Nice place."

"Isn't it?"

Vicky's two friends took off to dance, and Suda was left at the table alone with Vicky. A chance of a lifetime.

"Wanna dance?"

"Yeah." Suda's invitation was swiftly accepted by Vicky.

Suda hadn't had that much fun since he didn't know when. He forgot all his worries and concerns. He danced with Vicky. He danced with Cathy. He danced with Linda. And he danced with Vicky, again and again. Vicky was a great dancer, kicking her heels and moving her hips provocatively, and Suda wanted to think that she was doing all this just for him. He didn't remember much of the conversation, but they joked a lot and laughed a lot. And when everything was over, Suda found himself seriously infatuated with Vicky Royce.

Chapter 2

1

"Thanks, I had a great time," was what Suda said to Vicky at the end of the evening. "Me, too," she replied, and Suda believed she meant it. If he had asked to kiss her that night, and he had wanted to very badly, he was sure he could have. If he had invited her to his room, and he had wanted to do that even worse, she might even have come. But something stopped him that night. Or something stopped her.

A sign of getting older—suffering from muscle aches and fatigue—it took Suda a whole day to recover from the wild outing of the night before. Vicky had said she was going to have a couple of days off, and Suda wanted to see her again. After all, they didn't get to talk about Kentaro at all. But Suda decided to give it a day or two before he gave her a call. He didn't want to appear desperate.

There was no one but Sato at his desk at the Zatech office when Suda dropped in that evening. Just the man he wanted to talk to. Sato looked disquieted when he saw Suda come through the front door. Sato was the kind of man who looked down on anyone who he considered to be lower in social status. Suda figured that out the first time he had spoken with him. His bloodless face showed nothing but contempt when Suda stood in front of him.

"I was wondering if you could give me some time to ask you a few questions." The tone of Suda's voice was polite but imposing.

"I was just about to go home," said Sato wryly as he rose from his chair, precipitously picking up his burgundy leather briefcase off the floor.

"I won't take up much of your time. If you don't mind, let me buy you a drink. We can talk over a beer."

"No, thank you. I don't drink."

"In that case, let me just speak with you here."

Sato hesitated a little but reluctantly sat back down on his chair. Under the florescent light of the office, Sato's face looked paler than ever at night. Suda pulled a chair closer and sat knee to knee with Sato, who expressed his annoyance by a childish frown.

"I want you to tell me anything you know or anything you noticed about the disappearance of Mr. Suzuki," said Suda, still with a politeness that Sato might not deserve.

"I only know things you already know. Nothing else." Sato responded with calculated rudeness, crossing his legs and leaning back, glancing at his wristwatch.

Suda's dislike of the man quickly intensified. Sato reminded him of a boy who had lived in his neighborhood when he was a child. The kid, perhaps through no fault of his own but of his odious parents, almost never played outside among other kids. Presumably he studied all the time—at least he did a good job pretending since he stayed indoors all the time—as evidenced by his sickly face. The more he and his parents flaunted his good grades in school, the more he became alienated from the rest of the kids in the area. Suda often wondered how he was functioning as an adult in the society. Perhaps he turned out to be someone like this Mr. Sato, who sat grudgingly in front of Suda.

"Oh, come on, Mr. Sato…You worked with him for almost a year. Surely, you have something more to say."

Sato didn't look like he was trying to hide something intentionally. He gave an impression that he was just so preoccupied with himself that he didn't want to think about anything else. Whichever the case might be, Suda was fast getting tired of being a civilized man.

"All right, let me ask you more direct questions," said Suda brusquely. "What kind of a man was Mr. Suzuki to you?"

Sato's eyes wandered about uncomfortably, avoiding Suda's inquisitive and overpowering stare, until inevitably coming back to fix on Suda. He seemed to have given up on the idea of putting up a defensive wall.

"Well, he was a good company man," he said with no apparent conviction, rhythmically and restlessly twitching his free foot. "We are the same age, you know. We came to Zatech the same year. I didn't know him very well then. We became friends after we came to America."

"Were you close friends?"

Sato threw a pack of Camels and matchbook on his desk with studied casualness, slowly tugged out a cigarette and lit it in an affected manner, as if to test Suda's patience.

"We mostly talked about work, if that's what you mean," he exhaled nervously and moved a tin ashtray closer. "We didn't talk much about our personal lives."

"Did you notice anything unusual about him before his disappearance?"

"No."

"What do you think has happened to him?"

"I don't know."

"You must have some opinion." Suda persisted.

Sato looked away from Suda and flicked cigarette ash into the ashtray, clearly intent on expressing his irritation.

"Well?" Suda was not about to let him off the hook so easily.

"Mr. Suda, I don't think Mr. Suzuki is still alive. I think he was abducted and murdered by someone. I think Mr. Takeda suspects the Bartlet Corporation, but I don't think so. I think some of those local thugs did it...or..."

"Or?" Suda leaned toward Sato, who seemed to be looking for an appropriate expression.

"Or who, Mr. Sato?"

Sato stubbed out his cigarette, hardly smoked, and looked back at Suda askance.

"Well, Mr. Suda," said Sato, timidly, "I don't know much about this kind of thing, but I think the first thing to look for in a murder case is to identify who has the most to gain by committing the murder."

"So?"

"All I'm saying is that the Bartlet Corporation really has nothing to gain by killing Mr. Suzuki."

Clearly, Sato wouldn't come straight to the point. He was trying to weasel out of what he was about to say a second before.

"Because the Bartlet Corporation was paid by the city to shut up?" Suda raised his voice deliberately.

"I know nothing about such a deal." Sato looked genuinely surprised.

"Who do you suspect then? Tell me," demanded Suda.

"I've said all I want to say. Excuse me."

Hurriedly, Sato started to get up. Suda reached out and forcefully pulled him by his arm back down into the chair. The chair squeaked. So did Sato.

"What, what are you doing?" Sato's ashen face turned to stone.

"I'm not through with questioning you." Suda held tightly onto Sato's flabby upper arm.

"You..." Sato fumbled for words. "You're being unreasonable!"

Sato tried to stand up again, grimacing, but Suda wouldn't let him.

"Stop it! What the hell are you trying to do?"

Suda moved his face closer and spat out his words. "I want you to tell me who you think killed Mr. Suzuki!"

"Damn it!" Sato screeched like a woman, twisting his mouth.

Suda was evidently the stronger of the two. Sato was too proud for his own good, but he was not stupid. He was shaking with fear and anger, but prudently stopped resisting Suda's force.

"I'm gonna tell you what I think. But this is just my opinion. I don't want you to take it personally." Sato's eyelids twitched as he spoke.

"Let's hear it." Suda let go of his arm and sat back in his chair, smiling inwardly with satisfaction.

"Well, as I said, I think it's important to know who had the most to gain by having Mr. Suzuki killed."

Sato's voice came out quivering. He was still breathing heavily from the earlier struggle with Suda.

"I'm listening."

"I really hope you won't be offended."

"Who are you suspecting?"

Sato lowered his eyes in hesitation, but when he looked up, he had apparently made up his mind. To Suda's amazement, Sato's prime suspect was Miho. Sato had heard from Takeda about Suzuki's presumed affair with the mystery woman. Ever since then, he had suspected Miho.

"Mr. Suzuki had an expensive life insurance policy on himself," observed Sato. "Close to a hundred million yen, I think. If your sister had known about his betrayal and resented it, don't you think it would have been plausible for her to plot his murder and collect the life insurance money?" Sato asked Suda, still massaging his upper arm as if it had been injured.

There had been similar cases in Japan in the past. A man had insured his wife for a hundred million yen, brought her to Los Angeles, and allegedly had her killed by a hired hit man. An insurance saleswoman

42

allegedly poisoned her own mother to death to collect her hundred-million-yen insurance policy. A mother killed her own child to collect insurance money. And so on and so forth. But Miho?

Of course, Sato had no idea Suda was a private eye hired by Miho herself, but still, what a preposterous idea. Why would she hire a detective to investigate a murder she'd been responsible for? Or was she so confident that her killing of her husband was a perfect crime, and Suda would never resolve the case? Was it all a part of a cover up? Nonsense. Had she indeed planned all this, she should have been nominated for a master crime figure of the century. The idea seemed so ludicrous Suda began laughing.

"What's so funny?"

"Oh, nothing…Sorry…" Suda leaned back in his seat, his amused eyes fixed on Sato's apprehensive face. "But if she were the murderer as you think, didn't you think it would be dangerous to tell me that? I'm her brother, you know. I could kill you to shut you up."

Sato gave a violent start at Suda's words, his eyes swiftly surveying an escape route. Suda broke into laughter again, thoroughly relishing the moment.

"Don't worry, Mr. Sato," Suda said kindly. "Miho isn't a killer, I assure you. We don't really even know if Mr. Suzuki's dead, do we? Anyway, if she had anything to do with this, how would you explain the phone calls made by Mr. Suzuki on the Monday before he disappeared? He made a phone call to the lawyers in Atlanta, and he even called Mr. Takeda that day."

"I don't know…I didn't say your sister was the murderer. All I suggested was the possibility."

Sato was clearly afraid of Suda. As he spoke, his voice shook with fear although his eyes still retained plenty of hostility and resentment. Suda started to feel sorry for the guy. Perhaps Suda had been too rough on him.

"I understand," Suda relented with a conciliatory smile. "Thank you for your suggestion. I'll keep it in mind. Oh, one more thing…Don't tell anybody about this conversation, all right?"

Sato's idea was entertaining, but it was just that—entertaining. Miho, the cold-blooded killer. When Suda left the Zatech office, he left the idea behind along with the still shaking Mr. Sato.

2

Neither Lisa Parkins nor Jean Konopinsky provided Suda with new information the next day. Lisa Parkins simply corroborated that a phone call had been made to the office by Kentaro Suzuki shortly before his disappearance. She was the one who had received the call and relayed it to her boss, Takeda. Hitting a dry well in the Zatech office, Suda had apparently no alternative but to investigate the Bartlet Corporation. If in fact Kentaro had been abducted and murdered, Suda still believed the most likely perpetrator had been the Bartlets or someone connected with them.

Before he rushed into action, Suda hoped to consult with Vicky. Vicky was young, but she seemed bright and sensible. Suda had not seen or spoken to her since the night they danced together. If possible, Suda wanted to avoid going to the police station and risking another encounter with the inhospitable Sergeant John Brown. She was living with her parents at home, Vicky had said. Suda did not venture to ask for Vicky's cell phone number the other night nor did she volunteer the access, but finding out her home phone number would be a cinch. Suda picked up the remarkably thin City of Moeling telephone directory as his heart began to race like that of a teenager before his first date.

"Hello?"

A woman answered the phone. An older voice. Perhaps Vicky's mother. Suda took a deep breath.

"Hello, may I speak with Miss Vicky Royce, please," he said, sounding like an insurance salesman.

"May I ask who's calling?"

"Oh, this is Koji Suda."

"Who?"

"Koji. Koji Suda." Calm down, man, Suda said to himself. Just keep cool. He wished his name had been John Smith.

"Just a minute, please."

The minute seemed like an hour as some song once said. Suda's heart was fluttering as though he was about to engage in a 100-meter dash, and he couldn't believe he was experiencing such a feeling after all these years.

"Hello?"

It was definitely Vicky's voice. She was there.

"Hello. This is Koji." His voice was tremulous even to his own ears.

"Oh, hi."

Suda was on the verge of collapse. Keep cool, he said to himself again and stomped his foot.

"I just called to see if you have any time tonight," he barely managed.

"Tonight?"

"Busy?"

Come on. Don't be busy. Suda prayed.

"No...O.K....Where do you want to meet me?"

Slight apprehension in her voice, maybe. Suda gathered all his courage.

"Why don't I buy you a dinner?"

"Sounds good to me. Where?" Contrary to his near basket-case state, Vicky sounded utterly relaxed.

"Well, I don't know too many places in town, so..."

"Why don't I come pick you up then? I'll take you to a good place," suggested Vicky blithely.

"That'll be fine."

"What time?"

"How about seven?"

"That's fine. I'll see you at seven, then," she said cheerfully.

"Do you know where I am?" Suda added hastily.

"Yeah, I know the motel you're staying at."

Suda had told her about his motel the night they had danced together. And she remembered, to his thrill.

"I'm in Room 105."

"I'll see you then."

"Right."

"Oh, Koji?"

"Yes."

"Let me give you my cell phone number just in case."

"That'll be great. I'll give you mine, too."

Suda's hand shook as he took down her number.

"And one more thing," Vicky said.

"Yes?"

"Let's go casual, O.K?"

"Right."

The conversation had gone relatively smoothly, even though his heart pounded at a sprinter's pace the whole time, and Suda was immensely thankful for that. The anticipation of seeing Vicky again was exhilarating. The fact that she had given away her cell phone number to him was a testimony to her fondness of Suda, he convinced himself.

Vicky came to the door exactly at 7 PM in a crisp snow-white cotton shirt, oyster-colored slacks, and a pair of dark blue low-heels, carrying a small Gucci handbag. Her carefree smile stretched wide as she asked, "Are you ready?" Little did she know that Suda had been ready practically since he had gotten off the phone with her earlier.

"Yes, I'm ready," declared Suda, as he heard her red Mustang purring right outside the door.

Vicky took Suda to the only Italian restaurant in town, and it was not a Pizza Hut. This was one of the oldest restaurants in town, Vicky said, opened originally by an Italian immigrant's family at the turn of the last century. Despite its reputation and classy ambience, Suda had tasted better food before, but he didn't think about food that night. There was Vicky, across the table, with her milky white skin, wearing her lank hair loose, and smiling winningly. Her dreamy green eyes glanced at Suda almost bashfully, dazing him at will. She didn't want to talk about the missing man in the restaurant. There were too many ears, she said. Instead, she talked about her college days. She had studied criminal justice in college before she became a police officer. She wanted to work for the FBI in the future, she said. Suda soon found out that "Vicky" was a short for "Veronica."

"That's a beautiful name," complimented Suda.

"Do you think so?"

Suda truly thought it was a most beautiful name.

"I guess I have to thank my mom for naming me Veronica in that case." Vicky laughed, tossing her head and flashing her perfect pearl white teeth.

Suda talked about his college years, too. Then he talked about life in Japan, and Vicky seemed to be genuinely interested. When they finished eating, Vicky suggested they go for a drive in the country—somewhere quiet.

For a man like Suda, who was born and reared in Tokyo, driving at night on a rural highway in Alabama was a spooky experience. There were no streetlights to speak of. The sole source of illumination, aside from occasional houses that appeared and disappeared as they drove past them, was the head lamps of the very car he was riding in, which allowed him a limited view of the paved road directly ahead and nothing else. It seemed the only people on the road that night were Vicky and Suda. He wondered what would happen if the engine died suddenly or if they ran into some gang on the road, and prayed she had a shotgun in the car. If it weren't for Vicky, who looked entirely comfortable at the wheel of her Mustang, Suda would never have ventured out into what seemed like the heart of darkness.

Soon Vicky steered the car off a highway and onto an even darker side road, and Suda began to worry.

"Where are we going?" he asked imploringly.

"We're almost there."

The road had gotten narrow and bumpy. Suda glanced over at Vicky, who was silent and beautiful. A sense of foreboding prevented Suda from asking another question as to their destination. Abruptly, she stepped on the brake and pulled the car onto the shoulder of the road, slowly bringing it to a halt.

"We're here," she quietly announced, cutting off the lights and turning off the engine. "We're at Lake Martin."

It was very dark. In fact, when the lights of the car were cut off, Suda could not see a damned thing for a minute or two. Vicky got out of the car, and Suda followed her example. Without a word, she took Suda's hand and led him closer to the edge of the tranquil water. Her hand was soft and warm. Suda could see some faint lights across the lake, and when he looked up, the stars were numerous and stunningly bright unlike he had ever seen them before. A gentle warm breeze wafted in from the surface of the lake, and the scent of Vicky's hair sweetly teased his senses. If not for the frogs and crickets, this world would have been a soundless world.

"Do you know what they are?" Vicky asked quietly, still holding Suda's hand, referring to the noisemakers of the wild.

"Frogs and bugs, I guess." What a romantic statement. Suda could have stabbed himself.

Vicky stood near the water peering over the lake surface as if she had not heard what Suda had said. Suda could vaguely see her quiet profile and hear her sedate breathing. The night was deep and mysterious, seemingly demanding every attention.

"Let's go back to the car. We'll get bitten by mosquitoes here," said Vicky suddenly, turning to Suda, finally letting go of his hand, leaving only the sensation of the warmth behind.

Once they climbed back in the car, Vicky explained to Suda all about the lake. It was a man-made lake—the largest of its kind in the area.

Many people owned cabins on the shore as summerhouses, and boating and water-skiing were very popular sports on the lake. These days, young people liked to jetski instead. The water was murky almost all the time from algae, so it was not suited for scubadiving.

"When I was in high school we used to come here all the time to water-ski," Vicky reminisced. "You remember Linda, right? Her parents own a cabin here. They have a boat, too. We used to come and spend the night. Those were the good ol' days."

"You don't water-ski anymore?"

"I'd like to, but you've gotta find the time and someone who will drive a boat for you, and that's the hard part."

The singing of the frogs and insects seemed to have gotten quieter.

"Well, now that we are here, why don't we talk about your brother-in-law?" She bade Suda.

Suda pondered. He wanted her. He wanted her badly. But he didn't want to pressure her in any way. She sat only inches away.

"Vicky," said Suda with a silent resolve.

"Yeah?"

"Before we talk about him, I have to tell you something."

Vicky said nothing. He could see her big green eyes staring right at him, into his soul.

"I'm not his brother-in-law. I'm a private investigator hired by his wife to search for him," Suda spurted out, holding her stare and keeping his proverbial fingers crossed. He could not lie to her any longer. Whatever might happen between her and him, he wanted to be honest at least. Vicky breathed a huge sigh.

"Is that all? Why did you decide to tell me that now?"

"Because I like you very much. I just didn't want to keep on lying to you," Suda confided and immediately felt like a jerk.

"Did you ask me out just to tell me this?" Vicky didn't break her serious tone.

"No. I asked you out because I wanted to see you. I wanted to be with you."

Suda heard Vicky's sigh again. Her eyes searched Suda's face until they locked onto his earnest and imploring stare and lingered, anticipating, fearing. The moment seemed to last all night. Finally Vicky bravely and assuringly declared, "Well, you've got me tonight. I'm all yours."

Suda took her hand and gently pulled her into his sinewy arms. Vicky was trembling. When their lips met, she let out a tiny moan. Her lips were soft and sweet. Aided by the darkness of the night, she soon overcame her initial shyness. She boldly and willingly let her firm supple body open up to Suda's adroit hands and experienced lips. And she became his. Vicky was superbly beautiful. Suda took his time, and she responded ardently to touches and kisses that explored and probed every inch of her young naked body with no reservation. He existed only for Vicky that night. Her feverish gasps, her irrepressible groan, her writhing ecstasy, every moment was precious to Suda. She was a treasure to be cherished. Suda forgot the time.

Suda and Vicky came back to the motel while it was still dark. Vicky had to go to work in the morning. She didn't want people to know she was sleeping with him, she said.

"This is a small town. Rumors can get around very fast."

Suda understood exactly what she meant. Vicky didn't want anything disclosed that might compromise her career as a police officer. And a love relationship with a private eye from Japan might just prove to be that "anything."

As Suda sat in the motel room, he couldn't help thinking about Kentaro. Maybe Kentaro had run away with that mystery woman after all.

3

Suda spent all afternoon making love to Vicky. She had taken a day off so that they could be together all day at the cabin Linda's parents owned. She could borrow the key from Linda whenever the cabin wasn't in use. The cabin was perched on a wooded hill overlooking a portion of the lake. Most trees in the area were pines that had grown to thirty to forty feet in height, and through the woods led a narrow cobbled pathway down to the dock, where a motorboat was moored.

The cabin, a two-bedroom wooden construction with a shingled roof, was built simply to accommodate a small family. It was equipped with just about everything they would expect in a house in the city, including a large freezer-refrigerator with automatic defroster, a stereo-CD player, and a VCR-TV set with over 200 channels to choose from. There were a number of fishing rods in the closet ready to be baited, but Suda was not a big fisherman. There was also a ping-pong table out on the screened-in porch, but Suda was not big on ping-pong, either.

"Did you tell Linda about us?" asked Suda as he gently caressed Vicky's naked back, still glistening with perspiration. She lay beside him on the bed, seemingly out of energy from the long searing afternoon of pleasure-sharing with her newfound love.

"Yeah, I had to," Vicky answered, languidly lifting her head.

"What did she say?"

"She said 'Good luck.'"

And good luck, it was. Vicky had become a great partner not only in bed but also in Suda's investigation. She volunteered to obtain a copy of the police file for the case. But the file did not contain as much information as Suda wanted. In fact, not much had been done in the way of investigation by the police. They had no meaningful lead, and they had no suspect. They had not even interviewed anyone in the Bartlet Corporation. A composite picture of the mystery woman was in the file, however. Her picture, along with Kentaro's, had been distributed to the police departments and county sheriffs' offices all over the state of Alabama. And there were the names and addresses of the witnesses who supposedly saw Kentaro and his mistress together. The man in the gas station. The motel clerk and the waitress in Birmingham.

"I'll go to Birmingham with you," Vicky said as she rolled her delectable body toward Suda, pushing back her disheveled hair from her face.

"Can you?"

"Yeah, let's do it on my next day off."

Vicky didn't think Kentaro had run away, either. She believed that Kentaro was dead and that the key to solving this case was the mystery woman. Kentaro's face was all over television and the newspapers following his disappearance. The mystery woman must have seen it unless she was dead herself. Why didn't she come to the police?

"Either she was involved with the crime, or she is a married woman," observed Vicky as she rested her head on Suda's muscular chest.

"The question is where Kentaro met this woman. Those Japanese guys don't go out much. He must have met her somewhere in his line of work," Suda said, gently stroking her chestnut-colored hair.

"Birmingham police checked that out for us. They couldn't find anyone that matched the composite. Of course, the composite could be unreliable."

Suda was supposed to meet with the head of the Bartlet Corporation the next day. Vicky had been instrumental in arranging the meeting. Suda debated on the approach he was going to take. At first, he had thought of saying he was a purchasing agent from Japan interested in importing some of the garments produced by the Bartlet Corporation. Vicky thought the idea was lousy. After some ideas had been thrown back and forth, he decided to take an orthodox road. There was a limit to how long Suda could hide his true intention from everyone in the city. Sooner or later, it would come out that he was looking for the missing Japanese, and it would be much better to come out of Suda's own mouth than somebody else's. So he would introduce himself as he was supposed to be, a brother-in-law of the missing Japanese employee of the Zatech Corporation.

"Hey, maybe she was a mutual friend of the Suzukis. She could have been Mrs. Suzuki's friend. Isn't it possible that's how he met her?" Vicky asked, raising her head off Suda's chest and meeting his soft gaze.

"I think that's unlikely."

"Why?"

"Well, seems like for that kind of relationship to develop, it'd take time, and I don't think Kentaro had time for that. I'm thinking more along the line of a one-night-stand."

"Koji, it's not like we had that much time, either. I think it can happen to anyone."

Suda looked at Vicky. She was right. Suda didn't even know her just ten days before.

"All right...I'll send her the composite and see what she says."

Suda was still not about to tell Miho what the woman was supposed to be.

Exchanging ideas with Vicky was very helpful. Naturally, she knew much more about the local issues than Suda. She said that the theory of the city government paying hush money to the Bartlets was highly unlikely.

"The city budget is checked very carefully each year. If something like that went on, it wouldn't be just political suicide. Somebody could end up in jail."

Vicky was smart, and Suda liked that very much. Passionate in bed. Intelligent in discussion. Just like Caroline. Only difference was Vicky was down to earth, while Caroline had been somewhere above the clouds. Vicky reminded him of the red earth of Alabama somehow...

They went for a swim in the lake late that night. There was a little illumination outside, but it was dark enough that they didn't have to wear bathing suits. Mild wind was blowing, and it was a bit chilly on the dock, so they stayed mostly in the warm murky water of Lake Martin. The darkness was somewhat eerie, but Suda was not about to admit it. Vicky swam well, much better than Suda in fact, with a smooth freestyle and breast stroke, but she didn't venture too far from the shore for fear of getting hit by a boat. She had swum competitively in high school, she said. Suda loved Vicky's athleticism, and he enjoyed looking at her superbly balanced body. When laid out on the dock, Vicky reminded him of a mermaid, except, of course, she had a gorgeous pair of legs.

Occasionally a motorboat cruised by, humming in the distance, and the wake of the boat reached the dock and lapped gently against the wooden pillars that supported it.

"Some people like to fish at night," Vicky explained, gazing into the darkness.

"What can they catch?"

"Catfish and bass, I think."

A thought of a large catfish lurking underwater with its gaping mouth did not sit well with Suda.

"Hey, you know what? Let's take the boat out," said Vicky, her face brightening.

She was referring to the motorboat, which she had brought from the marina that morning.

"What do you mean?"

"I mean on to the lake."

"We have to put on clothes, right?"

"We'd better. We just might surprise someone if we didn't," Vicky said with a chuckle.

Vicky handled the boat like a veteran yachtsman. After checking a few things, she was ready to go.

"We can't go too fast at night."

The boat was not big—only 20 feet in length—but it could go as fast as 40 miles per hour. Reaching into the darkness, the lights of the boat reflected on the gray surface of the tame water as Vicky navigated the boat slowly and quietly.

"Let's go to the middle of the lake. Mosquitoes don't come out that far," she said in a half-whisper.

After about ten minutes, Vicky stopped the boat. She cut the engine off and turned the lights out. It became almost pitch black.

"I'm supposed to leave the lights on at night, but it's O.K. I can hear a boat coming."

Aside from the sound of tiny waves hitting the sides of the boat, it was a world of serenity and silence.

"Is it always quiet like this at night?" Suda asked looking around into the lightless world.

"Yeah…Sometimes we can hear a bird…Whip-poor-will…I don't know where they are tonight."

Suda held her closer as they sat in the boat. The scent of her burnished hair and the warmth of her lithe body had now become familiar to Suda. Vicky was apparently enjoying the quiet to the fullest, but Suda was getting a little scared. Maybe he'd seen too many horror flicks. Any moment some monster would rise out of the lake. Suda couldn't tell how much time had passed. When Vicky said, "Let's go back," it was fine with him.

Suda grilled rib-eye steaks on the bed of red-hot charcoal in the hibachi, and Vicky was in charge of baked potatoes and salads. A romantic dinner with candlelight. No television, no radio, no music. They were the only two people in the entire world. They existed in a vacuum. Suda relished every moment with Vicky. Her tender smiles pleased him, her cheerful carefree laughter delighted him, her loving gaze gave him comfort, and her long athletic legs turned him on. She made love without inhibitions, freely expressing her joy. She knew exactly when to be aggressive and when to be passive. She was a natural.

"I'm very happy I met you, Koji," said Vicky as she leaned her back against Suda's chest on the couch.

A moment of reflection passed after their perfect dinner. Suda put his arms around her shoulders, and nuzzled her ear. The sweet scent of her hair filled him with satisfaction.

"Do you remember the first time you saw me?" she asked with a lilt.

"You weren't very friendly when I walked into the police department," Suda whispered in her ear.

"I wasn't?"

"I thought you were great looking, though."

"I thought you were great looking, too."

"You hardly looked at me."

"I did, too."

"I love you, Vicky."

Vicky turned around and looked at Suda, perhaps a little surprised. That was the first time the word "love" had come out of Suda's mouth.

She gazed at him a long time, then grinned mischievously and said, "Prove it."

Vicky was more passionate, more ardent than ever that night, pushing and challenging Suda, and he responded in kind. He gave her everything he had, caressing her, kissing her, teasing her, driving her to ecstasy. Suda didn't let her go. It was Vicky that gave out first. The sun was already peeking over the horizon.

"I love you, too, Koji."

Vicky had become a very special person for Suda. She was gentle but strong. She was innocent but bold. And above all, she was a lover and a friend.

4

The gas station was located about a mile outside of the city limits—technically a county sheriff's jurisdiction. Everyone had to pass this gas station on the way to Birmingham if they took the main thoroughfare. A typical family business with the owner as the manager, it was a half full-service and half self-service station, with an attached convenience store. Any sort of full-service station was hard to find even in this part of Alabama nowadays. The owner-manager, Ralph Johnson, was a squat, bald, middle-aged man with a droopy mustache, sweaty face and beer belly, a kind of man, Suda assumed perhaps unfairly, who would belch in front of strangers unabashed. He was the man who had supposedly seen Kentaro and his blonde lover together.

Suda bought a bottle of coke and a can of cashew nuts in the store and initiated a conversation with Ralph Johnson, who stood, in a plaid cotton shirt and a pair of Dockers, rather lethargically behind the cash register.

"My brother came to your store sometime ago. Do you remember him?"

With a blank expression in his hazel eyes, the man looked at Suda's face as he picked up the coke and cashews off the counter to put them in a brown paper bag.

"Nope."

"I've been looking for him. He's been missing."

The man looked at Suda again with the same expressionless eyes.

"Are you his brother?" Johnson spoke with a "country" Southern accent, which was quite different from Vicky's more refined version.

"Yes, I am. You remember him?"

54

"I didn't see him." Johnson shrugged his round shoulders, punching the cash register. "He was sitting in the car. I think Joe saw him."

"Who's Joe?"

"He put the gas in the car. He used to work for us. Now, he's quit. That'll be three fifty five."

The account was different from what Suda had heard at the police department. According to the police record, it was the blonde woman who had been sitting in the car, not Kentaro.

"So did anyone come in to pay for the gas?" Suda asked, paying the man with exact change.

"A girl," Johnson replied tersely, twitching his nose.

"Did you know the girl?"

"Yeah. She's one of the Bartlet girls. I don't know which one."

Suda almost dropped the coke and cashews on the floor when he heard the name "Bartlet." Kentaro with a Bartlet woman?

"You mean The Bartlets?"

The man nodded his head.

"Did you speak to the police about this?"

"Yeah...I did."

Suda pulled out a copy of the composite picture of the woman from his hip pocket.

"Do me a favor," said Suda. "Please tell me if that woman looked like this."

The man took the picture in his hand and stared at it for a while, stroking his mustache with the free hand.

"Well, I reckon so," Johnson answered uncertainly. "But she had some of them dark shades on...She was a blonde. That's for sure."

According to the police record, she could have been as tall as 6 feet.

"How tall was she?" asked Suda.

"Oh...5'9"...5'10"...I don't know."

"Do you remember what kind of a car they were driving?"

"Well...It was a dark blue car, I think."

"What kind of car was it?"

"I can't tell you 'cause I don't know." Johnson raised his brows. "It was one of those late-model cars. Hell, they all look alike to me."

Kentaro's car was a 2003 Mercury Sable. It was certainly a late model, but the color was different. His car was silver. The car must have been the woman's car.

"How long ago was this?"

"Oh…This was a long time ago…April or May…I don't remember exactly."

"Where can I find Joe?"

"He lives in Goodwater."

"Which is?"

Ralph Johnson gave Suda the direction to Joe's house.

"He doesn't have a phone, but he stays home most of the time. I'm sure you can find him there."

Suda could not wait to see "Joe," the man who saw Kentaro in the woman's car.

"Vicky?"

Suda rang her cell phone once back in his car.

"Oh, hi."

She was at the police station.

"Busy?"

"Kind of. I'm dispatching right now. What's up?"

"I just spoke with the gas station guy."

"Yeah?"

"He says a guy named Joe saw Kentaro and the woman together. Joe lives in Goodwater, apparently. What kind of a town is it?"

"My dad has a business there. It's a real small town. You shouldn't have any trouble there. Are you going?"

"Yeah."

"Good luck. Don't forget I have the nightshift today."

A narrow two-lane highway took Suda straight to the rural city of Goodwater, a small town, even smaller than Moeling, largely supported by a single lumber business founded by Vicky's father. A good chunk of the population, Suda was told, worked for the Bartlet Corporation, however. One short strip of dusty paved street ran through the middle of the town with old rustic stores lined up on both sides. A couple of old churches with steeples and tiny cemeteries, a small supermarket with a pot-hole filled parking lot, a single railroad track that appeared unused for decades, and a gas station that reminded Suda of the one Gomer Pyle worked for in the Andy Griffith Show—a throwback to the mid-20th Century—that was the essence of Goodwater.

Joe's house was not hard to find although Suda had to make several twists and turns on bumpy narrow roads to get there. He lived alone in what could appropriately be described as a tarpaper shack in the predominantly black neighborhood of the town. It was clearly a poor neighborhood but seemed peaceful. Suda was used to associating poverty with violence, but apparently that was not the case here. According to Vicky, the people in Goodwater may be poor and uneducated, but they were nevertheless gentle and upright.

Joe Bodine, a skinny black man with stubby gray hair and an unshaven face, answered the door in a crinkled white cotton shirt and faded jeans marked with oil stains. Ralph Johnson said Joe was in his late sixties. He stood in the doorway, warily gazing at Suda, but when Suda spoke of Ralph Johnson, Joe moved out of the way to let the visitor into his house. He showed Suda to a reclining chair with torn vinyl upholstery, flopped on an aged wooden straight-back chair himself, and complained about the air-conditioner not working as if he were apologizing to Suda. His wife had died two years before, he said. He had a son living in Montgomery with his family, and he had a daughter who was married with two children, living in Atlanta, he said, and he pulled the photographs of his children's families out of a cookie jar and showed them to Suda one by one.

Suda was more fascinated by the interior of the house than the pictures of Bodine's family members, however. If poverty in America had embodiment, Joe Bodine's residence would surely qualify, with its warped veneer walls, torn furniture, and sagging linoleum floor. A painting of Jesus that hung on the wall seemed somewhat ironical.

"Mr. Bodine, I've come here to ask you a few question." Suda came to the point of his visit as he respectfully handed back to Bodine the pictures of his family. "My brother's been missing for more than a month now. I hope you can help me."

"Anything you say…uh…"

"I'm Suda…Koji Suda."

"O.K…Mr. Suda."

Joe Bodine looked older than his age, his teeth in disastrous shape. He must have lived a hard life.

"I believe you saw my brother at the gas station," Suda proceeded. "He was sitting in the car when you saw him."

"That's right," Bodine answered without hesitation as he neatly put aside the pictures.

"What did he look like?"

"What do you mean, now? He looked like you." He smiled faintly and lifted his dark wrinkled hand slowly and pointed at Suda's face.

"His face looked like mine?"

"Not exactly…But he looked like you."

"You mean he was an Asian?"

"Yeah…Korean or Chinese or something like that. Do you want coffee?"

"No, thank you, Mr. Bodine." Suda stopped Bodine who was about to get up. "Was he wearing glasses?"

Kentaro wore eyeglasses.

"Yeah."

"Was he tall?"

"Don't know…He was sitting in the car."

A reasonable answer. Bodine's mind was still sharp. Suda showed him Kentaro's picture.

"Yeah, this is him. He was sitting there," enthused Bodine, slightly tilting his bony head as he looked at the photo. Bodine's confirmation was not unexpected. The next question would be the critical one.

"What about the woman? Did you know her?"

"Never seen her in my whole life," replied Bodine firmly and handed back Kentaro's picture. The answer was mildly surprising to Suda.

"She was not one of the Bartlet girls?" Suda asked.

"You mean Teressa Bartlet?"

"I don't know. How many are there?"

"Well now, there's four Bartlet sisters that I know…" Bodine stuck out his right hand, his fingers curled down, and raised them one by one. "They used to stop by at the gas station."

"Did she look like any one of them?"

"Mr. Johnson says she was Teressa Bartlet, but I don't think so. Miss Bartlet ain't that tall."

"But she was wearing shades, right?" Suda pressed.

"That's right…But that wasn't Miss Bartlet…No way."

Suda wondered if Joe Bodine was protecting the Bartlets for some reason but decided not to pursue the matter at the moment. Instead, Suda produced the composite picture of the woman and handed to Bodine.

"Do you think this is her, Mr. Bodine?"

Bodine held the picture in his hand and immediately challenged, "Now you tell me. Do you think this looks like Miss Bartlet?"

"I've never seen her."

"I told the police what she looked like. I don't think this is her."

"How did she look different?"

"She had shorter hair. Her face was longer. I don't know. But this don't look like the woman I saw."

Based on whose description did the police come up with the composite picture? Not on Joe's at least. Was she Teressa Bartlet, or was she not? According to Bodine, the composite picture didn't even look like Teressa Bartlet. Where did Ralph Johnson get the idea that the woman was Teressa Bartlet?

A woman's face can change dramatically by simply changing her make-up or hairstyle. Her blonde hair could have been dyed for all Suda knew. In this case, the woman was even wearing a pair of sunglasses. Perhaps it was not surprising that the two witnesses came up with two different impressions.

"What about the car? What kind of car was she driving?" Suda asked.

"Oh, it was a Buick." The answer came back immediately.

"How do you know?"

"Oh." Joe Bodine chuckled under his breath. "I like cars, you see. So I remember."

"Do you remember what kind of Buick it was?"

"Century."

"Are you sure?"

"Yeah…Dark blue Buick Century. I saw it written there on the back of the car."

So the mystery woman drove a dark blue Buick Century, at least according to Joe Bodine.

5

A message from the police department was waiting for Suda at the motel. The spacey high school girl came running out of the office to personally hand him the hand-written note as he got out of his car. The message was from Shugert. Suda had not left his cell phone number with him. The note read, "Please come to the police department as soon as possible. Your brother's vehicle has been recovered." The girl stood there smiling inexplicably, filled with youthful curiosity while Suda read the message.

"When did you receive this message?" Suda asked the girl, who must have written it down since the handwriting was most definitely girly.

When he spoke to Vicky earlier on the phone about Goodwater, she said nothing about Kentaro's car.

"About an hours ago."

Suda thanked the girl and jumped back into the car.

The police station looked busier than the last two times Suda had made his visit. Vicky saw Suda but did not say anything. She only smiled at him with her eyes. Their relationship was to remain secret at least for the time being. John Brown was there also. Suda ignored his presence. The police department was clearly expecting Suda, who, upon showing his sun-tanned face at the station, was directed to the chief's office almost instantly.

Chief Shugert was talking on the phone behind his desk when Suda entered his office. He acknowledged Suda and, with his hairy arm exposed below the rolled-up sleeve of his white dress shirt, motioned him to sit down. Suda was anxious to hear the news. This might be the big break in the investigation.

"Well, we've found his vehicle," were Shugert's first words after he got off the phone.

The news could have been good or catastrophic, depending upon one's view. The discovery of Kentaro's car would be a step forward in the investigation, but at the same time, it could mean that the owner of the car was no longer alive. Shugert must have known this, and yet, understandably, he sounded excited to break the news to Suda.

"The Atlanta police reported it to us this afternoon," said Shugert, rising from the chair and bringing his stout frame around to sit on his desk, facing Suda. "A kid was driving it around and got picked up last night. He says he found the vehicle abandoned in his neighborhood, but they're still questioning him. They can't release the vehicle yet, but as soon as they're done with checking it out, you can bring it back here. Now I can send two of our officers to go pick it up, but since it's your brother's car, I thought you might wanna go pick it up. Would you like to do that, Mr. Suda?"

"Yes, I'll be glad to," said Suda agreeably.

"Good." Shugert clapped his fleshy hands once. "We still have to send one of our officers with you to sign out the car."

"That's fine. Anything else about the car?" Suda queried. "Any hint of what might have happened to my brother-in-law?"

"They'll be through with checking all that by tomorrow, I'm sure. They'll report their findings to me, or they'll even tell you if you ask them."

Apparently a 17-year-old kid had been arrested by the Atlanta police for DUI late last night. By matching the license tag and the vehicle identification number, they had been able to determine that the car had belonged to the missing man. Not much more could be found out at this point. One thing seemed to be clear, however. Kentaro had indeed gone to Atlanta, and he had disappeared after that. The focal point of the investigation might now have to be shifted to Atlanta. And that would mean an investigation a hundred times more difficult, as Atlanta was the largest city in the South. Suda didn't have a slightest idea even where to start. He decided not to let Miho know the latest news. Until something definite came out about the car, he didn't want to worry her unnecessarily.

Next morning, Suda was awakened by the telephone at eight o'clock sharp.

"Hello?" Suda lifted the receiver languorously.

"Wake up, sleepyhead. We're going to Atlanta!"

Vicky!

"I'm gonna come pick you up in thirty minutes," she declared brightly. "So get dressed and be ready."

Before Suda could ask questions, she hung up. His head was still woozy as if he were under water. He forced open his eyes and then closed them, hoping to go back to sleep a minute longer. Vicky's voice was still ringing in his ear. He wondered what Vicky would do if she found him asleep when she got here. While he wished she would crawl into bed with him, he knew her mind would be on business, instead. Suda sighed wistfully as he slowly got up to put his clothes on.

Vicky arrived in exactly thirty minutes, and Suda could have cursed at her punctuality. She was in plain clothes and driving her own car. Standing in the flooding rays of the morning sun, she looked so fresh and appetizing that, once again, Suda regretted that he couldn't undress her on the spot.

"Why are you driving your car?" Suda asked, peering at himself in the mirror over the dresser as he struggled to put on his tie.

"Shoot, they're not about to let me drive a squad car all the way to Atlanta, especially with me in plain clothes, but they're paying for the gas and meals. I'm still carrying the badge and the gun, so don't try anything funny," said Vicky jokingly and opened her white summer jacket to reveal the gun she carried underneath.

"All right, officer, please give me some slack," said Suda with a smile, meeting her gaze in the reflection of the mirror.

Vicky laughed at Suda's humorous tone. Little did she know he was feeling more amorous than humorous. Once Suda got in, the red Mustang took off like a jet while Suda strapped himself into the safety belt.

"How did you manage to get this assignment?" Suda asked, still knuckling his eyes.

"I volunteered. It's like a semi-official assignment if you know what I mean. Nobody wants to take a round-trip to Atlanta in one day."

This was a pleasant surprise. As it was, Suda was distressed about the prospect of having to move his investigation to Atlanta.

"So I'll be driving his car back today?"

"You don't have to, but I have to come back and file a report."

"No point in spending a night in Atlanta all by myself," said Suda discomfited. He had been hoping to spend the night with Vicky in Atlanta.

There was no direct interstate highway that linked the city of Moeling to Atlanta. They either had to drive northeastward on a country road two-thirds of the way, crossing the Georgia border, before reaching Interstate 85, or they could head southeast to the town of Opelika and get on the Interstate from there. Either way would take about the same amount of time, Vicky said, so Suda chose the former. Since time was not the issue, the local road was immensely more palatable than the interstate highway, as it wound through golden pastures and shady woods, occasionally offering a glimpse of matchbox farmhouses and postage-stamp communities. In these areas, not much appeared to have changed since the days of the Civil War, except that the road was paved with asphalt and that there were no more huge plantations with slaves.

"You know I spoke to the witnesses at the gas station," Suda said to Vicky.

"Yeah. How did it go in Goodwater?" She turned her head momentarily toward him.

"I forgot to ask you if you knew Teressa Bartlet."

"What about her?"

"Well, Ralph Johnson says the girl who was with Kentaro Suzuki was Teressa Bartlet."

"He's the owner of the gas station, right?"

"Yeah."

Vicky didn't look surprised. The car was going through the town of Roanoke, Alabama.

"I won't say it's impossible," said Vicky, her eyes alertly on the road. "But I think it's very unlikely. We went to the same high school. We were never close friends or anything. Teressa was in a grade above me. She was kind of wild. She's the youngest of the Bartlet sisters and a handful. I thought she left town and went to New York."

"How old is she?"

"Twenty-eight."

"Could the woman be any of the other Bartlet sisters?"

"She could…But I kind of doubt it. They're all married. If they'd been having an affair with Suzuki, they wouldn't have been advertising it by stopping at some local gas station."

"She came into the store to buy something, not Suzuki," revealed Suda.

"See?" Vicky shrugged. "Do you think she would do that and be recognized by everybody? Where would she have met him anyway? The Bartlets are kind of an exclusive family. They don't go around much. Do you think any of them would have an affair with some Japanese guy while the whole family is feuding with his company? I think they're kind of racist anyway. I don't think they'll even consider going out with a Japanese guy. Besides, the composite doesn't look like any of the Bartlets."

"What's funny is the other witness, this guy in Goodwater, denies knowing the woman. He says he had never seen her before, and he claims he knows what the Bartlet sisters look like. I thought maybe he was protecting the Bartlets for some reason, but you don't think so, huh?"

"I don't know." She shook her head, shooting a short glance over at Suda. "The whole thing just sounds iffy to me. She was wearing shades, right? I don't think we can count on either guy to identify her. We have to go to Birmingham and talk to the other witnesses. What did what's-his-name say?"

"Who's what's-his-name?"

"You know that Japanese guy in the company."

"Oh, Takeda."

"Yeah, that guy. He saw them together, too, right?"

"He told me he'd never seen the woman before, either. That's the question. Who made the composite picture? Whose description of the woman did you use?"

"Gee, you got me there." Vicky paused, chewing on her lower lip. "I don't know. I'll check on it when I get back."

"She drove a dark blue Buick."

"What?"

"That's what Joe Bodine told me. He says that the car was a dark blue Buick Century."

"It may be a little too difficult to track her down from the car, Koji. I imagine there are hundreds, if not thousands, of dark blue Buicks in the state of Alabama alone, and we don't even know who the car belonged to. If we had the license plate number, it would be much easier."

"No, I don't think we have that."

On a narrow country road with two-way traffic, Suda would have driven at forty miles an hour max, but not Vicky. Saying that she knew the road like the palm of her hand, she drove at sixty to seventy miles an hour. All Suda could hope was the palm of her hand was not too slippery. Soon the car had crossed the state line, and they were in Georgia. So this is Georgia, mused Suda. The scenery hadn't changed noticeably, but the sun was getting hotter.

"Let's put down the top," said Vicky.

She shut off the AC, and in no time the roof of the car came off, folded down neatly behind the back seat, exposing them to the pleasant wind and bright sunshine. Definitely beachside picnic weather.

"When we get to Newnan, let's stop and eat," Vicky suggested.

"It's about time."

"You didn't have any breakfast?"

"You kidding? You gave me only thirty minutes to get ready," Suda complained.

"Oh, I'm sorry…Poor hungry boy." Vicky reached for Suda and patted him on the head jokingly.

"I should have eaten you for breakfast. You looked very appetizing this morning."

Vicky blushed at his words, and Suda savored the moment like a cat that had caught a mouse.

As planned, Suda and Vicky stopped at a restaurant in Newnan, Georgia, near the entrance to the interstate expressway. From there to Atlanta would be much faster on the highway, Vicky said. Suda didn't dare to ask how fast she was intending to drive.

The combination of a young woman in plain clothes and an oriental man in a dark suit must have looked peculiar to many in the restaurant. Together, they attracted a lot of eyes as they took the table by the window looking out on the parking lot. The windshield of the Mustang glinted, as it faithfully waited for its owner in the outside parking lot, bouncing off the rays of the scorching sun, and the pine trees lazily wagged in the distance. All the indications suggested that it was going to be another searing day.

"Have you ever shot that thing?" asked Suda, pointing to the semi-automatic Vicky carried under her summer jacket.

"Of course. We had to pass a course in marksmanship," she said proudly then smiled.

"I guess you're pretty good at it then."

"I've never shot anybody. I hope I'll never have to."

Vicky ordered skim milk and salad, and Suda ordered a full breakfast with three eggs, over-easy, three strips of bacon, hashed brown potatoes, three pancakes, and a glass of fresh-squeezed orange juice.

"Are you gonna eat all that by yourself?" Vicky teased Suda, as she placed the cloth napkin on her lap.

"I'm very hungry," he confessed.

"That's kind of obvious." She giggled.

"What do you think? You think Suzuki went to Atlanta?" Suda asked, chomping down on a forkful of eggs.

"I think that's a safe bet."

"So it looks like he ran away."

"I didn't say that. He could have been killed in Atlanta. A victim of a car-jack or something."

"What do you think of those mysterious phone calls he made?" Suda was still hung up on the phone calls.

"You mean to the lawyers and the company?"

"Yeah, I just can't make any sense out of them."

"Are you thinking about moving to Atlanta to continue the investigation?" Vicky shot him a keen gaze.

"I may have to," he answered numbly.

"I won't get to see you very often then," said Vicky sadly, dropping her eyes to her half-eaten salad.

"I guess not..."

"I'll come to Atlanta on my days off."

He wanted to hug her. Suda didn't know how much longer he could stay in the U.S. Almost three weeks had passed since he arrived in Alabama, and his progress was slow. Neither the Suzukis nor the Nishiyamas (Miho's real maiden name) were wealthy. He could not stay in the U.S. indefinitely, but he didn't know what to say to Vicky. When the time came, he knew he had to leave her.

6

The report from the Atlanta police stated that at the time they recovered the car, there was no sign of foul play. Of course, it had been more than a month since the car was supposedly left abandoned, but at least there were no blood stains detectable anywhere in Kentaro's silver Mercury Sable. The 17-year-old boy who was picked up driving the car was apparently not the first one to drive it after Kentaro's disappearance. The boy, according to his official statement to the police, had been driving it for only a week. The police didn't know who had been driving the car before him and abandoned it in the boy's neighborhood. It was a poor section of the town with drug problems and a high crime rate.

Except for the boy's, no fingerprints could be lifted from the car. After the month of neglect and abuse it had endured, the Mercury was in pretty bad shape, with dents and scratches, not to mention torn upholstery. The glove compartment was empty. Whatever had been in the car, including his laptop PC and cell phone, at the time of Kentaro's disappearance were no longer there. In short, the police still had no clue as to what had happened to Kentaro.

As he followed Vicky's red Mustang back from Atlanta, Suda's heart was heavy as the lead-colored clouds that had formed above his head. He didn't know what to say to Miho. Whether Kentaro was alive or dead, the news would not be pleasant to Miho's ears. The question was whether there would be any valid reason to move his investigation to Atlanta. Suda was fast losing his confidence, as this case had started to look more and more like a dead-end case.

Suda called Miho that night. Sooner or later she had to know. Miho remained calm while she listened to Suda's explanation. He refrained from mentioning the possible infidelity of her husband, but he told her everything else that he thought was relevant.

"What do you want me to do with the car?" Suda asked Miho.

"Oh, I have no use. Do as you please with it."

"Well, in that case, maybe I should drive it and ditch the rental. That way you'll save some money."

"That'll be fine."

Miho hesitated.

"Mr. Suda?"

"Yes?"

"I have to talk with my husband's family to decide what to do from here on. I mean, personally I'd like you to keep on working on the case, but I'm not sure how Kentaro's parents feel."

"I understand. Did you have a chance to look at the composite picture I sent you?"

"Oh, yes. I don't think I know her. What did you say she was?"

"I'm not really sure," Suda mumbled. "The police thought she was one of the important witnesses, but if you don't know her, I guess she's not important."

"I see."

Miho sounded uncertain but, to Suda's relief, did not pursue the matter any further. Talking to Miho left Suda even more depressed. He felt frustrated at his progress. He felt inept. Suda was supposed to meet with the head of the Bartlet Corporation the next day, the biggest and baddest cat in town, according to Vicky and anybody else for that matter, Lansford W. Bartlet.

Lansford W. Bartlet was the third of the three sons of the late Charles H. Bartlet, the founder of the Bartlet Corporation. He, along with his two brothers, Charles H. Bartlet II and Richard W. Bartlet, had made the Bartlet Corporation the empire that it was, but it was he who had taken leadership from an early age. Unlike his two elder brothers who had been educated in the Northeast, he barely graduated from high school, and yet, by the time he turned thirty, he had virtual control of the entire corporation. Having fought in Korea as a marine sergeant, he had acquired the reputation of being tough and often ruthless. Even at the ripe old age of seventy-five, he was still very active and involved with all the aspects of the Bartlet Corporation while his two brothers enjoyed rich country club lifestyles in retirement.

The Bartlet Corporation had thus far managed to avoid many of the ills traditional American companies suffered in the 1980's and 90's. First, by guaranteeing higher wages and better benefits than its competitors, the Bartlet Corporation successfully shut out the influence of the labor unions. Second, they didn't choose executives whose ticket consisted exclusively of an MBA from Harvard or Stanford, but rather chose executives from among long-time, outstanding employees, regardless of their education. By doing so, the Bartlet Corporation was able to give its employees incentives to work hard. Third, through intensive lobbying in the Congress by the local politicians and hired former government officials, the Bartlet Corporation was able to establish an effective trade barrier to foreign competitors and, thus, avoid the harm caused by cheap imports. Fourth and perhaps most importantly, by establishing its own brand name and niche products, the company was able to specialize in athletic wear and specialty clothing items, which were now exported to major trading partners abroad. Thus, despite the passing of NAFTA, the Bartlet Corporation was able to stay "domestic" unlike many of its competitors, which had long since shipped their jobs south of the border or to China.

The Bartlets' names were seen everywhere in the city of Moeling. There were hospitals named after the Bartlets. Schools were named after them. Parks and recreation centers bore their names. A country club was owned by and named after the Bartlets. Their influence in the city was indeed tremendous.

Lansford W. Bartlet's family mansion sat on a beautifully landscaped hill overlooking the city. On some twenty-acre site, a massive traditional Southern mansion built of auburn-red bricks with white Corinthian columns supporting a sculpted temple front was impressive from a distance as well as up close. Lansford was the father of the so-called Bartlet sisters, one of whom was Teressa Bartlet. As a teenager, she had ridden a horse hell-bent through the manicured yard, Vicky had told Suda.

Suda's appointment with Lansford Bartlet was set at 2 PM, but by habit, he arrived at the house ten minutes early. While he waited in his car, parked in the shade of a majestic oak tree casting its gigantic shadow on the paved driveway, he was trying to picture what this man would be like. Vicky had given him a vague idea as to Bartlet's craggy appearance and temperamental personality, but basically he was a blank sheet of paper for Suda. A couple of plump peacocks came sashaying beside his car, sporting their feathers of rich iridescent turquoise spotted with a rainbow of eclectic colors. His beat-up Mercury Sable was indeed an eyesore in this magnificent yard.

Exactly at two o'clock, Suda stepped out of his car, walked up the driveway, up the stone steps to the solid oak double doors of the house, and rang the doorbell. Almost immediately, Suda was greeted by a bald-headed man at the door of the mansion whom Suda thought was a butler at first. When he introduced himself as Lansford Bartlet, it caught Suda off balance.

"You must be Mr. Suda," said Bartlet and extended his hand, his piercing eyes grippingly meeting Suda's.

"Yes" was the only word to come out of Suda's mouth as he exchanged a firm handshake with the old man.

Suda didn't expect to be greeted by the man of the house at the door.

"Well, come on in," said Bartlet loudly, placing his thick hand on Suda's shoulder and cracking a wicked smile for the first time.

Bartlet looked younger than his age. As Vicky had told Suda, he was not big in physique by any means, but still he was a strong looking old man. Wearing a wrinkle-free white polyester-cotton shirt with the first button unhooked and khaki cotton slacks, Bartlet, his broad shoulders somewhat hunched, led Suda into the belly of his spectacular mansion, which symbolically and undoubtedly expressed the heart of this man. There were numerous hunting trophies ranging from a crocodile skin on the wall of the hallway to a tiger skin rug on the marble floor, apparently acquired long before the Washington Treaty had come into effect. There were oil paintings glamorizing the American Revolution and the Civil War, and at the entrance to the study was a bronze bust of his late father, Charles H. Bartlet.

"How about a drink?" Bartlet asked with his penetrating voice as soon as Suda situated himself in a thick-padded suede armchair that faced Bartlet's solid ebony desk in his study.

"No, thank you."

Bartlet hand-gestured "Do as you please," and took a seat in his squeaky swivel chair behind his desk. An oil painting, depicting colonial America, hung above his head on an oak-paneled wall flanked by a couple of elegant windows that looked out to the front yard. The bookshelves that stretched from wall to wall were crammed with books ranging from Shakespeare to a field guide to birds. The dark wooden floor was burnished to perfection, partially covered with an antique Persian rug, and from the high golden ceiling hung a glittering crystal chandelier.

"So you're from Japan," said Bartlet as he pulled out a cigar from an etched silver cigar case next to a tiny bronze sculpture of a bucking horse on his desk.

"Yes."

"I suppose you don't smoke either."

"No, I don't, but I don't mind your smoking, Mr. Bartlet."

Bartlet smiled wryly and kindled his cigar, puffing out white smoke a number of times.

"I was in Japan twice. In 1953 and 1973," he said, studying the wet end of the cigar. "In 53, I was too young to appreciate the country, but in

1973, I took a little trip in the orient with my family. Japan was my favorite country in Asia."

"I'm glad you liked it there."

Bartlet smiled as he spoke, but his eyes did not smile. It was as though he was trying to look into Suda's mind.

"I knew then Japan was going to be a major threat to our country. Oh, I respect Japanese people. I respect any hard working people. But that does not mean I have to give you what you want."

Clearly, Bartlet was set to dictate the pace and the subjects of the conversation. He continued.

"I spoke to the President at that time and warned him to watch out for Japan. I told him if we don't keep our eyes on Japan, they will undermine the very foundation of our nation. Of course, several years later, my prophecy came true. Japan started beating us in our own game. Fortunately, you people got a little too cocky, and we, on the other hand, woke up to the national crisis. You know, a lot of people believe that it was good ol' American ingenuity that beat back Japan. The truth is, it was our protectionist threats that beat back Japan. The rest is the currency. We jacked up the yen so high that your exporters became unprofitable. Your auto companies had to move their factories here to stay alive. Sure we are ahead of Japan in information technology and services right now, but if we become complacent in protecting our trade interest once again, we will begin to lose again, probably this time to China. What do you think, Mr. Suda?"

"I understand you fought against the idea of Zatech opening a plant in this city." Suda went directly to the crucial point.

"We did. We fought against it because our principles were at stake... Mr. Suda, your country took advantage of our idiotic free trade policy and almost completely destroyed our economy while you shut your doors to foreign imports and investments. Why, then, do we have to give your corporations a tax exemption and other incentives to open a factory here? That's why we fought against it."

"But Zatech will be providing jobs for Americans, and I believe that the company is now thirty percent owned by foreigners, mostly American investors."

"You mean shareholders?" Bartlet furrowed his brows. "Mr. Suda, I don't consider those short-term investors as owners. I don't even consider them as investors as a matter of fact. They're nothing but gamblers and speculators. They might as well go to Las Vegas and gamble their money away. And as far as jobs are concerned, American companies can provide enough jobs for our citizens if it weren't for the free-trade nonsense."

"So you're still fighting."

"If a man gives up his principles, he's left with nothing, Mr. Suda." Bartlet's eyes glinted ominously.

"Would you stop the Zatech project at all costs?"

"We're still trying, as you said."

There was something insolent and vicious about the way he grinned. Suda felt a shimmy of fear crawl up his back. And yet, he was determined to venture further to find out whether Bartlet had anything to do with Kentaro's disappearance.

"I'm looking for my brother-in-law, Mr. Bartlet," said Suda, summoning his courage. "I think you know he's been missing since mid-July. I heard rumors in town that you might know his whereabouts."

Lansford W. Bartlet was no longer grinning. His energetic face turned stern and grim, but Suda didn't shy away from his piercing eyes. He did not want to be intimidated.

"That's why you're here," Bartlet leaned forward, bracing himself with his elbows on his desk, pinching the cigar between his fingers. "You think I did something to your brother-in-law."

"I don't know. That's why I'm here. To find that out."

As he sat across the room from Lansford W. Bartlet, Suda felt like a sacrificial lamb that had just walked into a lion's den. The confrontation with one of the most powerful men in the state of Alabama had come, and it was not easy.

"Mr. Bartlet, my sister's husband was a very good man," Suda forged on. "A hard worker. As you can imagine everyone connected to him is totally devastated as a result of his disappearance. I've been all over town asking questions, and everything seems to point to the feud between your company and Zatech. So I had to come to you. I had to know the truth of the matter from you."

Lansford W. Bartlet was still staring at Suda, but there was no longer a menacing light in his eyes. He tamped out his cigar slowly in the ashtray and leaned back against his chair.

"Mr. Suda," Bartlet bit out, still staring. "Suppose I tell you I had nothing to do with your brother's disappearance. How would you know I am telling you the truth?"

71

"I believe I'm a good judge of character, Mr. Bartlet. I may not believe you completely, but at least I would have some idea whether you're telling me the truth or not."

"And suppose I tell you I am responsible for your brother's fate?"

"Then I guess I would have to go to the police, provided that I got out of here alive."

Suda held Bartlet's stare. It was the only answer to the question he could manage. Suddenly Lansford Bartlet erupted into a roar of wholesome laughter, his deep blue eyes amused. Suda could not help but smile at Bartlet's reaction.

"Mr. Suda, you're an interesting man," Bartlet boomed. "And an honest one, I might add." His eyes smiled for the first time.

"Thank you." Suda felt more relieved than Bartlet could possibly have imagined.

"Let me assure you then," announced Bartlet in a serious tone of voice, as he leaned back toward Suda. "I had nothing to do with the disappearance of your brother-in-law. None of our family did. As I said, we're still working on driving Zatech out of this town, out of this country if we could. There are many ways of achieving our goal. But abducting your brother-in-law is not one of them. In fact, when I saw the story in the paper, I was intrigued myself. So he has not been found, yet…I see."

Bartlet narrowed his eyes, slightly inclining his head, apparently lost in his thought. To Suda's eyes, Lansford Bartlet was as sincere as he could have been. He was not a zany character obsessed with power as Suda was led to believe. He seemed wise and sensible. Would a man like this kidnap Kentaro, a small fish, and possibly kill him? For what?

"May I ask one more question, Mr. Bartlet?"

"That's what you're here for," said Bartlet opening his arms, slightly twisting his chair.

"If you could tell me where your daughter, Miss Teressa Bartlet, has been in the past six months, I'd appreciate it."

"My daughter is involved in this story, too?" Bartlet's brow creased.

Suda told Bartlet about the eyewitness account that she might have been the woman who was seen with Kentaro Suzuki on many occasions. Bartlet did not look either disturbed or surprised.

"Mr. Suda…I thank you for being so candid. If Teressa hears about this, she will be amused, I'm sure. She lives in New York, Mr. Suda. She's studying to be an actress there, and I can tell you she has not crossed the

Mason-Dixon line since last Christmas when she came for a short visit. If you have any doubt, you can call her right now and ask her yourself."

Suda declined the offer. Lansford W. Bartlet might have been ruthless to many of his rivals, but at least for Suda, he seemed to be a well-balanced and honorable man. Still, a twinge of doubt remained in Suda's heart, but he felt he'd gone as far as he could.

"I'm sorry I couldn't be of more help to you," said Bartlet as he walked Suda to the door. "I hope you'll be able to locate your brother soon. Take good care of yourself in the meantime."

Suda apologized for taking up his time and thanked him for his kindness. When Suda looked back, walking down the driveway, Bartlet was still standing at the door watching him. He looked sad for some reason.

Chapter 3

1

Suda received a phone call from Miho the next day. She, as well as her family and Kentaro's family, wanted Suda to continue his investigation a little longer. How much longer was uncertain, but Suda figured he would not have much more time. He had to gear up the investigation. He had to go to Birmingham as soon as possible.

On the way to Birmingham, Suda heard some interesting news from Vicky.

"Koji, I was told the composite picture was drawn almost solely based on the description provided by Takeda," Vicky said to Suda, as she sat in the passenger seat of his Mercury.

"Takeda?" He glanced at her in surprise. "Why? He only saw them come out of a movie theater at night. How could he be so accurate?"

"I know…But we tend to trust the opinion of people who have some sort of social status more than the ones who don't," Vicky said regretfully, her eyes on the road. "The motel clerk and the waitress in Birmingham are not exactly people in high positions, so I think they put more emphasis on Takeda's description."

"It's gonna be interesting what they say about the picture."

Indeed, it would be an interesting weekend. The main purpose was to see the motel clerk and the waitress who had witnessed Kentaro and the mystery woman together, but Suda had a side benefit of spending the whole weekend with Vicky. When he thought of the prospect of going back to Japan any day, he wanted to spend as much time as possible with her. Suda hadn't talked with Vicky about his having to leave the country. She didn't say a word about it either, but Suda was sure she had thought about it. Asking her to go back to Japan with him would be cruel. She had a life-long dream of becoming an FBI agent someday. But at the same time, it was unthinkable for him to stay in the U.S., relinquishing his job and life in Japan.

Vicky was impressed when Suda told her about his experience with Lansford W. Bartlet.

"I can't believe you asked him such things," she said, turning to Suda, her green eyes wide open, with a certain lilt of admiration in her voice.

"What else could I have done? I had to ask questions." Suda shrugged his shoulders.

"You know what I'm gonna call you from now on?" asked Vicky with an amused grin.

"What?"

"Mr. Intrepid."

The name sounded good, especially coming from Vicky.

"So you believed what he says?" Vicky asked Suda.

"Sort of…What do you think?"

"I'm not sure." She tilted her head. "I heard too many bad things about Lansford Bartlet when I was growing up. So I'm not the best person to ask. I'm too prejudiced to judge him."

For the time being, Bartlet was out of Suda's focus. He saw no reason to suspect the Bartlets any longer.

The motel Suda and Vicky checked into was supposed to be the one Kentaro had stayed in on occasion. It was not up to the standard Suda expected a Zatech employee to maintain for a business trip or otherwise, but this was where Kentaro had been seen with his alleged lover. The clerk who witnessed them together worked only at night. With unkempt dark brown shoulder-length hair and a mustache, the young man wore the motel uniform of red blazer uncomfortably on his willowy figure. He said, without being asked, that he went to college in the daytime. When Suda showed him the picture of Kentaro, he replied unhesitantly, "Yep…This is him. He's the one who checked in…I remember." He looked at Suda and Vicky in turn.

It was sometime in June, the clerk said. That was the only time he'd seen Kentaro and the woman.

"What about his physique? Was he tall? Fat?" Suda asked.

"He was kinda tall…Yeah, and kinda skinny."

The clerk had apparently not been taught how to speak properly to guests or maybe he didn't give a damn. Suda really didn't care in any case.

"How tall?"

"I'd say 6 feet. Maybe 6'1". I'm 5'10", and I think he was a little taller than me."

Kentaro was 5'11". Close enough.

"Well dressed?" Suda asked.

"He was in a suit."

"Do you remember his name?"

"How am I supposed to know that?" He shrugged, turning to Vicky for sympathy, which she was not prepared to give.

"Doesn't a guest have to sign in here?" Suda demanded impatiently.

"No way. We don't do that here. As long as we get paid, we're happy."

"Didn't he use a credit card to pay for the room?" Vicky broke in.

"No, he paid cash. Cold cash..." The motel clerk gave a good long stare at Vicky, who was in gym shorts and a tank top.

"You remember he paid cash?" she asked, as if she were in uniform, ignoring his lewd stare.

"Yeah...Not too many guests pay cash these days. So I remember."

Suda and Vicky exchanged glances. The reason for using cash instead of a credit card was obvious.

"You remember the girl who was with him that night?" Suda took over the questioning.

"Yeah...She was some hot chick...I just saw her waiting for the guy in the car." He lifted his chin faintly, pointing outside toward the parking lot.

"Do you remember what she looked like?"

"It was kind of dark out there...She was a blonde, though." The man winked at Vicky, smirking, the meaning of which Suda failed to comprehend.

"Do you remember the car? What kind of car was he driving?"

"I don't know...It wasn't an SUV or something like that. But all cars look the same to me."

Then the man drowned himself in a guffaw of laughter, veins swelling on his forehead. Suda saw no point in talking to him any further. The man was kind of flaky. Suda had hoped there would be other witnesses aside from the clerk among the motel workers. An inter-racial couple was not very common in a state like Alabama. Kentaro and the woman together must have attracted some attention.

"Looks like there were more than one reason why they used Takeda's testimony to come up with the composite picture," Suda said to Vicky as they left the motel lobby.

"Don't give up yet. We've just started."

The motel, although not a first-class joint, nevertheless stood in one of the wealthier sections of the city bordering Mountain Brook, which seemed to indicate that the woman was probably not some hooker Kentaro just picked up off the street.

The restaurant, Alta, was located only about five minutes away by car from the motel. The posh establishment that served continental cuisine was quite famous in the Birmingham area, according to Vicky. Elegantly landscaped and fronted with a row of towering palm trees swaying in the wind, Alta boasted the interior that was equally classy with tables arranged comfortably distanced from each other, with white linen table cloth and candles, and the subdued illumination creating a mature and relaxed ambience. Suda had checked by phone to make sure the waitress was working that night.

When Suda and Vicky got there dressed appropriately for the place, it was already well past dinnertime. Talking to the waitress would be easier this way. Her name was Mary Delmonaco, a strawberry blonde whose facial features looked a lot like those of young Melanie Griffith. She, too, was a student who went to school in the daytime and worked in the restaurant at night, but unlike the man, her head seemed to be screwed on tight. When Suda showed her Kentaro's picture, she said the police had come to ask about the same man.

"Are you sure this is the man you saw?" asked Suda, placing the picture on the table, as she came over, with the manager's permission, to sit with them.

"I think so," Mary replied, gazing at the picture.

"You mean you're not sure?" Suda peered into her young face.

"I can't say one hundred percent," said Mary. "It's dark in the restaurant."

"Was he tall or short? Do you remember?"

"Yes, he was tall for an oriental man, I thought," said Mary, moving her eyes off the picture to Suda's face.

"Do you work here every night?"

"No, I get two nights off. Usually not on weekends."

"And you saw them together here."

"Yes. I waited at their table one time."

"One time? Did they come here more than once?"

"Yes. I saw them together at least three times."

Suda and Vicky looked at each other. If she had seen them so many times, she might be the most reliable witness there was.

"About when was this?" Suda asked, leaning closer to Mary.

"Starting about January, I think," Mary answered after giving it a few seconds of thought. "But I haven't seen them for a while."

"Not before January?"

"I started working here in January, so I don't know."

"Do you remember if he used a credit card to pay for the food?"

"I don't remember. But he was stingy on tips. I remember that." Mary glanced at Vicky apologetically.

"But if he had used his credit card, it's easy to check 'cause we should have the record then."

"Yeah? Will you check on that later?"

"Sure, of course."

Suda had no doubt Kentaro had paid for everything in cash.

"Would you tell us what they were like? I mean, were they like friends or husband and wife or lovers?" Vicky asked.

"Oh, they were kind of strange. He talked mostly and she sort of sat there nodding every now and then."

Mary did not remember any part of the conversation.

"What did you think of them?" asked Suda.

"Well, we said she must be a hooker or something."

"Who is 'we'?"

"Me and Bonnie. She used to work here on weekends. She waited on them, too, a couple of times. She quit in July."

"Was Bonnie here before January?"

"Yes, she'd worked here more than a year."

Bonnie could be another important witness, but Mary said she didn't know where Bonnie had gone after she had left the job. She also said she'd told the police about Bonnie.

"Do you think anybody else here knows where Bonnie might be?"

"I don't think so. She didn't leave her contact number or anything. I can check with the manager if you like."

"What's her last name?"

79

"Laughlin. L-A-U-G-H-L-I-N."

Suda quickly wrote down the name in his memo book.

"What was the woman like?" Vicky asked Mary.

"She had pretty blonde hair and was kind of tall, too," Mary recollected. "Anywhere between twenty and thirty years old."

"How was she dressed? Like a hooker?" Vicky lowered her voice.

"No, nothing like that." Mary let out a short smile. "We weren't serious when we said she might be a hooker. She looked like a typical yuppie type. She was in a nice dress."

Kentaro would not have brought a woman dressed like a hooker to a nice restaurant like this. If she had been a prostitute, she would have had to be a high-class call girl.

"Do you think you would recognize her if you saw her again?" Vicky asked Mary, glancing at Suda.

"Oh, I think I'd recognize him, too."

Suda took out the composite picture from the inner jacket pocket and put it on the table.

"Please look at it carefully. Was this the woman?" asked Vicky.

"No," said Mary by giving it one look.

"Are you sure?" Suda asked although he had expected the answer.

"Yes. She didn't look like this," said Mary shortly.

"Now wait a minute, you said you weren't sure about the man, but now you're sure about the woman. Why?" Suda pressed.

Mary inclined her strawberry blonde head in thought, and answered, "I don't know, but his skin was kind of dark, and he was wearing glasses, so it was kind of hard to see the features very clearly."

There was no record of Kentaro's credit card usage left at the restaurant. Suda was not surprised but nevertheless disappointed. It was well past 10 PM when they parted with Mary, thanking her for her cooperation.

"What she says makes sense, I think," Vicky observed as they walked out of the restaurant. "Besides, you Asians all look alike to us."

"Thanks a lot. I look like all the others, huh?"

"I'm only kidding." She laughed, bumping her shoulder against Suda.

According to Takeda, Kentaro took numerous trips to Birmingham. He must have gone to other restaurants with the woman in question. They must have been seen by a lot more people than the few in the police file. Where are the rest of the witnesses?

"I feel like going from restaurant to restaurant asking whether they've seen Kentaro," said Suda as they headed back to the motel.

"That's gonna be like finding a needle in a haystack, Koji."

"I know."

Birmingham didn't compare to Tokyo in size, but if he'd gone restaurant to restaurant, it would have taken months if not years, and still he wouldn't have any guarantee that he would find a reliable witness or useful information.

"I'm sure all the restaurants near the motel were checked out by the Birmingham police," said Vicky to a skeptical Suda.

"What about Bonnie? I wonder if they checked her out, too."

"It wasn't in the report. I'll check on it when I get back to the department."

Bonnie Laughlin could be the next important witness, but neither the manager of Alta nor any of the employees knew of her whereabouts.

"I can check on her on the computer," Vicky offered. "If she's still alive and keeps her driver's license current, I can probably find out where she is."

Having a professional police officer as his aid proved to be more powerful than Suda had imagined. In particular, when the police officer was as attractive as Vicky, any help would be more than appreciated.

"You know what I think?" Vicky turned to Suda. "This one looks like one of those love triangle cases. Suzuki falls in love with a married woman. The husband finds out. He gets enraged and kills Suzuki or maybe his wife, too."

"In Atlanta?"

"Let's forget about where. If we think of it that way, we can make some sense out of those phone calls he made, too. The husband took Suzuki at gunpoint or something and forced Suzuki to make those calls. The reason is he didn't want anybody looking for him at that point. He needed the time to think about what to do with Suzuki."

Vicky's theory was perhaps not without merit. But it was still just a theory. There was nothing to substantiate the existence of a love triangle except for the fact that Kentaro had spent some time with the mysterious woman in the months preceding his disappearance.

"I know it's just speculation..." Vicky mumbled to herself.

In any case, the identity of the woman was still crucial to this case. The composite picture now appeared to be utterly unreliable. Mary told Suda and Vicky that the woman she remembered had shorter hair and a longer face. Suda remembered Joe Bodine had said the same thing. She had those bedroom eyes, Mary Delmonaco had said.

"What are bedroom eyes?" Suda asked Vicky.

"I don't know. Sexy droopy eyes, I guess."

"We need a new composite picture."

"That's for sure. I can't ask our artist to redraw the picture, but I'll try to find somebody that can draw once we get other witnesses and decide whose description of the woman is the best."

The effort to find more witnesses among the motel workers proved to be futile. Obviously Kentaro was doing his best to hide himself and the blonde woman from the eyes of people. Suda wouldn't have been surprised at all if Kentaro had worn a disguise when he went out with the woman.

2

Suda didn't see much point in moving his investigation to Atlanta. He would be even more lost there. But then again, he didn't have much to do in Moeling, either. He seemed to have exhausted every hand he could play. Almost out of desperation, Suda went back to Takeda again. The Zatech office was bustling as usual. Everyone except Sato greeted Suda. In fact, Sato stood up and left the office as soon as Suda walked in. Takeda was looking through some e-mail messages from Tokyo, but he was pleasant about talking to Suda. He invited Suda into his office and offered him a cup of hot Japanese tea.

"My wife sends me the tea every month. Good tea is hard to find in America," said Takeda, chuckling under his breath, as he poured hot tea from an electric kettle into a Japanese Imari teacup and slid it on his desk toward Suda. As Takeda said, the aroma suggested that it was high-quality green tea, perhaps grown and harvested in Uji.

"I was very surprised to hear that," Takeda said with concern on his face. The police had already notified Takeda about Kentaro's car.

"It doesn't look good, does it?" He took a sip from his cup as he sat behind his desk.

"I'm afraid not."

"This means he actually went to Atlanta, doesn't it?"

"Most probably," Suda replied and relished the exquisite taste of the tea himself. "Mr. Takeda, I went to Birmingham the other day, to the motel where my brother-in-law used to stay."

"Oh, I see."

"I was wondering if that is the only place he used when he spent a night in Birmingham. Do you know any other motels or hotels?"

"We don't have any official place where our employees stay. Besides, we really don't need to stay overnight in Birmingham if we go there for business. It's not that far."

Suda informed Takeda about the restaurant also. Except for the issue regarding the composite picture, Suda mentioned everything the waitress had said. Takeda looked surprised at Suda's report.

"Looks like he was really involved with this girlfriend of his," said Takeda tightly.

"Yes…The problem is we don't know who this woman is. You said you had never seen her before. I was wondering if you could think of any place where he could have met this woman."

"Well, I thought he might have met her in the law firm in Birmingham. Did you go check there?"

"No, I didn't."

"I see. Well, I certainly don't remember ever seeing her there, either."

Suda had no reason to do so since the composite picture of the woman turned out to be so unreliable.

"Isn't it possible he met her in some kind of a party-like situation?" asked Suda.

A Japanese man forming a relationship with a local American woman after meeting her in a party-like situation was a highly unlikely supposition, particularly in a small country town like Moeling. Suda knew that. He could not leave any stone unturned, however.

"I really don't know that much about his private life," said Takeda, sipping the tea. "If you are talking about the company party…Yes, we've had a few of them since we came here, but Mr. Suzuki always attended them with his wife…Besides I would have recognized the woman if I had seen her before."

"Would you tell me what she looked like when you saw her?"

"What do you mean?"

"I mean her appearance."

"Well…she was a nice-looking blonde," reflected Takeda thoughtfully, narrowing his eyes. "Tall and slender. I only saw her momentarily, so it's kind of hard to remember. I gave the police my description. They made a composite picture of the woman, you see. I believe they still have the picture if you'd like to see it. I'm sure they can accommodate you on that."

But that was the problem. His description was no good.

"So you think the Bartlets had nothing to do with this?" asked Takeda.

"I know you've suspected them, but I think they're clear on this one."

"I see." Takeda looked perplexed. "Mr. Suda, would you tell me what you think happened to Mr. Suzuki, then?"

"Well, it's clear to me the woman was involved in this case one way or another. That's why I'm desperately seeking her identity. Maybe Mr. Suzuki was in some sort of a love triangle situation. I don't know. But I think if this woman could be traced, we could find Mr. Suzuki."

"A love triangle…That's bad…"

Suda felt Takeda was more concerned about the reputation of the company than the safety of his employee. He realized the possibility, however, that he could be judging Takeda through a skewed perspective of a man who had developed an allergic reaction to Japanese corporate life and anyone that took part in it.

Another uneventful day would have passed if it hadn't been for Vicky. Suda was cutting his toenails in his motel room, halfheartedly watching the CNN evening news, when he received a phone call from her.

"Hey, what are you doing?" Her voice sounded like a song to Suda's tired soul.

"Oh, nothing much…I went to talk to Takeda again today."

"Any news?"

"No, nothing."

"I've got news for you."

"What is it?"

"Bonnie Laughlin still lives in Birmingham. So we can go back and hook up with her anytime."

"That was fast."

"Do you wanna hear another news?"

According to Vicky, Kentaro was a regular customer of some local tavern.

"You remember Cathy, right?" Vicky asked.

"Yeah. We went dancing together."

"Yeah, that Cathy. She went to this bar with a guy and overheard the conversation between the bartender and a customer. I thought you might wanna know."

"What kind of conversation was this?"

"She didn't hear the details. Are you gonna check it out?"

"Might as well. I have nothing else to do."

"I wish I could go with you, but I have to work tonight. This guy called in sick, so I have to take his place."

"That's all right. I can handle it myself. Where's this bar located?"

"Have you got a pen there?"

Suda picked up a pen and a memo pad.

"I'm ready."

"The bar's name is 'Old South Tavern,' and it's at the corner of Second Street and Robert E. Lee Avenue."

Suda jotted down the name and the address of the bar. Any lead would be helpful at this point. What interested Suda was the fact that no one ever told him that Kentaro Suzuki had a drinking habit, much less visited some local bar on a regular basis. Why? Didn't anybody know about it? Yet another dimension of the missing man was opening up in front of Suda's eyes.

The bar was located in the old section of the town, a few blocks off the main street. A hand-painted sign that dimly read "Old South Tavern" fronted the modest single-story establishment. It was apparently a popular gathering spot, as all the parking slots on the street in front were already taken, and Suda had to park his car a couple of blocks away. If Kentaro had come to this place, he must have brought his car. The bar was too far from the Zatech office on foot.

The interior of the bar looked like what could have been a tavern in the Old West, with the exception of a jukebox and a couple of big colorful neon signs above the bar counter with names of different brands of beer spelled out on them. Not very upscale, but not a seedy joint, either. A congregation of what appeared to be factory workers and local businessmen milled about, drenched in the purple mist of cigarette smoke. About a third of the customers were women, some middle-aged, some young. There were no minorities in the room. That should have been expected, considering the name of the bar. As usual, when he walked up to the bar counter, Suda felt all eyes converge upon him.

"What can I get you today?" the bartender asked Suda. He was the only one working at the counter that night.

"Beer, please," shouted Suda, as country-western music blared from the jukebox, hoping this bartender was the one that knew Kentaro.

"What kind?"

"Let me have a Bud."

The bartender was one of those guys who gave the impression that he had tasted all the hardships in the world already. Burly and thick-armed, he could have passed himself off as a bouncer if it had not been for his friendly brown eyes. Suda guessed his age to be around thirty despite his prematurely graying hair and the wooly beard.

The music roared through the stagnant air, and the conversations were utterly drowned in the rumble and the roar. Cathy must have good ears to have picked up the bartender's conversation in an atmosphere like this. Suda found an open stool at the end of the counter and perched on it. He looked for a chance to speak to the bartender, but it was not an easy task with men and women constantly coming up to the counter for drinks. Suda didn't drink much. He needed a clear head for talking to the bartender. The next day was a Saturday, and it was well after eleven before the crowd started to disperse, and Suda finally found an opportunity to talk to the broad-shouldered man behind the bar counter.

"Looks like you're doing great business here," remarked Suda, smiling congenially.

"Yeah...not bad. Of course, it's Friday, you know," the bartender returned, his voice hoarse, winking a friendly wink at Suda.

"Are you one of the Zatech people?" he asked Suda, handing a pitcher full of beer to another patron.

"Not exactly. Actually I'm looking for my brother-in-law. My sister's husband. He's been missing for more than a month."

The bartender looked taken aback a little. He stared at Suda's face for a moment before he spoke.

"He used to come here," he said low.

"Really?" Suda's feigned astonishment approached that of an art form.

The bartender said to Suda that Kentaro came to the bar for the first time sometime in mid-April. He came alone and looked as though he had stumbled upon the bar by accident, but he must have liked the place since, after that, he had come to the bar every now and then, all by himself. During the month prior to his disappearance, the bartender said, Kentaro's visit had become more frequent. Kentaro did not drink much—only a few beers at most, but he seemed to enjoy the music and talking to the bartender.

"It was like he needed someone to talk to. I mostly listened," said the bartender as he deftly polished the tumblers.

"What did he talk about?" Suda asked with affected casualness.

"At first he didn't say much. Then he complained about the company mostly."

"You mean Zatech?"

"Yeah."

"Do you remember anything specific?"

"He just wasn't happy working there. He didn't get along with his boss, I think."

Another side of the man was turning up. No one, including Miho and Takeda, ever told Suda that Kentaro was unhappy about his work. Of course, anyone could be a good company man and unhappy about his work at the same time. Suda had seen too many examples of that. But the news most definitely strengthened the possibility that Kentaro's disappearance could have been voluntary.

"What was it about his work he didn't like?" Suda inquired, gazing into his empty glass.

"He, uh, he didn't like being a small part of a big company, I reckon. I guess he didn't like taking orders no matter how unreasonable they might be. He said his company was like one big money making machine or something to that effect. Everyone's obsessed with money, and he didn't like that. It's the whole package that disgusted him, I think. He used to tell me he was nothing but one tiny screw that could be replaced by anybody."

Not an uncommon complaint from a Japanese worker or any worker, for that matter. Suda used to say the same kind of thing to his friends over a drink or two. What fascinated Suda was the fact that Kentaro apparently didn't voice such a complaint to anybody but this bartender.

"Did he talk about a woman?" Suda asked.

"Not that I remember...What kind of a woman?"

"Any kind. I was wondering if he talked about anything else."

"Like I said, he mostly talked about his work...He talked about Japan. He asked me about this place. Oh, yeah, one time, only one time, I think, he talked about his wife...I guess that's gonna be your sister."

"What did he say?" Suda leaned forward, full of curiosity.

"Well…" The bartender hesitated. Obviously what Kentaro had said about Miho was no wine and roses. In spite of his looks, the bartender showed some sensitivity, perhaps the mark of a good bartender.

"I don't mind. I won't tell her," said Suda with an assuring smile.

"He said she didn't understand him," the bartender confided. "She was sort of cold to him."

"Anything else?"

"No, that's all. I think he was in a bad mood that day. Maybe he'd had a fight with your sister or something."

Suda didn't know what to think. Was it just a simple gripe many husbands have about their wives? Or was it something deeper and more serious than that?

"Are you the only man he talked to? Didn't he make any friends here?" Suda asked, glancing around the almost empty space. A bar scene could have given Kentaro an opportunity to meet the mystery blonde in Tokyo, but in Moeling?

"He came here alone and left alone. He was kind of a quiet guy… Didn't seem to have any friends."

"Did he speak to any women?"

"He could have, but no one in particular that I can think of."

"Are you sure?"

"I can only tell you what I remember."

An image came to Suda—an image of a lonely man sitting at the bar alone, drinking beer and talking to the man behind the bar counter—quite contrary to the image of a hot shot international elite businessman.

"Did he ever get into an argument with somebody here?"

"Oh, no, nothing like that. People knew pretty much what he was and they sort of left him alone."

"It looks like many of your customers work for the Bartlet mill," Suda ventured. "Seems like some of them might wanna pick a fight with someone who works for Zatech."

"Why's that?"

"I don't know…Aren't they against Zatech moving here?"

"The mill workers aren't against Zatech," said the bartender with a knowing smile. "The owners may be, but the mill workers basically welcome the move. Now they'll have another place to work and get paid more. Of course they won't say it out loud—they don't wanna lose their jobs at least not yet, you know."

The conversation with the bartender essentially ended there. No more interesting fragments popped up. Suda thanked the bartender who was starting to put everything away for the night. At the end, the bartender introduced himself as "Bob" and shook Suda's hand.

It was past midnight when Suda left the bar and went out to the dark, empty street. A warm summer breeze was gentle to his soul although his mind was filled with the image of Kentaro, leaning over the bar counter, with a mug of cold beer in his hand. Did he really not meet anyone in the bar? Suda had to walk around the block into an even darker alley to get to his car. He only heard his own footsteps and saw his own faint shadow until suddenly, he felt someone was following him. He turned back. Several men, some thirty yards away, were fast coming his way. It was too dark to see their faces or what they were all about, but something told Suda that he was in danger.

Almost instinctively, he ran. He heard someone shout from behind. Looking back, Suda saw the dancing shadows gaining on him. He figured he couldn't outrun them and stopped in front of his car to conserve his strength. He wanted to reason with the men if possible but knew his chances were slim. Five men. Two with baseball bats. Three wore baseball caps. Quickly, Suda looked for knives and guns in their hands but didn't see them. He didn't recognize any of the men. They were all young white men.

"What do you want?" Suda called out as he pondered an escape route.

The men stood ominously, forming a warped semicircle of three yards radius around Suda. Suda's back was against the cold metal surface of the door of his Mercury, and further behind was a brick wall of flour and grain warehouse that stretched ten yards vertically and thirty yards horizontally. The empty street mercilessly led straight into the darkness to his right and left.

"We'll teach you a lesson, boy."

A thick rural Southern drawl. Suda couldn't tell who the voice was coming from.

"Goddamned Jap!"

"Look, I have nothing to do with Zatech. You've got the wrong man," Suda protested, barely controlling his quivering voice.

They said nothing. The glare in their eyes reminded Suda of mad dogs. They clearly meant business. Suda realized he might die here. He looked around for help once more in vain, but frightened as he was, there was some strange calmness in his heart at the same time. He prepared himself for a fight. Suda took a step forward. Simultaneously the man in front of him raised his baseball bat overhead. Suda jumped inside the man's arms and threw a knee at his groin. It was a clear hit. Spit flew out of the man's mouth with a gasp, and Suda saw him fall backwards in slow motion.

"Shit!" Someone spat out.

Suda turned and saw the other man with a baseball bat coming at him. The swing of the bat missed Suda's temple by a hair. The man with the bat lost his balance, and his face came only a few inches away from Suda. Suda didn't hesitate. He threw his right elbow at his face as hard as he could. The man staggered. Suda went for the baseball bat, but the man wouldn't let go. Suda threw his right fist to the bridge of his nose, and the man fell to his knees with a groan, still holding on to his bat.

"Goddamn it!"

Another man roared, and suddenly, Suda was pushed back against his car by a tackle to his hips. The tackler hit his head on the side mirror of the car and fell down, cutting his forehead, blood gushing out of it. Another man threw a hard knuckle at Suda's face, and Suda almost blacked out. Another punch glazed his chin. Suda didn't remember exactly what followed. He dished out punches and elbows like a boxer pinned against the rope until all of a sudden, he felt a dull pain in his stomach and fell to the ground.

Suda didn't know what had hit him. He tried to get up but couldn't. He was kicked in the face, and everything was going blank. Reflexively, he covered his head with his arms. He smelled his own blood. Pain shot through his spine. He heard something snap in his body but couldn't tell what part. He thought of his death. He thought of his life. He thought of Vicky. And somewhere far away, he heard the wailing siren of a police car.

Suda was not sure how much time had passed. He was on the pavement but conscious when his face suddenly came under the scrutiny of a flashlight. A young policeman looked into his eyes.

"Are you all right?" His inquiry had an urgent pitch.

Suda was happy to see the police officer's face but sorry it wasn't Vicky.

"We'll get you an ambulance right away."

Suda knew he was bleeding from somewhere. He also knew some parts of his body must have been broken. He felt no strength in his arms or legs. Fortunately, he felt no pain either. The ground felt hard and cold, but lying there was rather pleasant, smelling the mixture of asphalt and dirt. Strangely, Suda didn't worry about whether he was going to die or be paralyzed.

Another police car arrived, its brakes squealing, and two more police officers jumped out.

"Koji!"

One of them was Vicky. She came running over and tried to hug Suda.

"Don't move him!" Another police officer stopped her.

"Jesus Christ! Who the hell did this to you?"

Vicky was practically frantic. Suda didn't want to look ugly or pathetic in front of Vicky. A man's vanity knows no end. Vicky held Suda's hand and softly placed it against her cheek. She had tears in her eyes. Suda smiled at Vicky, or at least he tried to. He felt more embarrassed than hurt.

"You'll be all right, Koji…You'll be all right," Vicky said, assuringly, knowingly, smiling a forced smile as tears came coursing down her cheeks.

Suda appreciated that.

He wanted to say he loved her, but the words didn't come out. He wouldn't have minded dying in her arms with his head pressed against her breasts. The ambulance arrived with a whooping siren, and Suda heard the sound of the ambulance doors fly open and the EMS crew dash out. He heard Vicky saying something to another police officer. When Suda's body was gingerly lifted off the ground and put into the ambulance, Vicky jumped in with him. Suda saw her worried face looking down into his. Pretty green eyes, he thought. He smelled the sweet scent of her hair. He wanted to touch her but couldn't. Then he slowly lost consciousness.

3

Suda woke up flat on his back in a hospital bed with pain all over his body. He could see the bright blue sky outside the window to the right side of his head and wondered how many hours or days had passed. What had happened to him seemed only like a bad dream. He noticed his left arm was in a heavy plaster cast, but he was able to move his right arm with only mild discomfort. He felt relieved when he found he could move his legs, too. He wanted to turn his head, but it hurt too much to move.

The door of the room opened, and somebody walked in. Suda saw a nurse's white uniform at the corner of his eye.

"Oh, you're awake!" she exclaimed, looking at Suda, sounding astounded.

"I guess I am."

The voice didn't sound like his, but at least he could speak. He moved his tongue around in his mouth to check if any of his teeth were missing. They all seemed to be intact.

"How do you feel?" the nurse, a young African-American with gorgeous teeth and dark eyes asked, peering into his face.

"Pain...Just pain."

"Is it really bad?"

"No, I can live with it for now."

"It's gonna be painful for a while. If it's too bad, let me know."

"Am I gonna be all right?"

"Yeah. You're young and strong. Don't worry," said the nurse kindly. Suda couldn't see what she did, but she did something in the room and left silently.

Suda thought of what had happened to him. He wondered if Kentaro had encountered a similar fate. Except in Kentaro's case, it might have been a whole lot worse. He was aware of the irony of driving the silver Mercury, originally Kentaro's car. Suda had had close calls a couple of times before, but this was the first time he had gotten beaten up. It didn't boost his male ego for sure, but he was thankful to be alive.

He heard the door again, and somebody came in. Suda knew who it was by the sound of the footsteps.

"How're you feeling, Koji?" Vicky's smiling face came into Suda's limited view.

"Couldn't be better...Couldn't be better," Suda repeated in good humor.

Vicky laughed, but Suda couldn't laugh. It was too painful to move his stomach muscles.

"I must look terrible," said Suda in a more serious tone.

"You've seen better days," confirmed Vicky lightly.

Her gentle tone somewhat eased his pain. Her tender smiling face was the best medicine Suda could have.

"How long have I been here?" Suda asked Vicky.

"You were brought in last night."

Vicky was still in uniform. She said she hadn't gone home since the night before.

"You're lucky the only thing broken in your body is your arm," she added soothingly. "The rest are all cuts and bruises."

What happened to him was no laughing matter. Suda had feared for his life, and the incident might be a clear link to the fate of Kentaro.

"They tried to kill me, Vicky," said Suda solemnly. "Did you find out who they were?"

"Not yet. Do you remember what they looked like?"

"They were all young. All white. I'm sure I'll recognize some of them if I see them again."

"I'm sorry," said Vicky ruefully.

"For what?"

"If I hadn't told you about the bar, this wouldn't have happened."

"Don't be ridiculous. Thanks to you, I've found out some interesting things about Suzuki. I'm the one who has to apologize to you."

"Why?"

"Now the entire police department knows you're dating me."

"What are they gonna do? Fire me?" Vicky grinned defiantly.

"I was just wondering if those rednecks had anything to do with Suzuki's disappearance," Suda said to Vicky.

"I don't know." She shook her head thoughtfully. "But I think we should start thinking about this in that line."

"You don't think they're connected to the Bartlets, do you?"

"They might be mill workers. There're some roughnecks in the mill."

Suda didn't want to think that the attack had anything to do with Lansford Bartlet. He didn't want to be betrayed by his own judgment.

"Maybe you'd better start carrying a gun," Vicky suggested with a worried look on her face.

"I don't even know how to use a gun," Suda confessed.

"I'll teach you."

"Isn't it illegal for me to carry a gun?"

"Oh, don't worry about that. I'll make sure it's gonna be legit."

Suda didn't want Vicky to leave his bedside. He felt vulnerable for the first time in his life. He lifted his right hand slowly to reach for Vicky. She took hold of it, leaned over the metal bed railing and kissed him lightly on his swollen lips.

"I've gotta get back to work," she said with a compassionate smile. "Go back to sleep. And remember, don't get too friendly with the nurses."

Suda could not help laughing, and it hurt so badly.

Suda ended up spending four days in the hospital. The doctor advised him to stay for a week, but the mounting hospital bill convinced him otherwise. Besides, he didn't wish to waste more time lying in bed although he had to admit he was quite comfortable doing nothing but watching TV and staring at the ceiling. He was capable of driving a car but with great difficulty since his right ankle was still very sore when he stepped on the accelerator or the brake. The white bandage around his head made him look like a mummy, but the swelling of his face had gone down at least.

On the day Suda was released from the hospital, Vicky invited him to her home for dinner and to meet her parents. He was not sure if meeting her parents carried any significance, and he was sure he didn't want to go looking like a soldier who just came back from a battlefield in any case, but he figured he owed Vicky a favor or two.

Vicky's house was at the end of a road that wound through a hilly and densely wooded residential section at the southern edge of the city. The neighborhood was distinctly upscale and elegant. It didn't take long before Suda recognized that the area was where the Suzukis had lived and the Yoshikawas now lived. The house, built of mostly wood and painted in white, made a vivid contrast with the black pines that surrounded it. Suda liked the simple architecture that resembled the cabin of an old Mississippi riverboat. Ironically, the four-bedroom house stood across the street from a house owned and occupied by a member of the Bartlet clan.

Vicky's father was a heavy-set, physically powerful looking man in his fifties, with a balding head and kind, intelligent eyes behind the lenses of his spectacles. He had been a defensive tackle in his college days, he said. From the way he looked, Suda felt as though he could still play the position proficiently. He was one of the founders of the lumber company in Goodwater, to which he had devoted the past thirty years of his life. Vicky's mother looked like an older and heavier version of Vicky, with green eyes and a gentle smile. Like her daughter, she was cheerful and full of zeal.

"I remember talking to you on the phone," she said and smiled knowingly.

And they both welcomed Suda to their home as if he were already their son-in-law.

The roast beef dinner served with spinach casserole and sautéed assorted vegetables was superb, and the conversation was fun. If a mark of a good host or hostess is how well he or she can make the guest feel at home, Vicky's parents could not have been better hosts. Several times during the evening Suda almost forgot his left arm was still in a heavy cast. Vicky was clearly a good daughter to her parents and a good sister to her little sister, who was away studying in college. Suda saw another side of Vicky that night. She was no longer a cool, tough cop, and she was not a sexy and mischievous vixen, either. She was a daughter who cared about her family, and she was a young woman very happy to show off her new boyfriend even though he was covered with cuts and wrapped up in bandages.

"I think they really liked you, Koji," Vicky said joyfully as she drove Suda back to his motel. "They thought you were so handsome."

"For a man who got beaten up, right?" said Suda in jest in an attempt to hide his obvious delight in hearing what Vicky's parents had thought of him.

"Don't be silly."

Suda was happy to see Vicky's face so jubilant.

"So did I pass the test?" he asked, looking over at her.

"The question is whether they passed your test or not."

"Hey, if you ask me, you've got great parents."

"They can be a pain in the ass, too."

"Every parent can be sometimes. I envy you anyway."

Suda thought about his parents. As an only child, Suda had had a happy childhood growing up. His family was not wealthy but was surrounded by warmth and laughter. The happiness had seemed to last forever until the fateful day when his mother was diagnosed with a malignant tumor. For six months, Suda and his father had to watch her waste away slowly but steadily. She was brave. She didn't even shed a tear. The death of his mother was a rude awakening for Suda. Once he thought he was immune from all the ills of the world, but that no longer held true. He had witnessed a living hell on earth. How fast life had snatched happiness right out of his hand.

Vicky was worried about Suda. Concerned that the men who attacked Suda might come back, she insisted that Suda keep a gun in the glove compartment of his car at least.

"This is the easiest gun to operate. You just have to pull the trigger," said Vicky as she slowly pulled the gun out of her holster. "It comes with a full clip. You'd have to be a blind man to miss."

It was one of those semi-automatics Vicky carried when she was in plain clothes. Suda had never shot a gun in his whole life before. He was reluctant at first but decided to take Vicky's advice in the end. The attack on Suda led him again to look at the issues he once thought were no longer relevant to the disappearance of Kentaro. After all, Suda believed that he himself was almost killed by those men. What was there to prevent him from thinking that Kentaro had been attacked by the same men? Suda no longer suspected the Bartlets as Takeda once had suggested, but local thugs were another matter. The fact was that Zatech office did receive some threats over the past months, and those threats did not come from Japan. Kentaro had frequented the bar. He must have been an open target for those men.

Two distinct lines of investigation were now open. One—the mysterious blonde woman. Two—the local thugs. The two lines seemed as far away from each other as they could be, but perhaps Kentaro Suzuki stood where the two lines had crossed. Suda chose to leave the search for his attackers to the local police for now. He had to keep on tracing the line that should inevitably lead to the mysterious blonde.

Suda placed an overseas call to Miho Suzuki that night. What the bartender had told him about Kentaro had vexed him all through his stay at the hospital.

"I wanted to ask you about your husband's drinking habits," explained Suda, picturing Miho, with the receiver clutched tightly in her delicate hand, attentively listening to the voice from Alabama. "How often did he go drinking outside?"

"Not very often. He didn't like to drink much. Whenever he went out, he was with Mr. Takeda or Mr. Sato, and it was usually after work, before he came home."

Her response was delivered in a straightforward, no-nonsense manner, as if to say she knew all about Kentaro's drinking habit. Suda told Miho about the bar her husband had frequented alone after work.

"Alone? He never told me about it."

Miho sounded understandably surprised. She said whenever she had smelled alcohol on her husband's breath, he had always told her he was with his company buddies.

"Mrs. Suzuki, it seems he was not very happy with his job," Suda revealed. "At least that's what the bartender told me. Have you had any indication that your husband was unhappy with his work?"

"Well, he did complain about the way certain things were done in the company, but I think he was happy about his job in general."

"He never said he wanted to quit the job?"

"No, never. He enjoyed his work," said Miho without reservation. So there they were, the two sides of the man showing at the same time.

"What about his relationship with Mr. Takeda? Was it ever bumpy? Did your husband say anything about it?"

"As far as I know, they had a great working relationship," Miho reflected. "Mr. Takeda picked my husband personally to go with him to the U.S. When we were still in Japan, they played golf together and everything. Kentaro certainly never complained about him to me."

"What about Mr. Sato? Did your husband get along with him?"

"Well...he had a few problems with Mr. Sato. He thought Mr. Sato was kind of manipulative. But still it wasn't such a big deal. They got along fine, over all."

Suda pondered how to ask the next question without hurting Miho's feelings. When he had spoken to Miho before, she had given him the impression that the marriage between Miho and her husband was close to perfection, including their sex life. Apparently, the picture Miho had drawn was too pretty to be true.

"Mrs. Suzuki. I need to ask you one more time how your relationship was with your husband," said Suda.

"Why?"

"Please don't misunderstand. I'm not implying anything, but I need to know every detail of your husband's behavior, his relationship with his colleagues, and of course his relationship with you."

"But I told you everything I know already."

Miho sounded annoyed for the first time since Suda had been acquainted with her. What Sato had said about Miho crossed Suda's mind momentarily. Suda still did not suspect Miho, but he felt she was being less than candid. He decided to push on.

"I'll be frank with you, Mrs. Suzuki..."

Suda told her what the bartender had said. Miho seemed to be listening intently, collecting her thoughts at the same time. It took her a while before she began to talk.

"Mr. Suda." Miho paused. "Believe me, I loved my husband, and I have no doubt he loved me..."

"I'm not doubting that at all, Mrs. Suzuki," Suda said assuringly.

"But maybe I was a little too hard on my husband." She sounded contemplative. "I wanted him to succeed in the company. Maybe I wanted him to be a perfect company man. I thought it was one of my duties as a good wife to push him and cheer him on. My husband was not a very strong man. Mentally, I mean. He often needed someone to push him. He told me that once. But I didn't think I was being cruel or unreasonable in any way. I still don't. My husband certainly never said such a thing to me. I'm really shocked that he said such a thing to a bartender. I can't believe it."

As she spoke, her voice trembled. Suda felt sorry that he had to break the news, but at the same time the picture of Kentaro had become a lot clearer.

Kentaro must have been a tormented soul. In a bind between the job he didn't like and his wife's expectation, he must have felt like a drowning man at times. Obviously, he had realized quitting the job not only meant a tremendous disappointment for his wife, but also a virtual termination of his life in Japan, as he had known it. He would have lost all the prestige and social esteem that were only bestowed upon those who were elite company men. He would have forever lost the chance to become the best of the best by climbing up the corporate ladder to the top. Suda knew how he must have felt. Suda himself had spent many nights vacillating between the company life and the "free" life. In Suda's case, the decision had been made easier by the fact that he did not have a wife whose life he was responsible for.

Kentaro must have met the blonde woman at a time like that. For him, the blonde woman had represented everything his wife did not. In fact, she must have symbolically embodied the antithesis to the nation of Japan itself. His attraction to her might have grown rapidly until one day, he came to a major decision of his life—he decided to run away with the woman, casting aside everything he had possessed, everything he had known, everything he had cherished.

The story no longer sounded farfetched, and yet the same problems kept on coming back. The mysterious phone calls Kentaro had made the day before his disappearance. And why did he have to abandon his car in Atlanta? Was he involved in a love triangle as Vicky suggested? And how did the men who attacked Suda fit into this picture?

4

Suda went back to the Zatech office to meet with Takeda again. Takeda was surprised to see the bandage around Suda's head and the cast on Suda's left arm. To avoid a long explanation, Suda told Takeda that he had been involved in a traffic accident. The local newspaper had not carried the story of Suda's altercation with the local hoodlums.

Suda conveyed to Takeda what the bartender had said about Kentaro regarding his work, but Takeda denied strongly ever hearing any complaint from Kentaro.

"I believe I was not only a good boss for Mr. Suzuki, but also a very good friend," he contested, not hiding his vexation as well as bewilderment. "If he had harbored any resentment against me or the company, I'm sure I would have been the first one to know about it."

Suda saw no reason to talk to Sato, who was glancing at Suda with not-so-well-concealed hostility. He doubted Sato would tell the truth anyway. As for Lisa Parkins and Jean Konopinsky, it was preposterous to assume that they would know anything about the intricate relationship between the Japanese boss and his closest subordinate. So Suda bypassed Lisa's unfriendly face and Jean's friendly face as well.

Having nothing better to do, Suda decided to speak to Yoshikawa, the man who replaced Kentaro in the office. He had been quite friendly to Suda from day one, and in addition, had probably been associated with Zatech longer than anyone else in the office. Hopefully, he could shed light on the relationship between Kentaro and his boss.

"Hello, is Mr. Yoshikawa in?" Suda placed a phone call to his home thirty minutes after Yoshikawa had left the office for the day.

"This is he."

Suda apologized for the intrusion and explained to him that he wanted to speak to him about Kentaro. Yoshikawa sounded somewhat perturbed at first, but then invited Suda to dinner at his home that night.

"Are you sure? I can wait till tomorrow if you like," said Suda.

"No, it's quite all right. It's nice to have company for change." Yoshikawa laughed.

Suda felt a little awkward being in the house where Miho and her husband had shared their lives together. What was meant to be a love nest in America for them had turned into a house of nightmare. The elegant but simple interior of the three-bedroom house didn't show any sign of such misfortune, however. The house came furnished, with pictures on the walls included, Yoshikawa said, which meant Miho and Kentaro had used the same dining table, dresser, chest of drawers, and so on, and stared at the same pictures of flowers and landscapes on the walls.

Yoshikawa seemed to be a genuinely good man. A rare character in a competitive society. His wife resembled her husband in a similar sense. She was not beautiful in a conventional way, but she was clearly smart and good-natured. The two children were still too young to know the hardship of life. Looking at them, Suda couldn't help but pray they'd grow up to be like their parents.

"I don't have any interest in advancing in the company," Yoshikawa stated shyly as they sat around the dining table. "All I'm interested in is to do my best, and if I get promoted as a result of that, that's fine. If I don't, that's fine, too."

It had been a while since Suda tasted bona fide Japanese cuisine. The dinner was centered on boiled vegetables and grilled rainbow trout, accompanied by cucumber and radish pickles, miso-soup with tofu and seaweed, and of course, a bowl of steamed medium-grain rice, directly flown in from Japan. Nothing fancy, just simple Japanese cooking, and Suda savored every bite he took from the tips of his chopsticks.

"My husband is called a Swiss army knife in the company, because he can be used for many purposes. But that's exactly the problem, many people take advantage of him." Mrs. Yoshikawa, the chef of the evening, laughed modestly.

"It's nice to be useful," Yoshikawa said and winked at his wife.

This was not the first time for the Yoshikawas to be abroad. They had spent three years in San Diego, and prior to that they had been in London for two. Again, they said their major concern was the education of the children.

"When the factory opens, we'll have a lot more Japanese people coming to Alabama, and we'll open up a school for the Japanese kids," said Yoshikawa, glancing lovingly at his two children.

Suda remembered hearing about that somewhere. Talking to the Yoshikawas was fun. Their topics of conversation were not limited to the life of a company man. Yoshikawa said he liked fishing.

"I know there's a good lake here, but I've been too busy to go fishing since I came to America."

The Yoshikawas were fully aware of the reason why Suda came to the city of Moeling and why he came to their house that night. Of course,

Suda remained Kentaro Suzuki's brother-in-law as far as the Yoshikawas were concerned. When Mrs. Yoshikawa left the table to do the dishes and put the children to sleep, Yoshikawa suggested that they move to the living room where they could be more comfortable talking about Kentaro. Suda wanted to ask about the nature of Kentaro's work. Yoshikawa must have been performing similar duties as Kentaro's replacement.

"Mr. Suzuki was an expert in financial matters," said Yoshikawa. "I'm not near as able as he was. I didn't know him very well, but I heard he was one of the best among the younger generation of our company."

Yoshikawa's thick coke bottle eyeglasses gleamed, reflecting the yellow overhead light. Yoshikawa was ten years senior to Kentaro.

"What I'm doing right now does not exactly overlap what Mr. Suzuki was doing. I'm just doing a part of what Mr. Suzuki was doing. You see, Mr. Suzuki was also acting as a liaison between lawyers here and our legal team in Japan. So, I am handling most legal matters right now. The rest, especially the part related to finances, is under the control of Mr. Takeda at present."

"Was Mr. Suzuki's job particularly stressful?"

"Any work is stressful if you try to do a good job, as you know…But if you were asking me whether it was more stressful than ordinary, I'd have to say 'Yes' to that. Naturally this is my personal opinion, but I believe Mr. Suzuki's responsibility probably exceeded his ability more often than not. Mr. Suzuki was bright and able, but his job really should have been handled by at least two people, in my opinion."

"I don't know if you can talk about this, but how do you think the relationship was between Mr. Takeda and Mr. Suzuki?"

"I really don't know, to tell you the truth. Mr. Takeda is a good boss. He can be temperamental at times, but overall, I think he is a good man to work for."

Suda felt he could trust Yoshikawa's judgment. Suda had no doubt that Kentaro had problems with his work and possibly with his boss, Takeda. Takeda denied it. According to Yoshikawa, Takeda was a good boss. Certainly Kentaro's problems did not simply stem from his indulgence or imagination, or did they? Was Kentaro having some sort of nervous breakdown? Something was missing. Some crucial piece of information was lacking in the picture. Suda felt in his gut that he was overlooking something of grave magnitude.

A week passed without any incident or much progress. The bandage came off Suda's head, but the cast on his arm had to stay on two more weeks. Vicky came to see him every night at the motel. They talked about going back to Birmingham, but Suda wanted to wait until he was up to full-speed. So instead, they went out to eat together. They went to movies together. Vicky knew a lot of people in town, and she proudly introduced Suda as her boyfriend to each one of them. Suda felt as though he had known her for ten years, and apparently Vicky was perfectly at ease with Suda wherever they went, which pleased Suda to no end.

The day Suda had to leave Vicky came suddenly. Suda received a phone call from Miho one night. She told Suda it was a family decision.

"I wanted you to stay a little longer, but Kentaro's and my family both agree that it's best for the time being that you come back to Japan and leave the investigation to the local police," Miho informed Suda remorsefully.

Suda had dreaded this call for almost a month. What was worse was that he had to break the news to Vicky. Suda regretted he had avoided discussing the issue with Vicky before. Vicky was as blithe and bubbly as usual when she came to see Suda that night. It didn't take long, however, for her to realize something was wrong.

"What's up?" Vicky asked, looking into Suda's grim face.

Suda flopped on the edge of the bed and explained the situation to her while she sat motionless on the schlock motel armchair. He picked his words very carefully, and as she listened to him, she did not break her cool facade the whole time.

"So what're you gonna do?" she asked with forced calmness.

"I've gotta go home," replied Suda wretchedly.

"What about us?" she managed.

The notion of marriage had crossed Suda's mind a number of times. But marriage with Vicky would have meant either Vicky had to give up her dream of becoming an FBI agent and come to Japan or Suda had to give up his business and life in Japan and come to the U.S. to face an uncertain future. Neither one seemed realistic.

"Vicky," said Suda, meeting her uncompromising gaze. "We should have discussed this a long time ago. It's partly my fault 'cause I didn't wanna get into it. I wanna take you back to Japan if you'll come."

"Why can't you stay here?"

"You want me to give up my business?"

"You can find work here if you marry me."

Suda had not expected the word "marriage" to come out of Vicky's mouth before his. Apparently, Vicky had not either.

"Will you marry me?" Suda asked Vicky.

"Of course I'll marry you. I love you, you know."

It was not exactly the romantic proposition Suda had in mind. The words were simple, but there were a lot of emotions behind those simple words. And yet, Suda could not see his future in the U.S.

"You don't wanna come to Japan, I suppose," said Suda, feeling like a bumbling fool.

A look of disappointment blew over Vicky's face like a storm. She was clearly disappointed with the fact that Suda's response was not a simple "Thank you" or "I love you." Suda loathed seeing her like this.

"What am I gonna do in Japan?" Vicky returned heavily, lowering her eyes.

It was Suda who was disappointed this time. He wanted to hear "I'll go anywhere with you" kind of talk.

"You can teach English there."

Vicky shook her head as if to say, "I cannot believe he's saying this."

Suda couldn't see Vicky teaching English in Japan, either. Again, he felt like a biggest fool there was, and he cursed the moment.

"You have a college degree. You can get a job here," said Vicky imploringly.

"Doing what? Selling insurance?"

"No, you can do anything you want. You can be a private investigator if you want, or you can work for a police department like me."

"Do you really think people in Alabama will hire a Japanese private eye?"

"When I get a job in D.C., you can come with me."

"And you'll feed me."

The more they spoke, the more he felt they were drifting apart. Suda felt as though he were betraying Vicky's love for him. He felt bitter he could not repay what he had already owed to her.

"Let's forget it…You go back to Japan, and we'll see how we feel about it. We'll see what happens."

It was Vicky who cut off the discussion that seemed going nowhere.

"Let's just have fun tonight, O.K?" Vicky said gently as she came over to him, tears welling in her eyes.

Suda held her tight. He felt the soothing warmth of her body and smelled the sweet scent of her skin. As she pushed away the tears that wetted her cheeks, her face twisted in sorrow, and Suda knew he was cheating this wonderful woman. He knew he was treating her wrong. And yet, he simply did not possess the courage to take the giant plunge. He just could not commit himself to a life so uncertain.

Suda felt extremely low that night. Not only had he failed as a private detective, but also he failed as a lover and a man. He wanted to run away if he could.

5

The airport was deserted when Suda and Vicky arrived in the morning. The luggage felt to Suda as though he was carrying a block of lead, but his legs felt even heavier. His left arm was still in a cast, making matters worse. He didn't like anybody seeing him off at an airport usually, but it was different with Vicky. He wanted her there.

Suda and Vicky reached a mutual understanding. It was not comfortable, but it was the best they could do for the moment. They understood they loved each other, and at the same time, they understood it would not be easy to leave the lifestyles they were so accustomed to. So they decided to give it time—a cooling off period, so to speak—as Vicky suggested. If, as a result, they broke up, so be it. If they got back together, the love between them would only be deeper and stronger. The solution sounded like a cliche, but that seemed to be the wisest solution they could come up with.

Suda didn't sleep at all the previous night. Neither did Vicky. They stayed up all night making love. Vicky cried like a baby many times. Suda hoped the world would come to an end at daybreak. It was a misty September morning when they left the motel in Vicky's car.

Exactly forty days had gone by since Suda planted his foot on the red earth of Alabama. He could not complete the task he had come for, but he didn't come up short in the category of adventure. The people he met were nice to him in general, and he had a glimpse of local politics at work. He saw the poorest area in the region, and he met one of the wealthiest men in the state. He had a peek at the soul of a tormented man buried under a pile of duties, and he saw once again the heartless nature of corporate life. The dark side was that he almost lost his life. The bright side was, of course, that he gained Vicky.

Suda was tired, but he did not feel defeated. This was undoubtedly the most intriguing case he had ever put his hands on, and this was the first case he left unfinished since he became a private eye, but he didn't feel bitter somehow. It was perhaps akin to the feeling some athletes gained in competition. Sure, Suda would have preferred to win, but the losing did not get to him since he knew he'd done his best.

"Drop me a line when you get there," Vicky requested with a sad smile, as they sat on the vinyl seats in the waiting area.

Suda was to take the flight that would leave Birmingham and head for Dallas, and from there, a direct flight would carry him straight back to Tokyo.

"I'll call you," said Suda with a smile equally sad.

"Call me every day. I don't mind," she replied, grabbing on to his arm in jest. She knew how expensive it would be if Suda were to call her every day from Japan.

"We can set up one of those Internet phones," Vicky said.

"I'll send you e-mail."

"Good, write me every day." She was halfway teasing Suda, but he knew Vicky was hurting inside.

Waiting for his departure was not easy for either one of them. They didn't know what to say to each other, but silence would have been unbearable.

"I'll keep on investigating this case," Vicky said with forced cheerfulness. "Now you've got me really interested."

Suda's mind was so far removed from the case already. He was thinking about Vicky. How beautiful she was last night. How much he was going to miss her bright smile and gentle glance.

The time of departure came soon—much too soon for Suda. As he watched the line of passengers move slowly through the security gate, Suda sank deeper into distress. He and Vicky rose to their feet and walked slowly toward the gate. Suda felt like he was walking to a graveyard. They stopped, and they gazed at each other's eyes, groping for appropriate words.

"Well, soldier, on to the front," said Vicky jokingly.

Suda held her tight and kissed her good-bye. The warmth of her body flowed into his and entered deeply into his heart.

"I love you, Vicky." His words barely came out of his mouth.

"I love you, too."

Suda felt tears on her cheeks. He felt Vicky melt in his arms.

"Thank you for everything you've done for me," said Suda, standing straight like a soldier should.

"I thank you for all the excitement," Vicky replied, looking miserable. Suda couldn't stand to see her like that, though he was feeling just as miserable.

"It's not like I'm going to die."

Vicky cracked a smile, and her smile made Suda just a little happier.

"Take good care of yourself, my lady."

"You, too."

There was nothing more that could have been said. With an ephemeral smile, Suda turned and strode toward the gate as bravely as he could.

Chapter 4

1

Japan wasn't the same to Suda. He was back in the archipelago where he was born and raised, in the land of his mother and father, but the vacuum in his heart made him feel as though he were in a foreign country. Suda remembered that it had taken him some time to adjust when he came back from LA after college some years back, but this time it was different. He missed Vicky. He was fortunate she was only a phone call away; otherwise, he was sure he would have gone completely nuts.

Suda was to meet with Miho in two days. This was supposed to be the last meeting between Miho and him. He would tell her everything he knew about the case and get paid his fees and expenses. And that's that. The end. Supposed to be the end. But Suda found it terribly uncomfortable to have left the case unresolved the way he had. Of course, he couldn't have helped it. It was his client who had wanted to cut off the money. Sadly, human minds never worked so simply. The situation had continued to bother him from the minute he had set his foot on Japanese soil, and since then, he had gotten progressively and restlessly obsessed by it.

So before meeting Miho for the last time, Suda wanted to check one more time all the personal effects left behind by Kentaro, which Suda had in his possession borrowed from Miho. These items included Kentaro's memo books, appointment books, and company and family photo albums encompassing the last few years of his life. Unfortunately, Kentaro's laptop and cell phone had gone missing with his car, and when the car was recovered, they were nowhere to be found. Suda had gone over these items previously, but he wanted to make sure that he had not missed anything of importance.

Kentaro's memo books were filled with names and addresses. Some of them belonged to Zatech employees, company clients and dealers, bankers, and government officials. Others were Kentaro's college and high school friends. Suda had seen many of those whom he deemed significant but had come away with nothing.

The appointment books were filled with numerous appointments with bankers and the officials in the Ministry of Finance and the Ministry of Economy, Trade and Industry, indicating the fact that Kentaro was in charge of financial matters in his department. Unfortunately, there were no memo books or appointment books for the year Kentaro and Miho spent in the U.S. Both books, which Miho had confirmed Kentaro had always carried with him, were also missing along with him.

The rain had begun to pitter-patter against the windowpane some half-hour before. Suda sat on the carpet of his living room floor, performing the tedious work of going through the names and the list of appointments one by one. Beethoven's fifth piano concerto, along with a glass of iced coffee, served to save Suda from drowsiness somewhat. There were still some people in the books he wished he could have talked to, but he had no plans to do so now that he was not going to be paid any longer.

There were two volumes of company photo albums, and two volumes of family photo albums. Memories of his own days as an elite businessman came back to Suda as he skimmed through the company albums. Every time the company organized a trip, Suda had to go along to participate in a show of company unity. Everywhere they went, they took pictures. There was a picture of Kentaro grinning jubilantly, in a blue waterproof jumper suit, holding in his arms a large flat fish, balancing himself on the deck of a fishing boat. There was a picture of Kentaro in yukata, a Japanese bathrobe, in a hotel room with a group of his company buddies, lifting mugs of beer in unison, all smiling. It didn't take long before Suda found the familiar faces of Takeda, Sato, and Yoshikawa. The faces of corporate soldiers who were often willing to die for the company.

The first volume of the family album contained pictures taken in Japan. The optimistic faces of Miho and Kentaro certainly didn't show any sign of marital problems. There were many pictures apparently from their honeymoon. There were pictures with their families and friends. Who could have imagined Kentaro would one day become a target of investigation as a missing person?

The bulk of the second family album was allotted to their days in the U.S. Again, smiling faces stared right back at Suda. No sad faces, just happy ones. There was a picture taken in front of the Zatech office in Alabama with the other office workers. Iwao Takeda, Masao Sato, Lisa Parkins, Jean Konopinsky, and of course Miho and Kentaro. Looking for any clue that he might have overlooked the last time, Suda's eyes carefully roamed through the pictures until they landed on one and stopped. The picture was taken in front of someone's house. Miho, Kentaro, Sato, Takeda, and Jean Konopinsky were standing shoulder to shoulder smiling at the camera. Nothing unusual, except Suda's eyes were glued to the background of the picture. A car was in the background, a dark blue car! It might be a longshot, but it could have been the car the mystery woman presumably had driven.

Suda jumped up and dashed to his computer. An eternity seemed to have passed before his search engine showed up on the website.

Search: Buick

Return

Buick Century

Click

The distance and angle of the car in the photograph made it impossible to make a positive identification, but the car could easily have been a late-model Buick Century. Suda's hand reached for the phone immediately. He could no longer wait for two days to see Miho Suzuki.

Suda met Miho in a cozy cafe in the Shinjuku district, a meeting place Miho specified on the phone. Away from the bustling traffic of automobiles and pedestrians outside, the cafe was almost like an oasis in a desert. Artificial hibiscuses, oleanders, and cycad trees fittingly adorned the interior, and Mozart's piano sonata in the background was pleasant to his ears. But his mind was occupied with one thing—whether the dark blue car was a Buick Century, and if so, who owned it.

Seated across a walnut coffee table, Miho appeared tired and uptight. She looked outright haggard, in fact, having shed some weight since Suda had seen her last. Her long black hair had lost its shine, and her eyes wandered uncomfortably as Suda apologized for the inconvenience.

"I'm sorry I had to summon you like this, but I needed to see you as soon as possible."

"That's quite all right. I was trying to find somewhere to go anyway. I don't like to stay at home very much," confessed Miho, nursing a hot cup of Cappuccino and smiling weakly. The dimples on her cheeks had not changed.

Suda had already asked Miho on the phone whether she knew anyone who drove a dark blue Century. She could not answer the question because first she had paid no attention to who drove what, and second, she didn't know what a Buick Century looked like.

"It's this picture that I told you about on the phone. Do you remember taking this picture?" Suda asked as he put the picture next to her coffee cup on the table.

Miho moved forward to look at the picture, holding her hair in place, and immediately said, "Oh, yes. I remember."

"Whose house is this?"

"Mr. Takeda's. He had a party for all of us one day, and we took the picture in front of the house."

Suda's heart began to race.

"Do you remember this car in the background?" Suda asked, pointing to the vehicle.

Miho gazed at the dark blue car and shook her head slowly.

"Do you remember anyone driving this car?" he asked again.

"No, I don't...Sorry."

The car was parked in the driveway of Takeda's house. Suda knew Takeda drove a Cadillac, so the car must have belonged to one of the guests at the party.

"Was anyone else aside from the people in the office invited to the party?"

"No, it was just a little company gathering. So it was just the company people and their families."

"Was everyone from the company at the party?"

"I believe so."

"This is very important, Mrs. Suzuki," Suda leaned forward in his seat. "Please remember accurately. Was Lisa Parkins at the party, too?"

"Yes...Yes, she was at the party, I'm sure. I think she took the picture."

The tall blonde woman—Lisa Parkins! It had to be her. An affair between co-workers was a common story whether you were in Japan or America. Ever since Suda had found out about the car the mystery woman was driving, he had kept his eyes open for the dark blue Buick. He certainly had not seen it the parking lot of the Zatech office. In fact, he remembered Lisa driving a dark green Accord. She must have traded cars.

"When was this picture taken, Mrs. Suzuki?" asked Suda, hardly able to contain his excitement.

"Sometime last spring, I think. April or May."

Suda immediately realized problems with his conjecture. First of all, if the woman Kentaro was involved with had been Lisa Parkins, Takeda would have recognized her as his own secretary when he saw her with Kentaro coming out of the movie theater in Birmingham. Was Kentaro involved with more than one woman? Secondly, it seemed Lisa Parkins would have said something to the police when she had found out that Kentaro was missing. Did she want to keep her affair with him a secret? Or was she involved in the disappearance of Kentaro herself in some way?

"Does this have anything to do with my husband's disappearance?" Miho asked impatiently, gazing into Suda's face.

"As a matter of fact, Mrs. Suzuki, yes," Suda replied bluntly, meeting her inquisitive gaze.

Suda told Miho everything he knew and suspected about the case. This could be the last time he might see Miho. Suda felt it would be best for her to know everything even though the facts were unpleasant. Miho listened to Suda's explanation intently and reflectively. She didn't hide her shock and embarrassment when she heard about the possible affair between her husband and the woman, who could have been Lisa Parkins.

"So there is a chance my husband's still alive," Miho murmured, apparently bemused, looking down at the empty coffee cup on the table.

"Yes," Suda replied emphatically.

"And there is a chance my husband's with the woman," she said, gently caressing the rim of the cup with her hand.

"I think so."

Miho sighed deeply. This must have been the last place she wanted to be, Suda thought.

"Are you saying that the woman is Lisa?" Miho looked up at Suda's face, determined, with the same upward glance he had seen when he had first met her in his office.

"Not definitely," Suda said, holding her gaze. "But I suspect she is the woman. We can check it very easily."

Miho shook her head faintly and said, "I don't think I'm in a position to ask you to do that since we're no longer paying you. I'm looking for a job right now. As soon as I find one, I'm sure I can pay you some money."

Miho was a desperate woman trying to cling to the last ounce of hope she had, and for now, Suda was her only hope. Suda felt nothing but sympathy for this beautiful woman.

"You don't have to worry about that, Mrs. Suzuki. I won't be able to help you as much as I want to, but I'll see what I can do."

"Mr. Suda, all I care about at this point is for my husband to be alive. I don't care if he's with another woman. I want him alive and well. I want him happy."

Tears brimmed in her eyes as she expressed her feelings toward her missing husband. Apparently, Miho's devotion to her husband didn't sway an inch even after she had heard about the possible existence of another woman in his life. It was hard to believe Miho could have been a burden to Kentaro.

"I did a lot of thinking ever since you told me about what my husband had said about me to the bartender," confessed Miho introspectively. "I realized I'd made some mistakes. If I had another chance, I would do things very differently. My father has been a good company man all his life. I grew up watching him climb up the corporate ladder. I respect him for what he's accomplished. I've always admired his effort. But now I realize there are other ways of living. There should be other ways. There are other things that may be a lot more important than being successful in a company. I know I sound corny, but it's true. Now I realize how limited I was in looking at life."

Many housewives in Japan felt compelled to compete with one another by comparing their husbands' jobs, their husbands' companies, and their husbands' positions in the companies. Who had the best job and the highest position in the most respectable company became the measure of their social status.

If they couldn't compete using their husbands, they used their children instead. Whose children went to the best school became the measure of their own value. By doing so, they tried to satisfy their cooped-up frustration of keeping a household together while their husbands rarely came home early enough to have a dinner with the family. It was a trap set by the Japanese society, which still gave women lower salaries and fewer opportunities to work outside their homes. It was a trap Miho Suzuki, along with millions of Japanese housewives, had fallen into.

"Right now I just want a chance to apologize to my husband." Miho choked up as she uttered these words. "Hopefully, we can start a new life."

Miho was taking the whole thing way too hard, Suda felt. She was not on trial, after all. Nor was her relationship with her missing husband. He regretted telling her what Kentaro had said about her. Miho was clearly a good-hearted woman oppressed by the system called Corporate Japan. A woman like Miho did not deserve to suffer so much, but then, life was never a good dispenser of fairness.

"Mr. Suda, do you think the local police will be able to find him?" Miho asked almost desperately.

"They're doing their best, Mrs. Suzuki. I'll let them know about Lisa Parkins right away." Suda thought about Vicky.

Every step they took, Suda commiserated with Miho as he walked her through the unremitting rain to the nearest train station.

"Thank you very much...I just hope he's alive. That's the only thing I care about right now," said Miho and glanced up at the rainy sky as they parted at the station.

He watched Miho's small shoulders disappear into the herd of colorful raincoats. He hoped Kentaro was alive, too. For Miho's sake, Suda prayed that Kentaro was still alive.

2

To be a good detective, you have to forego your sentiments, Suda's father had once told him. In many cases, Suda had been very successful at that. After all, he was getting paid to do a job, not to feel sorry for a client or the subject of his investigation, and yet, this time the case really got to him. Miho Suzuki's charm as a woman and his sympathy for her may have had something to do with it, but there was something else that drove Suda in this case. Perhaps it was his background as a failed corporate soldier that drove him, or perhaps it was his professionalism that was being tested for the first time, or maybe it was his involvement with Vicky.

Suda didn't want to encourage Vicky to pursue the investigation on her own. Ever since the attack that took place on the dark alley that night, Suda felt uncomfortable about the investigation, much less letting his loved one continue with it. He had to let Vicky know over the phone about Lisa Parkins, however. It was the only chance if he had wanted to have this case resolved at all.

"But that's not gonna work." Vicky was quick to recognize the problem. "How could she be Lisa Parkins? Takeda said he didn't know her, right?"

"I know, Vicky," Suda conceded readily. "But it's possible that Suzuki was out with a different woman that particular night in Birmingham."

"You mean he was with a hooker or something?"

"I don't know. I feel anything is possible at this point. Just tell whoever's investigating this case what I told you. I think Lisa's the woman Kentaro was having an affair with."

"I'll go check it out myself."

Vicky was understandably excited about the potential breakthrough in the case—the very thing Suda didn't want to happen.

"Vicky," said Suda seriously.

"Yeah?"

"I don't know if that's a very good idea. Those men who attacked me haven't been arrested, right?"

"So?"

"Look, I almost got killed by those men. You don't know what they're gonna do next. I just don't want you to get into something dangerous."

Suda heard Vicky laughing.

"What the hell is funny?"

"I'm sorry. I didn't mean to laugh. Thank you for worrying about me, but all I'm gonna do is to take the picture of Lisa Parkins to Birmingham and ask the waitress if she recognizes her. If she's the woman, I'll just turn it over to the other guys and tell them to follow the lead."

"Are you sure?"

"Hey, I may not impress you as a brain, but I'm not stupid. If you're so worried about me now, what's gonna happen when I join the FBI?"

"Just be careful. I just want you to be careful."

"Yes, sir."

The composite picture of the woman had been a major stumbling block of the investigation since, according to Mary Delmonaco, the waitress, it didn't look anything like her. Using Takeda's quick impression of the woman for the picture was ridiculous to begin with. If Mary could identify Lisa as the woman who accompanied Kentaro, the case just might be halfway solved.

"You remember Joe Bodine?" Suda asked Vicky.

"Yeah, the gas station guy. He lives in Goodwater."

"That's right. Take the picture to him, too. There's a chance that Suzuki was involved with more than one woman. Also, if you can get in touch with Bonnie Laughlin, that would be great."

"I'll try. Send me Lisa's picture as soon as you can."

"I'll send you a few. Take whichever you think is the best picture of her."

Up until about 48 hours before, Suda had been hoping to take a nice vacation away from all the troubles of the world. The discovery of the dark blue car, which could have been the very Buick that Kentaro's lover had driven, in the album made it less likely that he was going to be able to, but now Vicky's involvement in the case made it practically impossible. At least, Suda was happy for Miho that Vicky was personally handling the case.

Suda sent the pictures of Lisa Parkins via overnight courier to Vicky as promised and anxiously awaited an e-mail message from her in return. The first message came back in a couple of days.

Hi Koji,
Received the photos. Taking them to Joe Bodine this afternoon. Will let you know the outcome as soon as I can.
Much love,
Vicky

The second message came back four hours later.

Koji,
Well, we may have the woman. Joe Bodine says Lisa looked a lot like the one he saw at the gas station. But, don't get too excited yet. Remember she was wearing sunglasses that day. At least this is a positive outcome, I think. I will drive to Birmingham tomorrow and try the waitresses. I miss you terribly. Do you miss me? I love you, Koji.
Thousand kisses,
Vicky

The next message came as a phone call.

"Well, you've got it. I think the woman is Lisa." Vicky sounded downbeat for a messenger of good news. "I checked with Bonnie, too, so now we've got the opinions from the three different witnesses. I think we have a positive identification now."

"Great!"

"But there's a problem."

"Yeah?"

"We don't know where she is."

"What're you talking about?"

"Lisa Parkins quit the job twelve days ago, and nobody knows where she's gone."

"What?"

"She didn't leave a forwarding address or anything. She just up and left. We're still checking on her friends and relatives."

There was good reason to be downbeat after all.

"So you didn't see her."

"No, but she used to drive a dark blue Buick Century. Her co-workers confirmed it. She got a new car sometime in July. We're checking all the auto-dealers in town to see exactly when she traded her old car in. She drives a dark green Honda Accord now."

"Damn it."

"Yeah."

"Did you tell Takeda that she might be the woman who was dating Suzuki?"

"Not yet. Do you think I should?"

Suda was curious what Takeda would say. Was it possible he didn't recognize his own secretary? Or was there another woman aside from Lisa Parkins?

"I'll leave that up to you."

"All right. Looks like we're finally on the right track. I'll keep you posted, Koji."

"You do that. Thanks a lot. I love you, Vicky."

Tracing Lisa Parkins shouldn't be too difficult. She could be easily traced by the car she drove. Zatech must have had the record of her previous employment and the names of the schools she attended. They might even have her home address.

Suda's thoughts jumped to the possible connection between Lisa Parkins and the men who attacked Suda. Maybe it was Lisa who told those men that Suda was sniffing around for Kentaro Suzuki. That might have been the reason why Suda was attacked. The two lines appeared crossed. But not so fast, Suda told himself. There was no evidence, yet. In any case, finding Lisa Parkins would have to be the first priority. At least now Suda knew for sure why Lisa had never smiled at him.

Suda had to wait two more days before he received another phone call from Vicky.

"We're still looking for Lisa Parkins."

"Any new discovery?"

"Not really. It's not like she's an escaped con, you know. People don't have time to look for a missing woman, especially when it's only us who are looking for her. It's hard to get other police departments to cooperate with us on this case," Vicky griped.

"What about the car dealers?"

"That's another thing. She didn't buy her new car in town. My guess is she probably went to Birmingham or Montgomery. She could have even gone as far as Atlanta or Mobile or even down to Florida. We're checking all the Honda dealers in Alabama, Georgia, and Florida, asking them if they sold any dark green Accords last July. That's gonna take some time. Accord is a popular car."

Lisa Parkins' background check was on a bumpy road also. Lisa was an out-of-towner who had lived in an apartment all by herself. She had many acquaintances but no close friends. She had moved from Birmingham to Moeling around the time the Zatech office opened in the city, and she had worked for Zatech since then. Lisa graduated from a high school in Birmingham and went on to graduate from a junior college there. When she was thirteen years old, her parents had gone through a bitter divorce, and her mother moved to Baltimore and remarried soon afterwards. Her father was an alcoholic and died in Birmingham two years prior to Lisa's move to Moeling. Lisa had worked in a bank in Birmingham since her graduation from the junior college, but no one in the bank was ever close enough to her to know her whereabouts.

"I'm still checking on her high school and junior college friends," said Vicky.

Lisa had an older brother living in Tampa, Florida, but according to him, he had not seen Lisa or heard from her since she graduated from high school, Vicky told Suda.

"This isn't gonna be easy." Vicky sounded tired. "By the way," she continued. "I told Takeda that there was a good chance Lisa was Suzuki's girlfriend."

"Yeah?"

"He looked really surprised. He said she wasn't the woman he saw at the movie theater, though. Do you really think there were more than one woman involved in this?"

"It looks that way, doesn't it?"

"I don't know…"

"What are you thinking?"

"I wonder if Takeda's telling the truth."

"Why would he lie?"

"I don't know. I just wondered about it. He's the only one who witnessed Suzuki with the other woman, right? Everyone else says he was with Lisa."

If Takeda had lied, he was probably trying to cover up the scandal in his office. He might have feared the marital infidelity between his workers could damage not only the company reputation of Zatech, but also his career as a manager. But would he have lied to the police to cover up such a minor scandal?

Hi Koji,

I called you earlier, but your phone seemed to be switched off. So I'm just dropping you a few lines to let you know what's going on over here. We're still looking for Lisa Parkins without any lead or clue to where she might be. One problem is Shugert is not really willing to spend more money looking for Suzuki or Lisa. We're a small city with a limited budget and resources.

I'm pretty much on my own now as far as this investigation is concerned. I'm doing my best, but please understand I have other duties as a police officer. And please don't worry about me, either. I'm not out looking for those men that attacked you, even though I want to find them and ring their necks for what they did to you. I miss you, Koji. Since you went away, I am leading a kind of a boring life. I know we have to give our relationship more time so that we can think about it. I just hope when all is said and done, we'll be back together again. We had so much fun together, didn't we?

Love always,

Vicky

Suda read the message when he got back from shopping in Ginza. He did have his cell phone switched off while he was riding the subway, as it was considered "impolite" to speak on the phone on the train in Japan. He missed Vicky terribly. Thanks to modern technology, he could get in touch with her almost anytime he wanted to, but that wasn't enough. He wanted to hold her and kiss her. He wanted to caress her and make love to her. Suda wondered about his future. Vicky was like a fresh breeze to his mundane everyday life. She was a ray of hope and a source of enormous joy. Without her, his life seemed almost meaningless.

The fact that the city police was tapering off its search for Kentaro disturbed Suda greatly. He knew missing person cases were not considered priority for the police unless the person was someone of significant stature. That was the reason he was hired for this case in the first place, but for Miho's sake, he wished things could have been different. If Zatech had put enough pressure on the local officials, they could have had a much more thorough investigation into this case—they could have even brought in the FBI. Zatech must have spent millions of dollars hiring lobbyists and lawyers in Washington to influence the politicians. Why couldn't they have flexed some of that enormous financial muscle for Kentaro?

The longer Lisa could not be located, the more it seemed that she was connected with the disappearance of Kentaro and possibly with Suda's attackers. The two lines appeared in front of his eyes again. The parallel lines that seemed to stretch endlessly like a railroad track. But they must have crossed somewhere along the way.

3

Suda was awakened by the ringing of his cell phone one early morning in mid-December. It was still dark outside and even darker inside. As Suda staggered to get to the phone, he hit his head so hard against the bookshelf he almost swooned.

"Hello?" said Suda, gripping the cell phone.

"Koji!" It was Vicky. The tension in her voice alarmed Suda. "The body turned up! It's probably his body!"

Vicky was practically screaming over the phone. It took Suda a second before he realized what Vicky was shouting about. They had found his body. Kentaro Suzuki's body had turned up. The circumstance surrounding the discovery of his body was not very clear even to Vicky. Apparently, his body had been found in a plastic bag tied to an anchor at the bottom of Lake Martin. Already the fish that had gotten through the torn plastic bag had eaten most of the flesh off the body, and whatever the fish had left had decayed away into the murky water of the lake. Only the clothing on the corpse suggested that the body was that of Kentaro.

"We notified the Zatech office to send us his dental record so that we can make a positive ID," Vicky explained. "I think it's him, Koji."

The news Suda had feared so long became reality like an odious intruder. They would make the positive identification in a day or two and notify the family members. He could not bear to think of Miho's reaction when she heard the news. The man she longed to come back to her would now come back only as gruesome skeletal remains.

Suda stayed in his office all day, restlessly waiting for another call from Vicky. The phone call came late at night.

"It was him, Koji," Vicky revealed darkly. "I'm sorry."

Suda's stomach sunk even though he had expected it all along. Maintaining his composure was not easy. He had never known Kentaro personally, and yet it felt as though he had just lost a close friend.

"Did you notify the family?" Suda asked Vicky.

"The Zatech office had already relayed word to the Tokyo office. I'm sure they'll soon notify the family in Japan if they haven't done that already."

"It's a clear-cut homicide case now."

"That's right. We're still waiting for a report from the coroner's, but it looks like somebody bashed him in the head."

"Did you actually see the remains?"

"Not me, but my fellow officer told me about it. What're you going to do?"

"I don't know."

Undoubtedly, the police would be much more serious about investigating this case from here on. There was bound to be media hype about this case on both sides of the Pacific Ocean. Perhaps going back to Alabama would be pointless for Suda.

"You keep me informed, Vicky."

"I'll do that."

Suda debated whether to call Miho. Expressing some form of condolence to her seemed only appropriate but not easy. Before he could make up his mind, the cell phone rang again. It was Miho.

"Hello, Mr. Suda? My husband has been found. He was found dead." Miho's familiar voice sounded calmer than Suda had feared. He realized she must have been in a state of shock.

"I heard the news. I was going to call you," said Suda in a subdued tone.

"I guess I expected it pretty much. I just wanted to thank you for all your help."

"I don't know what to say…I'm very sorry."

"Thank you…I'm flying to Alabama tomorrow with my husband's parents…"

"Please do take care of yourself."

"Thank you."

A bitter taste came up from Suda's stomach. Not only had he let down his client, but also he let himself down. Never before had he felt so helpless in this profession. Never before had he felt so defeated as a private eye. Suda felt for Miho—at the same time Suda felt burning anger. The anger was partially directed toward himself for his impotence, but the anger was chiefly directed toward the unknown killer—the killer who had made Suda feel inept, the killer who had deprived Miho and Kentaro of the happiness they rightfully deserved.

Koji Suda was on a plane the next day. He didn't give much thought as to what exactly he was going to do once he got back in Alabama, but at the same time, he knew he wouldn't be worth much of anything had he stayed back in Japan. He had to go back to Alabama. He had to see this case through. He had to…

There were a number of ways to get to Moeling from Tokyo. Miho, with Kentaro's parents, took a flight into Houston from Tokyo. From Houston, they would fly to Birmingham. Suda avoided Miho's flight since he did not wish to intrude in a moment of such sorrow. He instead took a non-stop flight into Dallas. The flight to Dallas was crowded with business passengers as well as people who were making an early exodus out of Japan, with Christmas break fast approaching. Suda felt alienated from the jolly tourists, probably headed for Florida using Dallas as a transit point. Except for seeing Vicky again, he did not look forward to this excursion at all.

A prim stuck-up woman in her mini-skirt, with a tasteless Louis Vuitton bag, sat next to him. She complained to a stewardess that she wanted a business class seat instead of economy. Tough luck! Suda felt bitter and gloomy all the way, but at least there were no babies on board this time.

Chapter 5

1

The coroner's report attributed Kentaro Suzuki's death to a single blow to the head. The blow was apparently made by a dull object such as a rock or a baseball bat. When he heard the report, Suda's thoughts immediately harked back to those men who had come after him with the baseball bats. The report also stated that determining the exact time of death was not possible, but the estimate from the degree of decomposition of his body, or what was left of his body, came out to be sometime around the month of July.

An intense investigation had already begun. A couple of homicide specialists were brought in immediately from the Alabama Bureau of Investigation, commonly known as the ABI. Following Vicky's lead, the search for Lisa Parkins and the men who had attacked Suda were going to become the focal point of investigation. Naturally Suda expected that he would be an important witness for the case.

The news of the discovery of Kentaro's body had spread through the media like wildfire. The city of Moeling had not seen a murder in twenty years. Needless to say, the town newspaper treated it as top news. The TV news in Birmingham and Montgomery reported it at the beginning of their evening broadcasts. The network news, as well as CNN and Fox, picked it up, and Suda had no doubt that it was widely publicized in Japan as well. Soon it was disclosed that the FBI was going to be in charge of the investigation. Considering the fact that the incident carried international significance, FBI's involvement seemed only natural.

Vicky was very happy and surprised to see Suda since he hadn't told her about his returning to Alabama. Equally surprised was Miho. She introduced Suda to the parents of Kentaro, who, as distressed as they were, had enough presence of mind to thank Suda over and over again.

"I was summoned here as a witness to the case," Suda lied to Miho although it just might turn out to be true. He did not want Miho to think his being there had anything to do with his relationship with Vicky.

There was a certain kind of uneasiness among everyone. The air was heavy and black, and yet at the same time, there was certain tension and, for a lack of a better word, a kind of excitement, a kind that only grave and tragic circumstances could bring about. The Suzukis checked into the motel where Suda had stayed before. The last thing Suda wanted was to run into the family in the motel lobby or restaurant. Fortunately, Suda didn't have to think long on how to avoid the awkward situation.

"Why don't you stay at my house?" Vicky suggested. "We have a guestroom downstairs where you can stay."

Suda had no reason to refuse Vicky's offer.

A simple funeral ceremony was promptly held for Kentaro, with his wife, Miho, and his parents in attendance. Iwao Takeda, Masao Sato and his family, the Yoshikawas, Shugert, and the mayor of the city were just some of the people gathered to pay their respects to the victim and his family. No one could overlook the insolent presence of TV and newspaper reporters and camera crew swarming in the area, either. A formal funeral service, along with a memorial service, was to be held in Japan when Kentaro's ashes returned to the place of his birth.

The day was a beautiful winter day, sunny and mild, which served only to accentuate the tragedy of the situation. Suda could not bear to watch Kentaro's mother crumble to the ground as she cried out for her dead son. As she was helped up by her husband, Miho remained motionless as if she had lost all her vitality. The pain Suda felt when he lost his parents all came back to haunt him. The pain of losing your loved ones—myriad had gone through it before and myriad would go through it in the future—would never become easier to bear even after a long time.

A hectic two days passed like a storm, as Kentaro's remains awaited cremation pending FBI approval. Miho spent the days being a subject of intensive questioning by the press as well as the police and the FBI. Suda had anticipated being questioned by the men from the FBI, but for some reason, perhaps because they figured they already had enough information from Suda via Vicky, he was excused from the whole rigmarole. As for the news media, Suda avoided them for good reason—he was in town under false identity as far as most people were concerned.

When the Suzukis finally left town with Kentaro's ashes, Suda for the first time had a chance to sit down with Vicky in the living room of her house for a long talk.

"An amateur fisherman discovered the body. It was wrapped in a black plastic bag and tied to an anchor at the bottom of the lake," Vicky informed Suda grimly, furrowing her brows.

Lake Martin, like most of the lakes in the vicinity, was a man-made lake created in 1926 by damming the Tallapoosa River in order to provide the area residents and industries with electricity. In the summertime, the water of the lake was kept at its maximum level for recreational reasons, but in the wintertime, by an agreement with the local electric company, the water level of the lake was dropped by some 15 feet. The dropping of water began after Labor Day and went on until mid-February when it reached its lowest level. As a result, during this time, a substantial portion of the lakebed became exposed, often with its shoreline receding as much as 50 yards in some areas.

"That's why he was never found in the summer," Vicky expounded further. "Lake Martin can be as deep as 500 feet at its deepest area, but Suzuki's body was not at the deepest level. Otherwise we would never have found him."

The fact that Kentaro was found as a gruesome skeletal carcass was still shaking Suda. He feared Lisa Parkins might have encountered the same fate.

"We're thinking along the same line, too. You know we've been looking for her for nearly three months, now. I think the reason why we can't find her is that she is dead," said Vicky.

"Are you going to look for her in the lake?"

"That's practically impossible, Koji. Lake Martin has a shoreline of 750 miles and it's 40,000 acres in area. Unless we have some concrete idea of where to look, it's impossible."

"Do those guys from the FBI have any suspects at this point?"

"Well, I told them everything I know. They have all the information we collected so far, but they haven't told me anything one way or the other."

The murder was the work of locals, Suda felt. Probably the same group of men who attacked Suda. For out-of-towners like Suda, who were so unfamiliar with the local geography or culture, this crime would have been too much to handle. Vicky concurred with Suda, and she didn't forget to mention that if some local thugs had indeed killed Kentaro, they probably would be still hanging about the area.

"Those guys just don't leave the area much, Koji. I know you've seen their faces, but it was dark, so they probably figure you won't recognize their faces even if you run into them on the streets. Besides, if they took off all of a sudden, it would be like telling the whole world that they are guilty."

Being back with Vicky again was nice. She didn't ask Suda why he came back, and he didn't say why, either. Vicky did not hide her happiness being in his arms again. Suda made love to Vicky that night for the first time since he came back to Alabama. He tried his best to forget the tragic image of Miho and Kentaro's parents at the funeral, but somewhere in the back of his head the image kept on knocking at the door of his consciousness.

Vicky took Suda down to the lake the next day. The dense forest that extended along the roadway like great parallel walls had long since lost its luscious glow, and the dazzling golden rays from the sun that had reflected off the scorched surface of asphalt had turned into the mild illumination of winter. Only the evergreen needles of towering pine trees reminded Suda of the brilliant summer that once was.

"If Lisa has been killed and buried somewhere in these forests, we would never find her," Suda said to Vicky as they strolled along the shoreline.

In general, a killer has a very tough time disposing of a dead body, Suda was once told by a professional homicide detective. If you bury it, a dog or some other animal might dig it up unless you bury it very deep. But to make a hole big enough to accommodate a human body is an all-day job. If you burn the body, the peculiar smell of burning flesh travels very far, and again it is an all-day job. To carry it around would be too conspicuous. So in many cases, a killer decides to cut it into pieces just as a butcher dissects a pig or an ox. "That way it's much easier to get rid of the body," he said to Suda.

Suda remembered a heinous case where a husband had killed his wife and put her through a wood chipper to get rid of her body. What had given him away was a wisp of the hair that was stuck at the shaft of the rotating blades. Chills had run down Suda's spine when he had heard the story. How cruel and callous a man could become.

From the serenity of the lake, it was hard to believe something as horrible as the murdered body was found in the water only several days before. The shoreline had receded markedly as Suda had been warned, but the lake still retained a significant body of water. Vicky took him to the location where the body was found. He had to walk some fifty yards on the mushy lakebed to get there.

"It was only about twenty feet from here," said Vicky, standing at the edge of the water and pointing to the approximate location where the body had been recovered.

"Did the man know it was a human body?"

"At first, he didn't. He saw something showing from a hole in the plastic bag. He looked at it for some time before he realized it was a human head."

The visibility in the water must have been only about a couple of feet. Seeing the body in the summertime, when the water level was some 10 to 15 feet above the present level, would have been virtually impossible. Why the murderer had sunk the body of Kentaro in the lake was obvious. He wanted this case to be only a missing person case. He did not want the police investigation to intensify.

"Officer, is this where the body was found?"

Suda turned back to the voice and saw an old man with a fishing pole standing behind Vicky and him. He was talking to Vicky who happened to be in her uniform.

"Yes, it is," Vicky responded politely.

"I live right over there." The man pointed toward the woods nearby. "It's scary something like this could happen," said the man glancing at Suda skeptically.

"Did you see anyone suspicious sometime in July around here?" Vicky questioned the man.

"No…Just a bunch of kids having fun, that's all. A police officer came to my home yesterday and asked me the same thing. I think if anybody had done a thing like this, he must have done it real late at night. When we were all asleep, you know. Because in the daytime there are too many people around here," the old man remarked, peering over the still surface of the lake.

"Right now we're going door to door looking for witnesses. When you and I came out here for a swim at night, we saw some fishing boats, right? There might have been someone who saw or heard the murderer dump the body in the water," Vicky later explained to Suda.

"If the murderer had pretended to be a fisherman himself, it would have been awfully hard to tell what exactly he was doing," observed Suda.

"I know."

That was why Suda suspected some local thugs to be the perpetrators, particularly the ones that ganged up on him. They could have pretended to be fishing while disposing of Kentaro's body without being suspected by anyone. Still, they had apparently been cautious enough not to go too far off shore. The further they had gone, Suda speculated, the more time it would have taken, and thus, the more likely they could have been witnessed. The body had been dumped only about 50 yards away from the shoreline. The problem was that the lake was too shallow there.

2

Christmas was just around the corner. Even to a town still shaken by the discovery of the murder, the jolly season was coming very much like every year. Lines of colorful lights were stretched around area houses and streets, and the whole town took on the aura of a dreamland, as families gathered in holiday spirits and businesses and shops prepared themselves for the biggest do-or-die sales occasion of the year. Suda helped Vicky trim a seven-foot tall Christmas tree with lights and tinsel in the house. He also put out wreaths on the front and back doors, and the house was ready for Christmas.

Lisa Parkins had yet to be found, and there was no suspect for the murder of Kentaro. The homicide detectives from the FBI left town for the time being. They wanted to celebrate the Christmas holidays with their families, too. Suda and Vicky came to the mall to pick out Christmas presents for each other and for Vicky's parents and sister. The mall was jammed with the hordes of last-minute Christmas shoppers scurrying back and forth, carrying armfuls of gift items. The day was unseasonably warm, and the sky was bright, not at all like the cold northern sky above the land where Christmas might have originated. Suda could get by with a T-shirt if he had wanted to.

"What is your sister's name, again?" Suda asked Vicky as they approached the entrance of the mall.

"Virginia. You can call her Ginny, of course."

Virginia was supposed to arrive back from college the next day. She was a law student intending to be a prosecutor in the future.

"She's the brain of the family," said Vicky jokingly.

"What's this about you and your sister? You make an arrest and your sister's gonna prosecute?"

Vicky laughed.

Suda and Vicky split up in the mall so they wouldn't know what they picked out as Christmas presents for each other. Uplifted by the steady flow of Christmas music from the loudspeakers, Suda's feet were light and his spirit was merry. The shopping was a smooth-sailing experience. Suda found a designer tie for Vicky's dad and an antique cameo brooch for her mother. He didn't have trouble finding presents for Vicky and her sister, either. He purchased a beautiful pair of sterling-silver earrings for each of them. For one precious moment, Suda left behind the death of Kentaro and the dreadful sorrow that had gripped his wife and the family. Suda was to meet Vicky at the entrance of the mall in exactly one hour. With fifteen minutes left at his disposal, he decided to browse. He wanted to look at tennis shoes in the sporting goods store, though he had no plans to buy a pair.

A man in a baseball cap was loitering in front of the shoe rack when he got there. Suda didn't pay much attention to the man, except to his dirty long red hair that jutted out below the rim of his oil-stained baseball cap. In the corner of his eye, however, Suda saw the man glimpse at him and take a few steps back as if he were jolted by an electric shock. When Suda turned to him, he was already walking away with his back turned toward Suda. How peculiar, Suda thought. Then it hit him. The man was one of them! He was one of the attackers who almost killed Suda that dark summer night!

Without a moment's hesitation, Suda took off after the man. He was about ten yards ahead of Suda, evidently not aware that Suda was following him. Suda hastened his steps. The distance to the man became eight yards. Seven yards. Six yards. Suda debated what to do with the man. Perhaps it would be better to keep a distance and see what he would do. Taking down the license plate number when he got to his car would be far better than confronting him on the spot.

"Koji!"

Shit! Vicky's voice came from nowhere. Before Suda could respond to Vicky, the man ahead of him made a dash. He must have seen Suda. Suda had no choice but to run after him.

"Call the police!" Suda shouted to Vicky wherever she happened to be.

The man was fast but not fast enough. Suda caught up with him in no time and grabbed him by his shoulder. The man turned around, obviously intending a counter-attack. Suda didn't give him the chance. With a twist of the upper body, he landed a straight right smack on the man's conspicuous red nose. The man staggered. Suda heard the screams. He didn't ease up. He tackled the man, and together they crashed through a show window and plunged into an apparel store. Suda got on top of the man and wrestled him to the floor. The man spitted out something, but Suda didn't understand what he said. The man was bleeding profusely from his nose and his head. He was stronger than Suda, but Suda had the advantage of position. There was one thing Suda had learned in his high school Judo class: how to hold down a man who was twice as big as you.

"Koji! What is it? Who is it?" Vicky caught up, her face red with agitated confusion.

"Did you get the police?" asked Suda while still struggling with the man on the floor.

"Yeah!"

Vicky was not in uniform. She had no handcuffs. Suda was doing his best trying to hold the man down. He noticed his hands were bloody from cuts he must have received when he and the man broke through the show window glass.

"Help me out, will you?" Suda shouted at Vicky.

Vicky quickly took one of the man's arms so that he wouldn't be able to push Suda off.

"Are you all right?" Vicky asked Suda, looking into Suda's face.

Suda heard the heavy breathing and saw the blood gushing out of the man's nostrils. His body odor was almost intolerable.

"This is the guy who attacked me…One of the guys." Suda could barely talk out of his mouth. He didn't have any saliva left.

The mall security guards came running.

"All right, you guys, break it up!" One of the guards ordered with authority.

"I'm a police officer! This man's under an arrest!"

Swiftly Vicky pulled her police badge out of her pocket and held it high on display above her head.

The man's name was Joe Montcrief. He worked as an auto mechanic in Goodwater. He was twenty-five years old and married with two children. He had no previous conviction or arrest record. Although he admitted to the police that he was a frequent customer at Bob's bar, he kept his mouth shut when asked about the attack on Suda. Suda had no doubt that Montcrief was one of the attackers. As far as Suda was concerned, Montcrief's reaction toward him in the mall proved that he was one of the men. Be that as it may, it would be one man's word against another. Joe Montcrief just had to be let go on the condition that he would voluntarily come back to the police station on a later date for more questioning.

"That's preposterous!" Suda raised hell in the police station. "He may be the one who killed Suzuki, and you're letting him go?"

"That's just the way the system works. You're lucky you didn't get charged for assault." Sergeant John Brown admonished Suda with a sneer.

"You're out of your mind. You're making a serious mistake!" Suda contested ferociously.

"Who are you calling 'out of mind'?" Brown raised his voice, glaring at Suda.

"Let's go, Koji. We have to go." Vicky pulled Suda to the side and whispered. "You can't make enemies here. You need all the friends you can get."

"I never thought Brown was a friend of mine."

"Come on. Let's go."

Vicky took Suda's arm and literally pulled him outside.

"All right, what's going on here?" Suda said once they got into Vicky's car.

"Koji, you have to listen to me." Vicky held his hands reassuringly, looking into his eyes. "I know you're upset and everything, but this is not Tokyo. This is Alabama. People don't look at you kindly if you beat up on the local boys."

"What the hell are you talking about?" Suda snapped, pulling his hands away from Vicky's. "He's the one who almost killed me. He could be the one who killed Suzuki."

"I know, but we have to let him go now," Vicky replied calmly. "We know now where he lives, right? We'll check on him later."

"What if he skips out of town?"

"He's not gonna do that. Think about it. That's gonna be like admitting his guilt. We just have to wait for those homicide guys to come back after Christmas. They'll know how to interrogate him, believe me."

Suda was fuming, but Vicky had a way of appeasing him.

When they returned to the house with the Christmas presents, Virginia surprised them by coming home a day early.

"Ginny, when did you come in?" Vicky hugged her little sister warmly as she climbed out of the car.

"About two hours ago. Did everything go all right?" Virginia peered at Suda inquisitively.

Vicky had called the house and explained the situation so that her parents wouldn't be worried about them.

"Yeah…This is my little sister Ginny." Vicky turned to Suda and introduced Virginia.

"Hi, nice to meet you," she said jovially.

Virginia looked like a young Vicky except her face was rounder and she had hazel eyes. She didn't look quite as athletic as her older sister, either. She gave a softer milder impression overall.

"Hello, we've finally met," Suda returned the greeting, smiling a friendly smile.

"How are your hands?" Virginia was looking at Suda's hands all wrapped up in bandages.

"They're all right. Just minor cuts." Suda lifted his hands in front of his face and wiggled his fingers.

"I heard all about it from mom and dad. I hope everything is all right," said Virginia with a concerned look.

"Me, too." Suda shot a protesting glance at Vicky. He still couldn't believe that the police had let the man go.

"How come you decided to come home early? We were expecting you to get here tomorrow," Vicky said, ignoring Suda's glance.

"I know. I just couldn't wait to see your new boyfriend," said Virginia and playfully winked at Suda.

"Call him Koji," Vicky said to her sister as they walked to the house.

"O.K. Vicky told me a lot about you, Koji."

"A lot of nice things, I hope."

"No, I told her all the bad things," Vicky teased Suda.

It was nice to see all the family members united that night. Suda was thankful and flattered that he was included in this family reunion on a special occasion. Suda felt the effort made by everyone in the family to make him feel at home. He had encountered the same kind of hospitality almost anywhere in the United States. America was a contradiction for Suda. Americans at times seemed obsessed with violence and power as though they were driven by a demon, and yet Americans could be the kindest people in the world.

Suda would have really enjoyed the night if it had not been for what had transpired earlier in the day. He just could not shake off the idea that they had let the murder suspect go so easily. The night had deepened, and everyone said "Good night" to each other. Suda tucked himself in the guestroom bed and waited for Vicky as usual. Her parents knew that they were sleeping together, but Vicky said she wanted to be discrete since they weren't married or even engaged. Suda didn't mind feeling like a teenager sneaking off from his girlfriend's parents.

"How do you like my sister?" Vicky asked in bed, resting her head on Suda's chest.

"She's neat. She looks like you."

"What did you think? She's my sister."

Suda was thinking about what had happened in the mall. The way Vicky pulled out her badge and declared that she was a police officer was just like watching a scene from a Hollywood movie.

"You know you were really cool, today," said Suda.

"Me? Why?"

"The way you got your badge out. If I hadn't been in love with you already, I'd sure have fallen in love with you then."

"And here I thought you were the coolest guy I ever met."

Vicky looked up at Suda with her liquid-green eyes beckoning for love. Suda put his lips against hers, holding her closer. He smelled the sweet scent of her hair and the seductive scent of her love. He wanted to forget everything that night, and forget he did by burying himself in a wild and beautiful creature named Veronica.

3

Joe Montcrief confessed to the police the attack on Suda that took place on that September night. Apparently his lawyer advised him to do so in order to avoid getting tagged with the more serious crime: the murder of Kentaro Suzuki. Once Montcrief had admitted his guilt in the attack, it became a matter of time to find the four other attackers.

INTERROGATION OF JOSEPH P. MONTCRIEF

Suspect: Joseph Paul Montcrief
Age: 25
Sex: Male
Race: Caucasian
Criminal Record: None

Police: When did you see Koji Suda for the first time?
Montcrief: I saw him in the bar talking to Bob.
Police: Bob is the name of the bartender, correct?
Montcrief: That's correct.
Police: Why did you decide to attack him?
Montcrief: I don't know. We just got together and decided to beat him up.
Police: Who are "we"?
Montcrief: (Silence)
Police: What did you all talk about when you discussed beating him up?
Montcrief: I don't remember.
Police: Did you decide to beat him up because he was Japanese?
Montcrief: I guess.
Police: Did you try to kill him?
Montcrief: No. We just wanted to rough him up, that's all. We just wanted to scare him a little.
Police: You needed baseball bats to scare him?
Montcrief: Why not?
Police: So what happened? You almost killed the man.
Montcrief: Well, we just wanted to scare him a little, but he became violent, swinging his fists and kicking us. So we had to fight back.
Police: So you beat him unconscious.
Montcrief: We just roughed him up. That's all.
Police: How often do you go to Bob's bar?
Montcrief: Oh, maybe once a week, once a month. It depends.
Police: Bob says you're one of the regulars there.
Montcrief: Whatever he says.
Police: Have you ever seen this man in Bob's bar? (Kentaro Suzuki's picture is shown to the suspect.)

Montcrief: I don't know.

Police: Are you sure?

Montcrief: Yeah, I have seen the man.

Police: What did you think of him?

Montcrief: Nothing much.

Police: What do you mean by that?

Montcrief: I mean nothing much.

Police: You mean he was "nothing" like dirt or something.

Montcrief: (Silence)

Police: How many times have you seen this man?

Montcrief: Twice or three times, I don't remember. It was a long time ago.

Police: Did you beat him up like you beat up the other Japanese guy?

Montcrief: No. Never.

Police: How about your friends? Did they beat him up?

Montcrief: I don't know. I don't reckon so.

Police: Did you hear about anyone beating this guy up and killing him?

Montcrief: No.

Police: You saw the news on TV that this guy was missing, didn't you?

Montcrief: I don't recall.

Police: Where were you on the night of July 13th?

Montcrief: What day is that?

Police: It was a Sunday.

Montcrief: I was at home with my wife and kids.

Police: You remember what you were doing that long ago?

Montcrief: I don't remember exactly, but I'm usually home with my family on a Sunday night.

Police: What about on the night of July 14th, Monday.

Montcrief: I don't remember exactly, but I reckon I was with my family also.

Police: July 15th?

Montcrief: The same.

Following Joe Montcrief's interrogation and a background check on Montcrief's circle of friends, the rest of the men who had participated in the attack on Suda were apprehended within days by the police. Suda was called in and asked to identify his attackers among the lineup. He had no confidence in identifying the men before he saw their faces, but to his surprise, all the memories of the night came back to him vividly. Apparently, fear had a way of engraving the images on his cerebrum like photography. The information on the four men was released in the town paper the next day.

Name: Jonathan Parker Campbell
Age: 30
Occupation: Carpenter
Marital Status: Divorced

Name: Michael Jackson Barnhardt
Age: 35
Occupation: Unemployed
Marital Status: Married

Name: Timothy Russell Getz
Age: 22
Occupation: Mill worker
Marital Status: Single

Name: Ronald Herbert Depriest
Age: 23
Occupation: Mill worker
Marital Status: Divorced

The men admitted to the assault on Suda, but they all firmly denied having anything to do with the disappearance of Lisa Parkins or the death of Kentaro Suzuki. Lack of physical evidence and the uncertainty in the time of death of the victim made it impossible to link any of the men to the death of Kentaro or the disappearance of Lisa. Suda was frustrated. His hatred for the five men had long reached the pinnacle, and yet, Suda was forced to watch them walk away with an assault charge or attempted murder at best.

"You know you may have a tough time convincing the jury that they tried to kill you," Vicky advised Suda.

"Why's that? You saw me the way I was. So did the other police officers and EMS guys."

"I know. You looked pretty bad, but remember, the only thing broken was your left arm. You had a minor concussion and cuts and bruises, but that's all."

"Damn it, Vicky. Whose side are you on?"

"I'm just stating the facts. The jury would think if those guys had really wanted to kill you, they would have used guns or knives. Don't forget you're faced with local boys. And they're all Caucasian. More than likely, the jury's gonna be all white. I'm not saying you can't convict them. I think the jury would find them guilty, but don't expect them to get the maximum sentence. That's all I'm saying."

One of the men, T. Russell Getz, had been charged with assault before but never been convicted. Three others had been arrested for DUI, and yet Suda knew what Vicky told him would probably turn out to be true. Although he had never experienced it personally, Suda had seen such examples over and over again in America. There lay another contradiction of America. People who profess to believe in fairness and equality often shut their eyes to racial prejudice or other forms of bigotry.

The only thing Suda could do at this point was to dig up some witnesses who had seen any of the men at the lake sometime last July or seen them with Lisa Parkins at any time. Even then, it was improbable that the murder of Kentaro Suzuki would ever be attributed to these men. Suda debated whether to press charges against his attackers. Even if they were found guilty, as Vicky said, chances were they would never be charged with attempted murder. More than likely they would be charged with assault and come out of jail in less than a year at most. Suda didn't fear their retribution, but he feared that Kentaro's murderer would become even harder to catch as a result. Even a child knows that generally the longer you wait, the harder it becomes to solve the case.

4

In late January, the case took a strange and unexpected turn. The sheriff's office suddenly produced several witnesses who linked one of the five men, John Campbell, directly to the murder of Kentaro Suzuki. One witness even claimed to have seen John Campbell actually dump what appeared to be Kentaro's body into Lake Martin on the night of July 14th of last year. Suda was flabbergasted when he heard the news from Vicky. The city police with the cooperation of the homicide teams from the FBI and ABI working together had tried their best to find witnesses and failed. The discovery of Kentaro's body had been widely publicized, and yet no witnesses had ever stepped forward in all this time. Why did they come out now?

John Campbell was rearrested and charged with the murder of Kentaro Suzuki immediately following the testimony by the eyewitnesses. The news of his arrest reached all over the nation and across the Pacific Ocean to Japan. The Zatech headquarters in Tokyo and the government of Japan praised the effort made by the local police and FBI. The question the public asked was no longer whodunit, but whether John Campbell would be convicted and if he was, what kind of sentence he would receive.

"The eyewitness account alone may not be enough to convict him," Vicky said to Suda.

"What other witnesses are there besides the guy who saw him at the lake?"

"Well, there are a total of three witnesses. One is the guy you just mentioned. Another one says he saw Campbell driving Suzuki's car toward Atlanta, and the last one swears he saw Campbell arguing with Suzuki on the Saturday before his disappearance."

"How reliable are they?"

"I don't know. What do you think? The key witness is the guy who claims that he saw John Campbell at the lake actually dump the body, right? But it was at night, and the body was wrapped in the black plastic bag as it was. How could he have seen it so clearly? It probably won't stand up in court."

The day after John Campbell had been rearrested, the sheriff's office came up with the physical evidence that could well stand up in court. They found a rope in Campbell's barn that was identical to the rope used to tie Kentaro's body to the anchor. No one knew where the anchor had come from. No stolen anchor had ever been reported by any of the boat owners at the lake.

"But there are hundreds of identical ropes, aren't there?" Suda questioned Vicky.

"Apparently it's the way the rope was cut. The edge of the rope that was around Suzuki's body matched the edge of the rope that was in John Campbell's barn."

John Campbell was a big man—6 feet and weighing over 200 pounds, and being a carpenter, he had strong arms, too. He could have pulled off this hideous crime all by himself with ease. The murder weapon had never been found, but Campbell's toolbox was full of tools that could have been used as a murder weapon.

"Well, what do you think? Is he guilty?" Vicky asked Suda.

"It looks that way. What do you think?"

"I don't know."

Vicky did not look at all convinced that this case was over. Suda didn't feel particularly good, either. Perhaps he, just as everybody else who was connected with this case in one way or another, was simply tired of the case and wanted it to come to a conclusion, but at the same time, could not believe the case was coming to its end so swiftly and simply.

MIHO SUZUKI'S LETTER

Dear Mr. Suda,

It has been almost two months since I last saw you in Alabama. I was surprised to find out that you are still there. And it has been almost two months since I had to come to terms with my husband's death, too. I must confess for some reason, I did not feel a great deal of sorrow. Perhaps I was prepared for his death. Perhaps I was angry at his betrayal. Or perhaps I did not love him as much as I thought I did. I feel sadder about the fact that I did not feel very sad about my husband's death.

I do not mean to dwell on my personal feelings. I am writing to you to thank you for all your help. I am delighted that the murderer was finally caught. I spoke to one of my husband's colleagues in the company the other day. He told me Mr. Takeda had a lot to do with the arrest of the murderer. Mr. Takeda pressured the Zatech headquarters to get tough with the local and state officials there. I thanked him on the phone the other day. He is the one who told me you were still there, in fact.

I find it rather ironical that my husband, who really did not like his life as a company man, was helped by his company in his death. I guess I am supposed to be grateful to the company, too. I'm sure there will be more and more Japanese people arriving in Moeling soon. It's funny I feel a certain pride in them although I have nothing to do with Zatech anymore. They tell me once a corporate soldier, always a corporate soldier. Perhaps it is true that once a corporate soldier's wife, always a corporate soldier's wife.

Please accept the enclosed check from my family and me as a token of appreciation. I do not know whether we will ever see each other again, but I wish you all the happiness in the world. Please take care of yourself.

Sincerely yours,
Miho Suzuki

The trial date for John Campbell was not yet set. Suda would have to have his authorized stay in the country extended if he had wanted to stick around for the trial, but the prosecution no longer needed him as a witness. Apparently, they felt confident enough with the combination of the physical evidence and the witnesses they already had.

Suda felt he couldn't stay in Moeling much longer. What worried him most was that his long absence from Japan would erode the foundation he had established as a private eye. It could mean the end of his career.

"I heard something interesting in the office today," Vicky said to Suda one day as she ironed her uniform in her room. "Do you know there are some people who believe that John Campbell was framed for a crime he didn't commit?"

Suda was not surprised at Vicky's words. He expected the voice of dissention in one form or another.

"Do they have any facts to back it up, or is this just one of those many opinions of theirs?" asked Suda as he flopped down on her bed, playing with the handcuffs.

"I don't know. I'm just telling you what I heard in the office today. I thought you might be interested."

Vicky had not said anything openly, but she was obviously unhappy with the outcome of this case. The talk of the town was that John Campbell would be convicted and would receive a maximum sentence.

"All right, Vicky." Suda tossed the handcuffs down on the bed. "Let's hear your opinion. What do you think about the whole thing?"

"What do you mean?"

"You obviously don't think John Campbell is the killer."

"That's not true."

"What is it, then?" Suda was vexed by Vicky's indirectness. "I've been feeling these strange vibrations from you."

Vicky stopped ironing and looked up, with certain determination, at Suda's face.

"I just don't feel right about the turn of events," she said. "Don't you feel it's strange that all of a sudden those witnesses showed up? The whole business about the rope cut in a certain way—that's a bunch of BS, I think. I think it's phony. You know it's not us who came up with that evidence. It's the sheriff's office."

"Is that how your police buddies talk about this case?"

"You don't have to be the police to notice something funny's going on here."

"If it's funny, why don't you go talk to the proper authority?"

"Shugert doesn't want to cause waves without any evidence. We can't go against the sheriff's office and the DA's office without any concrete evidence."

Suda was thinking about the letter from Miho. The letter clearly stated that there was some pressure on the local officials from the Zatech headquarters. A curious silence by the FBI and ABI agents since Campbell's arrest was intriguing and disturbing also.

Understandably, Zatech was not very enthusiastic about pursuing their missing employee in the beginning. They had probably been informed of the rumor of the illicit affair between Kentaro and Lisa Parkins, and wanted to keep it as quiet as possible. Equally understandable was why Zatech appeared to have suddenly changed its mind after Kentaro was found murdered and decided to become aggressive about the search for the killer. They probably feared the adverse effect it might bring to the morale of the Japanese employees at Zatech-Alabama if the killer were never caught. If John Campbell had been framed as Vicky suggested, the perpetrator would have been none other than Zatech Corporation itself.

The question was whether the local officials would succumb to pressure from Zatech so easily, especially to the point that the sheriff's office would manufacture false witnesses and evidence to convict an innocent man. They would be risking a major scandal by going along with Zatech if they had done so.

"There's nothing to it." Vicky didn't hold the local officials in the same light as Suda. "A false arrest is not that uncommon. Even a false conviction is not that uncommon. Witnesses can always say 'Oops, sorry, we had it wrong' without worrying about serious repercussion. In the same way, all the police or the sheriff's office has to do is to say 'I'm sorry we had a wrong man.' It's almost impossible to prove malicious intent on the part of the witnesses or local officials in a case like this since everyone is in it together. Just about the best we can hope to do is to prove their negligence."

Suda could have just sat back and relaxed. The killer of Kentaro Suzuki was arrested as far as most of the world was concerned, and Suda had gotten paid handsomely by his client. The problem was, however, that there were such things as honesty and fairness, which Suda happened to believe in, and of course, there was Vicky overtly displaying her dissatisfaction.

"What do you want me to do?" Suda asked Vicky.

"What do you mean?"

"You think I should do more on this case, right?"

"I just don't wanna send an innocent man to the death row, Koji," said Vicky. "And you're the only one who can stop it. We're not free to investigate Zatech the way you can. You can look into Zatech and tell the world if anything's wrong with it without jeopardizing your job or reputation."

Easier said than done. Suda heaved a long sigh. But at the end of the day, Suda couldn't say "No" to Vicky. He couldn't say "No" to his conscience.

"Where do you think I should start, Vicky?"

"Why don't you talk to John Campbell? If you think he's guilty after that, you don't have to do anything else."

"Is that possible?"

"Leave it to me." Vicky smiled confidently.

5

Suda felt uneasy about seeing John Campbell's face again. Since his arrest, Campbell had consistently denied killing Kentaro or knowing the whereabouts of Lisa. Suda was fearful that his own prejudice would preclude a fair judgment on ascertaining Campbell's guilt or innocence, whichever the case might be. After all, as Suda believed, Campbell was one of the men who almost killed him.

The meeting took place in the county jail where John Campbell was incarcerated after his bail had been denied. As Suda sat across the Plexiglas divider, facing Campbell, he could not help but think about the night he was attacked by the five men. This was the first time Suda had come face to face with Campbell since that night, and Suda remembered him all right. He was one of the two men who carried a baseball bat in his hand.

Campbell sat in front of Suda with a sneer on his face, his ice-blue eyes glaring at Suda defiantly. His thin blonde hair was uncombed and dirty, and his sandy white skin looked more like that of a reptile than a human being. Anger came up from deep within, but Suda kept his cool demeanor. He was not here to condemn the man. He was only here to judge him.

"I suppose you remember me," said Suda quietly.

Campbell said nothing. He kept on glaring at Suda as if he were going to attack any minute if given a chance. To feel so much hatred from a man he hardly knew was shocking, but Suda did not wince.

"I came here to talk to you, Mr. Campbell. I came here to ask you questions."

Campbell's face was still as Suda stared right back at him.

"Why did you kill Kentaro Suzuki?" Suda asked.

Campbell's expression remained motionless. This could very well be a big waste of time, Suda thought.

"Why did you attack me?"

Obviously, Campbell was determined not to respond to any questions he was asked. Perhaps he was instructed by his lawyer not to talk to anyone before the trial. Suda had hoped he might be able to have some form of conversation with this man so that he would not have to go home empty-handed. He gave up on the idea of direct questioning and decided to change angles.

"I'm not a Zatech employee." Suda forced a smile. "In fact, I'm a private detective hired by the wife of the man you killed. The reason I took the job was because I felt sorry for the wife and his parents. I don't know about you, but I've lost my loved ones before, and it really hurt. So I came here, to Alabama. You know I was kind of worried at first. I thought Alabama must be such a racist state that I might get chased away on the first day I arrived here. Well, I was wrong. The people in this state had been extremely nice to me. Of course, there are people like you who hate Japanese."

"I have nothing to say to you." John Campbell opened his mouth and interrupted Suda.

It was the very voice Suda had heard the night of the attack. A thick rural Southern accent that sounded almost musical. Suda felt a shudder run through his body. Stay calm, he said to himself.

"Mr. Campbell, I was hoping we could have a frank talk today. It looks like you're not prepared to do that."

"I have nothing to say to you. You dirty Jap! You framed me. You goddamned framed me."

Spit flew out of Campbell's mouth and landed on the glass divider. His eyes glared with hostility.

"Mr. Campbell." Suda raised his voice a notch higher. "I'm not connected with Zatech. I have nothing to do with framing you."

"Shit! You Japs are all the same. You sneak. You cheat. You steal. You lie. You ain't telling me no shit!"

"No. We are not all the same, and I'm not lying to you. Just like there're many different Americans, there're many different Japanese."

Campbell scoffed at Suda's words. Suda searched in his face for a trace of civility—or something that could give him a chance to mollify Campbell's unceasing rage and hatred.

"Mr. Campbell," said Suda, again, lowering his voice and looking into his eyes. "If you had really killed Kentaro Suzuki, then I would never forgive you. I'd hope you would receive a maximum sentence and receive a good dosage of lethal injection. But if you did not kill Kentaro Suzuki, and if you have been framed like you say you are, then I'd be on your side. Tell me, who do you think framed you? Zatech?"

John Campbell looked away from Suda as if he had not heard him at all.

"Tell me the truth, Mr. Campbell," demanded Suda with authority. "Did you kill Kentaro Suzuki?"

Campbell, with his face deadpan, had apparently decided not to talk again. Suda stood up. He saw no reason to continue his efforts. As he turned toward the exit, he heard the voice of John Campbell again.

"I didn't kill no Jap."

Suda turned to Campbell. He was looking at Suda in the same angry hostile manner.

"Can you prove it?" Suda asked as he came back and sat down. Campbell shook his head side to side.

"I'm the only one without an alibi," he mumbled weakly. "So they tagged this thing on me. I'm clear, man. I didn't kill the Jap."

"You were never out on the lake that night?"

"No. I don't even have a boat."

Suda gazed at the man, long and hard. Is he telling the truth?

"What were you doing that night, then?"

"Like I told the police already. I don't remember. I'm being honest, man. I mean who would remember what he was doing some six months ago?"

"But the rest of you, I mean the rest of the men who attacked me… They all remember where they were on the night of the 14th of July."

"I don't know how they remember. They could have made it all up. What do they care, huh? All they're interested in is to frame me and make me the murderer. I didn't do it, man. I didn't kill him."

"Who are they? Who do you think is trying to frame you?"

"Those Japs, man," Campbell growled. "The Zatech scum, and the police are going along with it. They need the business, you know, so they made me into a sacrifice. I'm a sacrificial lamb."

"Did you tell that to the police?"

"Yeah…Why would they listen?" Campbell shrugged, twisting his lips. "They're not on my side."

"What about your lawyer?"

"Yeah, but I don't trust him. He's just like the rest of them."

"Who do you think killed the Japanese?"

"I don't know. I honestly don't."

"Could it be one of your friends who attacked me?"

"I really don't know. If I knew, do you think I would be sitting here keeping my mouth shut? Think about it, man. I ain't stupid."

The great hostility that once engulfed John Campbell's face had subsided. The man who faced Suda was no longer a loathed beast but a desperate human being. Suda had no intention of making peace with him, nevertheless.

"Can you back up your claim in any way?" Suda asked Campbell.

"Back up what?"

"That you're framed by Zatech."

"Shit, if I could do that, I wouldn't be sitting here talking to you," Campbell snarled.

"Where did you get this idea, then? Did someone tell you?"

"I ain't no dummy."

"Did you think about talking to the press about this?"

"They ain't gonna listen. There's no proof to what I'm saying, you know. I think everybody in the state of Alabama is in on this. From the Governor on down to the local police. Everyone's in on this conspiracy. They all want the Jap factory and Jap money. Big business always talks, you know? Hell, we go to war so that big corporations can keep on doing what they're doing. I'm a sitting duck ready to be shot."

Suda did not trust John Campbell any more than he trusted the others who assaulted him that night, but there was some degree of plausibility to his story, particularly in the light of the rather odd turn of events in the last few weeks. Even if Campbell were lying, the story seemed worth looking into.

"Can you really help me?" asked Campbell, his face harboring a look of a cornered animal. Suda felt uneasy being asked to help the man who nearly killed him.

"I'll see what I can do," replied Suda without conviction as he got up to leave.

"We really didn't mean to kill you, you know."

They were faint but distinct words that came out of John Campbell's mouth. Suda refused to believe him.

"You know you broke my nose, too."

As John Campbell kept on, Suda turned around and walked away from the glass wall that seemed to have existed between them since the beginning of time.

Motivation plays a key role in the success of any activity, and a criminal investigation is certainly no exception. After talking to him, Suda was not at all convinced that John Campbell was innocent of the murder of Kentaro Suzuki. Suda had expected him to deny his guilt, of course, but he was hoping he could read something in Campbell's expression. Unfortunately, all he could see was a man of desperation and anger, looking more and more like a mad dog, which Suda believed he was. Suda didn't think Campbell was necessarily guilty of the crime, either, but it was difficult for him to bring himself to work hard just to save the neck of the man he so despised.

"Well, what did you think?"

Vicky was standing by her car outside the jailhouse, arms crossed in front, waiting for Suda.

"I don't know, Vicky." Suda shook his head in ambivalence.

He knew he had to keep the investigation alive, if anything, for Vicky's sake. The question, however, was how alive?

"You still think he's guilty?"

"Like I said, Vicky, I don't know. He was barking at me like a mad dog, though."

"Koji, don't feel like you have to keep at this case on account of me."

"I didn't say that, Vicky."

"Then what is it?"

Vicky stared into Suda's eyes as if she were trying to read his mind. Ordinarily, those big green eyes could play magic on Suda's mind, but this time he felt nothing but irritation from her long stare.

"Vicky, I don't know whether the man is guilty or not," said Suda, avoiding her eyes. "At this point, I don't think I really care either way. I hate this guy, Vicky. He's nothing but a racist pig. I hope you still remember this guy almost killed me. How am I supposed to feel sorry for a man like that? You tell me, huh?"

The last thing Suda wanted to do was to disappoint Vicky, but sooner or later his true feelings had to come out.

"I don't blame you for feeling that way," said Vicky quietly. "I don't particularly care about John Campbell, either, you know."

"I'm not saying I'm quitting. It's just that I don't feel very enthusiastic about helping that son of a bitch."

"I know," she acknowledged readily, and then walked around her red Mustang and opened the door.

"Hop in!" she commanded.

"Where are we going?"

"I'm taking you somewhere."

"Where?"

"Just come with me."

Vicky's tone of voice carried certain force. As usual, the Mustang took off like a bat out of hell as soon as Suda buckled himself in the passenger seat. In no time, the vehicle was on a country road that twisted like a tapeworm through the walls of pine forests. Vicky did not say anything. Neither did Suda. He still felt disturbed from his earlier meeting with John Campbell.

The somewhere Vicky took Suda was an old wooden shack that stood on about a half-acre lot tucked away from a narrow country road. The weeds, apparently uncut for months, grew wildly in the front yard, where old rubber tires and children's plastic toys covered with mud lay scattered about. A couple of automobiles sat decrepitly parked in the yard as well— one clearly inoperable and the other an old Chevy truck with a rusted tool chest in the back. A run-down barn, with its half-rotted roof and crooked front door halfway open, barely stood some ten yards from the main house. The white smoke billowing out from the auburn brick chimney indicated that the place was inhabited, but poverty was written all over the place.

Vicky stopped the car in front of the house and cut off the engine.

"Whose house is this?" Suda turned to Vicky.

"John Campbell's."

"Why the hell?"

"This is where he was born and raised. Do you know who lives here now?" Vicky continued solemnly, ignoring Suda's question. Suda raised his brows, faintly shaking his head.

"His mother and two children," she revealed, looking over toward the house.

"I didn't know he had kids," said Suda.

"I didn't either until the day before yesterday."

Suda was beginning to see Vicky's intent.

"John Campbell's father died when John was twelve years old," Vicky went on. "His mother was not very healthy, so he had to work in order to support his family. In addition to his mom, he had to take care of his two younger sisters and a grandmother who was bedridden. John Campbell married his childhood sweetheart, Liz Atkinson, at the age of twenty-three, but the marriage didn't last too long. His wife ran off with a preacher, leaving two children behind. They are five and three year olds now."

"Are you telling me that I should feel sorry for John Campbell?" said Suda testily.

"No, I'm not telling you to do anything. But I spoke to his mother yesterday. He's been a good son for her and a good father for the children. She says it was impossible for him to have killed Mr. Suzuki. She says he was too good a man to have committed such a horrible crime."

"And you believed what a mother says about her son."

"I think I do," she answered tersely.

"Come on, Vicky, don't be naive," Suda objected. "This guy was gonna kill me, remember? If what his mother says is right, who the hell was holding a baseball bat in his hand that night?"

"I spoke to John Campbell, too." Vicky was unmoved.

"So?"

"You've read Joe Montcrief's confession about the night they all attacked you."

"You showed it to me."

"Do you remember what he said?"

"Yes." The conversation was getting old for Suda. "He said they didn't mean to kill me. Do I believe him? Absolutely not!"

"Koji, John Campbell said the same thing to me. He said they just wanted to scare you off. But you started to fight back so hard that they had no choice but to rough you up."

"Bullshit!"

"I'm not kidding. You know you broke John Campbell's nose. A couple of the other guys got their ribs bruised and jaws busted. You put up a hell of a fight that night, Koji. If they had really wanted to kill you, they could have. But they didn't. What does it say?"

"It says you guys got to me before they could finish me off."

"Koji, you're being intentionally obtuse."

Suda had to admit rather reluctantly that Vicky might have a good point. It still didn't mean John Campbell was innocent, but it might mean Suda was looking at him a little too harshly.

"I know they're racist pigs like you say," relented Vicky. "And I hate them for what they did to you, Koji. But I still think John Campbell is a human being and he deserves justice."

A thin old gray-haired woman in her long dark brown dress came out of the house with two children. She recognized Vicky and waved at her, smiling.

"Hello, Mrs. Campbell. How are you today?" Vicky waved back and got out of the car to greet John Campbell's mother. "I've brought the man I was telling you about yesterday. He's the man who might be able to help your son," Vicky announced and nudged Suda to get out of the car as well. He did, mustering an awkward grin.

As Vicky introduced him to Campbell's mother, Suda was looking at the old woman's skinny shoulders and bony hands. They were a testament to the hard life she had led. In contrast, the children were as cute as angels. It was hard to comprehend such precious things were fathered by a man like John Campbell.

"Miss Vicky tells me you're a very good man," the old woman said with a gentle smile, her country accent sounding very much like her son's, and lowered her aged head slightly. The children hid behind their grandmother's long skirt and sheepishly peeked at Suda and Vicky.

John Campbell was scum as far as Suda was concerned, but Vicky's point was well taken. Suda always believed that a man should not get punished for a crime he did not commit, but perhaps now Vicky added a little more conviction behind the belief.

6

Due to the international implication of the incident, the U.S. government itself was probably eager to see the end to this case as soon as possible. Suda would not have been surprised if Zatech, through diplomatic channels, had in some way influenced the FBI investigation. In fact, from Miho Suzuki's letter alone, Suda had no doubt enormous pressure from Zatech had persuaded the local officials to arrest and indict someone for the murder of Kentaro. As far as Zatech was concerned, and perhaps some high-ranking federal and state government officials were concerned, that particular someone could have been anybody. John Campbell, with his tough luck, just happened to be an easy target. Proving the existence of such conspiracy, however, would be a formidable task. Suda could quite possibly have the entire state of Alabama turned against him if he stepped on the wrong toes.

The best thing to do was to find the true killer if indeed Campbell was not the one. That, however, was the very thing neither Suda nor anybody else, for that matter, could do so far. The second best thing, then, was to show that there was a reasonable doubt about Campbell's guilt, thereby preventing his conviction. In order to do that, first, the jury selection could not be biased, and second, John Campbell must be represented by a better lawyer, possibly one from outside the influence of Zatech's economic clout. Suda could not have achieved such an objective by himself, and there was only one man whom Suda could turn to—Lansford W. Bartlet.

"Lansford Bartlet is in the hospital. He's dying from cancer."

"What?"

Vicky's words jolted Suda. Suda remembered how sad Lansford Bartlet looked as he stood at the door of the mansion to see Suda off. He probably knew that he was dying then.

"How close is he to death?" Suda asked Vicky.

"No one knows. Most people don't even know he's in the hospital."

"I wonder if I can go see him."

"For what?"

"I think he's the only one who can influence this case. At least he's the only one I know."

"I don't know, Koji," said Vicky, faintly shaking her head. "You'll be walking on thin ice."

Vicky's reluctance aside, Suda had already made up his mind. He was certain Bartlet would offer his help.

Lansford W. Bartlet was hospitalized in the building that bore his own father's name, one of two hospitals in the city of Moeling. The old-fashioned red brick building stood surrounded by gorgeous pines on the tract alongside the land occupied by the Bartlet Corporation. The air was chilly and breezy outside, but Suda had to take off his jacket once inside the building. The interior looked surprisingly modern, which was a testament to the hospital's state-of-the-art facilities.

"I'd like to see Mr. Lansford Bartlet," said Suda as he walked up to a middle-aged receptionist who sat behind the counter in the nurse's outfit. Suda had brought with him a bouquet of flowers.

"I'm sorry, sir, but Mr. Bartlet is not receiving any visitors," the thin-lipped receptionist coldly said to Suda.

"Would you please tell him Koji Suda's here to see him?" Suda pressed.

"I'm sorry, sir. He will not see anyone outside the family." She didn't even look at him this time.

In a sense Suda felt relieved that he was refused permission to see Bartlet. He remembered how his mother had wasted away from cancer. He did not wish to see a man like Bartlet all wasted away. Just when Suda had turned around to go back in defeat, holding the bouquet dangling upside-down by his side, a woman strutted into the entrance, and Suda's breath almost stopped. A tall blonde! Lisa Parkins? Suda took a second look and realized that she was not Lisa Parkins although there was some undeniable resemblance. She must be one of Bartlet's daughters, Suda thought. Then it dawned on him. Teressa Bartlet!

Suda followed the woman with his eyes. As he had guessed, the receptionist greeted the woman as if she were some sort of a royalty. Suda didn't hesitate to walk up to her.

"Excuse me, but you must be Miss Teressa Bartlet," he said.

The receptionist looked at Suda with a frozen expression on her face.

"Yes, I am. And you are?" Teressa's sleepy blue eyes met his as she pirouetted to face Suda. Standing in front of Suda, Teressa looked over six feet tall in her heels. As Vicky had informed him once, Suda could see certain wildness in Teressa's eyes.

"My name is Koji Suda. I've come to see your father," declared Suda succinctly, with a slightest smile etched on his face, looking up at her beautiful expressionless face.

"I'm sorry Miss Teressa, I told him Mr. Bartlet is not receiving any visitors, but…"

Teressa Bartlet paid no attention to the receptionist, who was apologizing profusely.

"Is he expecting you?" she returned, deadpan.

"When he hears my name, I think he'll want to see me."

Teressa Bartlet gazed into Suda's face suspiciously. Suda recalled what Lansford Bartlet had said about his youngest daughter.

"Your father told me you're studying to be an actress in New York."

The timing was immaculate. And the ice thawed.

Teressa broke into a wide-open smile and said, slightly cocking her elegant head to one side, "I'll tell him you're here. Please wait for me, O.K?"

Suda ignored the annoying glance of the receptionist, as he paced about the lobby of the hospital while he waited for Teressa. A gorgeous magnolia tree overshadowed a bronze bust of Charles H. Bartlet, the founder of the hospital, just outside the entrance, and a couple of squirrels played hide and seek scurrying in between the bust and the magnolia tree. In less than five minutes, Teressa Bartlet came back down.

"My dad wants to see you," she announced with a friendly grin.

Teressa carried with her the same kind of confidence that some contestants in a beauty pageant carried. She stood tall and walked elegantly with firm strides. Suda wondered, as he often wondered about those beauty pageant entrants, how she had acquired such poise and elegance at such a young age.

"Don't you hate hospitals?" Teressa said to Suda in the elevator, turning her head to look into his face. She spoke with the same genteel Southern accent as Vicky's, though more slowly.

"Yes, I do. Both of my parents died in a hospital."

"I'm sorry to hear that. I lost my mom in this hospital." She frowned.

"Do you know Veronica Royce?" Suda asked.

Teressa's face brightened at the mention of Vicky's name.

"Yeah…Are you a friend of hers?"

"Yes. She told me you used to ride a horse in your yard."

And her eyes twinkled in mirth.

"You know I'll be in town for a while. Tell Vicky to come see me sometime. We went to the same high school."

"I know."

"I was a big time tennis player in school, and she was a big time swimmer. We sort of kept our eyes on each other."

Apart from a certain physical resemblance, Teressa was nothing like Lisa Parkins as Suda remembered. Lisa had neither the personality nor the brain of Teressa Bartlet. Suda could tell Teressa was as smart as a whip. As they approached the hospital room, Teressa became quiet, and Suda could not help feeling the mounting tension in his body.

"I've brought your friend, Daddy," said Teressa, opening the door quietly.

Suda was afraid he might see a skeleton-like figure on the bed. To his pleasant surprise, Lansford W. Bartlet, as he sat up in bed being fed intravenously, with an oxygen mask at his bedside, did not look nearly as bad as he could have. He had clearly lost some weight, but not that much. His face was somewhat pale, but still showed signs of rugged masculinity. The room could have passed as a hotel room with a full set of expensive furniture along with all conceivable amenities, including a television set, telephone, fax machine, and a personal computer.

"Hello, Mr. Suda...Not exactly the best place to receive a guest." Lansford Bartlet's genuine smile greeted Suda as Teressa took the flowers from Suda's hand to put them in a vase. "What brings you here today?" His voice was still strong, and so was his handshake.

"Mr. Bartlet, I've come here to ask for your help," Suda confided as he pulled a chair up to the bedside as directed by Bartlet.

Suda was blunt and direct in his approach. Lansford W. Bartlet listened to Suda's concise but thorough explanation with great interest. As the time went on, Suda saw the energetic color gradually come back to Bartlet's face. It seemed as though Bartlet was trying to gather strength, when he had so little left.

"So you believe Zatech is behind all this," said Bartlet after hearing Suda out.

"Most definitely."

"I see. It seems what I've feared all along has come true. A foreign influence making mockery out of the integrity of our nation."

Bartlet lowered his head, apparently lost in thought for a moment. When he looked up, Suda saw almost a cheerful and certainly a spirited expression on his face.

"Well, I must thank you for telling me all this, Mr. Suda. You see ever since I became ill, people stopped telling me what's going on in the city," confessed Bartlet and glanced at his youngest daughter's face in jestful admonishment. "They think it'll put unnecessary stress on me. They just don't realize I've always thrived on competition."

Bartlet's laugh was interrupted by a series of violent coughs, which seemed to embarrass him more than to upset him. By a sweeping hand gesture, he stopped Teressa from rushing to his bedside to rub his back.

"Mr. Suda," said Bartlet, regaining his upright posture. "If what you've just told me is true, this just might be the kind of scandal we need to stop Zatech. I'll direct my staff to look into this, and I'll see to it that man, Mr. Campbell, will get proper legal representation."

As Suda shook the old man's hand good-bye, he felt the warmth of Lansford Bartlet's heart. Perhaps it was the side of the man Lansford Bartlet almost never allowed himself to show, but Suda felt it deep in his gut.

"Mr. Suda," Lansford Bartlet called Suda, as he was about to exit the room. "I understand you're courting Royce's girl."

When Suda looked back surprised, he saw the father and the daughter with playful grins on their faces.

"When I'm cooped up in a room like this, all I hear is gossip. She's a wonderful girl. Take good care of her."

"I'll do that, Mr. Bartlet." Suda smiled back, sensing this was probably the last time he would see Lansford W. Bartlet alive.

Chapter 6

1

Inadvertently, Suda found himself going head to head with Zatech Corporation, a company that could single-handedly represent the post-WWII economic miracle of Japan. As a man who turned his back against Corporate Japan long before, Suda should have had no second thoughts about exposing Zatech's underhanded tactics concerning the present case, but as a man who was born and raised in the uniformity of Japanese culture, he could not help feeling like a traitor.

Suda could never understand how so many Americans disregarded the national interest of their own country and lobbied for their foreign industrial clients, apparently without feeling any remorse. Japanese could not get away with such acts without getting branded economic traitors and banished for life from Japanese society. There was nothing illegal about lobbying for foreign interests, but what was legal and what was socially acceptable were two different things.

"Koji, Lansford Bartlet died."

It was a dark rainy day when Vicky broke the news to Suda. Suda had met Lansford Bartlet in the hospital room only two weeks before. The death of the man came much earlier than Suda had anticipated. The announcement that the trial of John Campbell had been postponed indefinitely came a day earlier. Suda didn't know whether Lansford Bartlet was conscious enough on his deathbed to appreciate his last victory. Suda had met the man only twice in his life, and yet he felt a great loss at the news of Bartlet's death. When a man dies, he takes a large chunk of history with him. If only the circumstance had allowed, Suda would have liked to talk to him about his illustrious life and colorful experiences. Lansford W. Bartlet would certainly have told many interesting stories.

Although the press had never reported it, obviously a great deal of political tug of war had been going on behind the scenes of John Campbell's forthcoming trial. Time would only tell how the death of Lansford Bartlet might tilt the equation. For Suda, what needed to be done was to find the real murderer of Kentaro Suzuki, and it had to be done with great urgency. Vicky had been working day and night trying to come up with a thread that could connect Lisa Parkins with the rest of the five men who attacked Suda. Suda had been to Birmingham and Atlanta, searching for witnesses who could have seen Kentaro anywhere anytime. Despite their valiant effort, nothing of substance had yet to come from it.

The rain fell constantly into the night as if to mourn the death of Lansford Bartlet. Suda and Vicky had stayed by the fireplace in the den almost all day without doing anything much. They were both very tired.

"You know what I was thinking," said Vicky as she leaned her back against Suda's chest on the couch. Suda had just finished building a fire in the fireplace.

"What?" He put his arms around her waist and pulled her closer.

"The murderer who killed Suzuki," she murmured.

"Yeah?"

"I don't think whoever killed Suzuki is one of the locals."

"What?"

Vicky gently undid Suda's arms and moved away from Suda to face him. Suda looked into Vicky's face. She was dead serious. All this time, the assumption was that Kentaro had been murdered by someone who was well versed in the local geography and culture.

"The murderer sank Suzuki's body in the lake hoping that the body would never be discovered. If the murderer was one of the locals, he wouldn't have dumped the body in the lake like that," Vicky said.

"What do you mean?"

"Anybody who lives in the city knows the lake water goes down in the wintertime. They wouldn't risk having the body exposed knowing about the lake water going down in the winter. They wouldn't have dumped the body that close to the shore."

The fire logs popped, spewing sparks. Vicky turned to the fire, showing her profile, radiant, reflecting the color of the flickering flames from the fireplace. The room had warmed up to a comfortable temperature.

"Well, Lisa Parkins was an out-of-towner…" Suda mumbled.

But Lisa couldn't have pulled this thing off, at least not by herself. She wasn't strong enough.

"Koji." Vicky paused, shifting her expressive eyes to Suda. "This may sound outrageous, but don't you think Mr. Takeda looks like Kentaro Suzuki?"

The fire logs popped again. It had never occurred to Suda. Takeda was tall and lean, and so was Kentaro, but the resemblance stopped there, Suda had thought. Kentaro was younger than Takeda by some eight years, and he looked meek as opposed to the energetic Takeda. Of course, Suda had not seen Kentaro in person, but judging from the picture, Kentaro had bigger and gentler eyes than Takeda, and Kentaro's lips were fuller than Takeda's thin lips.

"Yeah, but both of them wear eyeglasses, right? It's no joke when we say y'all Orientals look alike, you know. Y'all really do," Vicky said.

"Do I look like Takeda, too?"

"Come on, you know what I mean."

"So what're you suggesting?" Suda looked into Vicky's green eyes.

"Well, I was just wondering if we'd been going after the wrong guy," she said. "Suppose it was Takeda who was having an affair with Lisa Parkins. I don't know about Japan, but in the U.S., an affair between a secretary and her boss is very common."

"Why did Suzuki have to get killed as a result of that?"

"I don't know…Maybe Suzuki found out about Takeda's affair with Lisa and blackmailed him or something."

"So Takeda killed Suzuki?"

"Something like that."

Blackmailing his boss would have been very uncharacteristic of Kentaro, Suda thought, but then again, he didn't forget he had been wrong before. But Takeda killing Kentaro? All Takeda had to do was to deny having an affair, and then it would have been one man's word against the other's. Or did Kentaro have some concrete evidence that his boss was having an affair? Did he have a photograph or recording of some sort? Would Kentaro have gone that far to get at Takeda? Highly unlikely. Even if he had, what would Kentaro have gained by blackmailing Takeda? Money? Kentaro was not poor by any means. He had a well-paying job in a prestigious company. Blackmailing his boss would have been suicidal for his career. Would Takeda have killed Kentaro for such a reason, anyway?

All questions aside, Suda found himself quickly drawn to Vicky's new theory.

"If we think of it that way, everything makes sense," Vicky continued. "That story about Takeda witnessing Suzuki with some blonde woman in Birmingham was a complete fabrication. That's why his description didn't match that of Lisa Parkins. That was his smoke screen. And…"

"Wait a minute," Suda interrupted. "Which came first, Takeda's testimony or the waitresses' testimony?"

"Takeda's."

"Right. Because of Takeda's testimony, the police started looking around that motel, right? And they found more witnesses there. Why would Takeda have falsified information that could possibly incriminate himself? It makes no sense."

"The first witness was the gas station attendant." Vicky did not retreat. "Because of him, we went to talk to Takeda to ask whether he knew anything about the suspected affair between Suzuki and the blonde woman. For Takeda, it was a very convenient misunderstanding. Instead of his affair getting exposed, he decided to substitute Suzuki in his place. That way it looked like Suzuki just eloped with the woman. But he had to make sure the identity of the woman was hidden, so he made up that stuff about seeing Suzuki and the woman in Birmingham and gave a totally wrong picture of the woman. It makes a lot of sense, I think."

"Yeah, but how did he know those waitresses wouldn't give away his identity?"

"He didn't know. But that's the gamble he took. Remember it was dark in that restaurant. Maybe Takeda knew he looked like Suzuki. Maybe he was mistaken for Suzuki in the past. Anyway, he almost won."

Suda had to watch himself being swayed by Vicky's enthusiasm. He could not forget that there were still questions to be answered.

"You were going to say something else, weren't you?" Suda asked Vicky.

"Oh, yeah…The phone calls, you know the ones Suzuki supposedly made to the lawyers in Atlanta and…"

"To Takeda."

"Yeah. Maybe those phone calls were made by Takeda himself."

"How did Takeda call himself?"

"No, dummy, just listen. We only know Takeda received the call from his testimony, right? Maybe he made it up. He never received a phone call from Suzuki that day."

"In fact, Lisa told me it was she who received the phone call from Suzuki and relayed it to Takeda," Suda acknowledged.

"It makes sense. She was only collaborating with Takeda."

"What about the lawyers?"

"How would the lawyers have known the phone call was from Suzuki? It could have been made by Takeda. You see, Koji, it makes sense that way. Suzuki's wife never got a phone call from her husband that day, right? The reason is she would have recognized immediately the caller wasn't her husband."

"Why did he have to make the phone calls at all?"

"I don't know about that. But I can think of some reasons. Maybe he needed alibi in case Suzuki's body turned up sooner than he wanted. Maybe Takeda killed Suzuki and didn't know what to do with the body, so he needed the time. Suzuki's disappearance was not reported to us until Wednesday, July 16. If the lawyers had not been notified of the cancellation of the meetings, they could have called the Zatech office raising hell by the afternoon of the previous Monday, July 14. Let's suppose Takeda killed Suzuki on Sunday and didn't know what to do with the body. He wouldn't have wanted anybody looking for Suzuki until he disposed of the dead body, so he had to postpone the disappearance of Suzuki as long as possible."

"But Miho Suzuki could have called Kentaro at any time. She had his cell phone number," Suda said.

"So? You know as well as I do that cell phones can become out-of-range or run out of battery all the time. I don't think that was a factor at all in Takeda's mind."

"Maybe you're right, but I think those lawyers would have recognized the difference between Takeda's voice and Suzuki's voice," Suda persisted. "From what I understand, they'd been dealing with the lawyers for quite some time. I've never heard Suzuki speak, but I imagine there was a difference."

"You think so?"

If what Vicky had conjectured was true, it would make one hell of a crime story. Vicky's theory was certainly entertaining if not intriguing. Still, it was too early to give any credibility to it since the theory lacked any factual basis. First and foremost, Suda did not see any reason whatsoever for Takeda to kill Kentaro. The only thing that led to the mushrooming of the speculation was that Vicky thought Takeda looked like Kentaro. That hardly constituted viable evidence, but be that as it may, Suda believed some things definitely needed to be checked out.

"Vicky, why don't you talk to the lawyers and see if they're really sure that the call they received was from Kentaro Suzuki?" Suda suggested. "I'll take the picture of Takeda to those waitresses and ask them if they think Takeda could have been the man they saw with Lisa Parkins."

"O.K."

"I wonder if we could check the phone records of Zatech and Takeda's residence."

"We can't really do that without a court order, and they aren't gonna give it to us right now. We don't have any evidence to charge Takeda with any crime."

"I think I may just enter Takeda's house without a court order, then. I may be able to find something interesting if what you're saying is true."

"You can't do that," said Vicky seriously.

"I can do anything I want to," Suda returned jokingly.

"You're talking to a police officer."

"Are you gonna arrest me?"

"Don't risk it."

Suda knew this was no joking matter. He would not only jeopardize Vicky's career but also risk himself getting arrested if caught committing an unlawful entry into a private residence. Furthermore, Suda knew that any evidence obtained illegally would be inadmissible in court. The judge might even decide to throw out the entire case as a result. The temptation, however, was too great. If Takeda had been the perpetrator of this horrific crime, he must have left a trace somewhere that could point to his involvement. The best place to start the search for such a trace, Suda felt, was Takeda's house.

2

Suda met with the two waitresses, Mary Delmonaco and Bonnie Laughlin, in Birmingham at a popular restaurant near the college Mary attended. Both women had been cooperative from the beginning, but this time Suda felt obligated to reward them with a free lunch. This was the first time Suda met Bonnie, a chunky, jolly brunette, whose chipmunk teeth peeped out adorably whenever she laughed. The two women sat side by side in front of Suda, somewhat taken by the gravity of the situation since they were now fully aware, from all the media attention the incident had received, of the significance of their testimony.

"I want you girls to remember what the man looked like one more time," said Suda, gazing at the attentive young faces. "Bonnie, I want to ask you first."

Bonnie nodded and shot a quick glance at Mary. Suda turned to Mary. "Mary, would you please close your eyes for a second?"

Mary shut her Melanie Griffith eyes tightly on command.

Suda pulled a picture out of his inner jacket pocket and placed it on the table. It was the picture Suda had borrowed from Miho, the picture taken in front of Takeda's house with Miho, Kentaro, Sato, Takeda, and Jean Konopinsky standing side by side.

"Tell me," said Suda to Bonnie. "Do you see the man you waited on in the restaurant in this picture?"

"Yes." Bonnie did not hesitate to answer, looking down at the photo.

"Which one is he?" Suda asked.

"This one." Bonnie's finger stopped on Takeda's face.

"Thank you, Bonnie," said Suda and turned to Mary. "You can open your eyes now, Mary."

Suda's heart was pounding fast. What Vicky had said was coming true before his eyes.

"Now, you heard the question, right? Point him out for me, Mary."

It took a while for Mary to make a decision, but her finger landed on Takeda's face, too.

"Why did it take so long, Mary?" inquired Suda.

"I was trying to decide between this guy and this guy," Mary pointed to Kentaro and Takeda. "They look alike."

"Yeah, they look like brothers," remarked Bonnie.

"So what made you decide it was this guy?" Suda asked Bonnie, pointing to Takeda.

"Well, it's kind of hard to say, but he has the same kind of mood, you know, like kind of dark and mean." Bonnie turned to Mary, seeking her consent.

"Yeah, he wasn't cheerful and nice like this other guy," Mary agreed with Bonnie, fingering Kentaro.

Both Kentaro and Takeda were smiling in the picture, but Suda understood what the girls meant by such adjectives as "dark," "mean," "cheerful," and "nice." Takeda did carry a rather grim and serious atmosphere with him.

On the way back from Birmingham, Suda stopped by at Joe Bodine's house in Goodwater. The visit was unplanned, but Bodine welcomed Suda into his cozy dwelling like an old friend. A copper kettle let out steam on top of an old wood-burning stove, heating up the room and fogging up the windows. Suda flopped on a half-torn vinyl armchair next to the stove and took out the picture to show it to Joe, who was kindly pouring a cup of coffee for Suda.

"Mr. Bodine, do you recognize the man you saw that day in this picture?" Suda passed the picture to Joe Bodine.

"Well, I'll be." Joe scratched his head, taking a good long look at the picture. "These fellows sure look alike, now, don't they?"

"Which man is the man you saw in the car that day, Mr. Bodine?"

Joe Bodine kept on staring into the picture for another half a minute and then looked up at Suda with a smile intended to hide his embarrassment. He said, handing back the picture to Suda, "He was one of these fellas here in this picture, you see. I can't recall exactly. I think he was one of those men, though."

Neither Mary and Bonnie's impression nor Joe Bodine's statement proved Takeda was the man who had been having an affair with Lisa Parkins, but it showed Vicky's speculation was correct to the extent that the man could have easily been Takeda, and not Kentaro. Suda was used to looking at Japanese faces. For Suda's discerning eyes, Kentaro Suzuki did not look anything like Iwao Takeda. It probably had never occurred to Miho, either. She had certainly never mentioned to Suda the resemblance between Takeda and her husband.

Just as the new information provided by the waitresses and gas-station attendant was enough to cast the shadow of a doubt on Takeda, the statements given to Vicky by the lawyers in Atlanta did nothing but to reinforce the suspicion.

"There're four lawyers altogether. Only one of them spoke to the caller directly that morning. And of course, the secretary. Neither of them could definitely say that the caller was Suzuki. The caller could have easily been Takeda, Koji," Vicky said with excitement in her voice.

"Don't they have recordings of the calls?" asked Suda.

"I checked that, but no."

"Now it really looks like I have to break into his house."

"Looks that way."

"You mean you don't object."

"Just do it when I'm assigned to that area for patrol. I don't want you to get caught."

Two important questions remained after Takeda had surfaced as a clear suspect. One, what was the motive? Two, what happened to Lisa Parkins? There were several options, not mutually exclusive, available to Suda at this point, but going to the police with the new information was not one of them. With the tremendous political pressure seemingly put on the police department by Zatech Corporation, Suda could no longer trust the police to conduct an effective and fair investigation at this point, especially after the death of Lansford W. Bartlet. They needed much more concrete and convincing evidence before they could overcome the pressure. Vicky agreed with Suda.

The first option was for Suda to simply keep his eyes on Takeda and hope he would expose himself as the perpetrator of this crime. If Lisa Parkins were alive and hiding somewhere, she had very likely been in touch with Takeda one way or another. Takeda could have been secretly seeing her all this time. John Campbell now arrested and indicted, Takeda, if he had been indeed the murderer, must have his guard down, so to speak. The man could become careless and reveal Lisa's whereabouts. Waiting for Takeda to make some mistake exposing him as the murderer was the orthodox course, but a rather passive one. In extreme cases, it could take years before Takeda made any mistakes.

The second option was a more aggressive one. Suda could tap Takeda's telephones and set up a microphones in his home as well as in his office. This would be a risky move on Suda's part, but it could bring a great deal of benefit. Takeda could have been in close contact with Lisa through his telephone. Even if Takeda had been using his cell phone to maintain his contact with her, chances were that he was placing the phone calls in his home. Hidden microphones should pick up any such liaisons. In addition, and perhaps more importantly, his phone conversations with the Tokyo office or anyone for that matter could possibly reveal Takeda's motives for the crime.

Rather than hiring someone to do the break-in and have the tapping device set up, Suda wanted to do it himself. That way, he could make sure that the jobs was done right and, at the same time, conduct a search of Takeda's home and the Zatech office. Suda did not think Takeda would have left any clue as to his motives, but it was worth a try.

Yet another option was to attack this case from the Japanese side. It was only natural and reasonable to assume that Takeda's motives were related to company matters, however indirect they might be. The very fact that Kentaro was complaining about his work and his boss, Takeda, shortly before his death seemed to indicate there was some problem on the job front.

Suda did not believe Kentaro had expressed his dissatisfaction only to Bob, the bartender. Kentaro must have spoken to his colleagues or friends in Japan. All Suda had to do was to hunt them down although they might not be willing to talk for fear of jeopardizing their job security. To take this approach, either Suda had to go back to Japan again or ask one of his friends to conduct the investigation on his behalf. Either way, it could cost a lot of money. Suda wondered what Miho would say if she were told that Takeda not only could have been the man who was involved with Lisa Parkins but also could have been the man who murdered her late husband.

"I don't think she's clear on this yet, Koji," Vicky objected to Suda's talking to Miho on this matter.

"What do you mean?"

"I don't know whether she was completely innocent like you think. I think it was one of the Zatech people who said she might have had a motive to kill her husband, right?"

Vicky was referring to the insinuation made by Masao Sato that Miho could have killed her husband to collect the life insurance money. Needless to say, Suda still gave no credibility to the idea.

"I don't think we need to be concerned about that, Vicky."

"Yeah, but what if she was in on this? What if she and Takeda planned this thing together? A million dollar seems like a good enough motive to kill the man to me. They get five hundred grand each."

"This is one way to check that, then. If she had been somehow connected with Takeda, she would tell Takeda what we're up to. Aside from us, nobody will know we're after Takeda except Mrs. Suzuki. If we see any sign of an information leak, we'll know for sure Miho Suzuki was involved."

"I don't know if I agree, Koji." Vicky shook her head, unconvinced.

After some contemplation, Suda chose to take all the options possible. A man in Kokusai Detective Agency owed Suda a favor or two. Hajime Kohmoto was his name. Suda had helped him a great deal in one of his most difficult cases. He was diligent and able, and he could be trusted, so instead of going back to Japan himself, Suda decided to call on Hajime

Kohmoto. But before anything else, Suda wanted to talk to Miho one more time.

"I want to ask you more about the day your husband disappeared," said Suda as he put a memo pad by the phone on the desk. "A person in charge of your husband's case in the police department in Moeling asked me to speak to you."

"I don't understand," Miho replied, clearly befuddled. "I thought the murderer was caught."

"Mrs. Suzuki, I'll be frank with you. I don't think he's the murderer of your husband."

Suda could have heard a pin drop over the telephone. It took a while before Miho digested what Suda had just told her.

"Mr. Suda, I'd like to thank you for your concern," she said uncertainly. "But since we're no longer paying you, I don't feel it's right for you to continue the investigation. It'll be a while before I get the insurance payment for my husband's death."

"Mrs. Suzuki, if we don't catch the real killer of your husband, an innocent man could be sent to the electric chair," Suda explained hotly. "I don't think you want that either. I'm not calling you to ask for more money. All I ask of you is a little cooperation."

"Do you have any suspect?"

Suda wondered whether to mention Takeda's name. It boiled down to the question of whether to trust Miho or not. Suda chose the former.

"Mr. Takeda?" Miho did not conceal astonishment in her voice.

"Not only that, I think he was the man who was having an affair with Lisa Parkins, not your husband."

Suda swore he heard a gasp on the other side of the phone.

"Oh, Mr. Suda, I don't know what to think," Miho said after a long pause.

"Can you think of any reason why he killed your husband?"

"No, I can't." She paused again. "I'm sorry I'm just so shocked."

Suda gave Miho a little more time to collect her thoughts until she said quietly, "I'll be glad to answer any questions you want to ask."

"Please remember carefully one more time. On July 13th, Sunday, your husband left the house to go to Atlanta in the afternoon. Tell me everything that happened afterwards. Anyone you spoke to. Anything you did."

Miho traced her memory step by step. Suda tried his best not to overlook anything out of the ordinary.

"You said your husband left the house around 1:00 PM."

"Yes, he had lunch with me, and it was soon after that," reflected Miho.

"This wasn't the first time he was going to Atlanta, correct?"

"That's correct. He'd been to Atlanta a few times before, all for business."

"Wasn't 1:00 PM a little too early to leave to go to Atlanta? It takes only about three hours to get there. He only had meetings the next day, correct?"

"I imagine he had something to look over when he got there. I don't know. I didn't question him."

"You didn't notice anything unusual about his behavior?"

Suda had already asked the same question a thousand times before, it seemed.

"No, not at all."

"Did he say he was going to meet with anyone before he went to Atlanta? Did he go by the office before he went to Atlanta, for example?"

"Not that I know of."

"When your husband did not call you two nights in a row, what did you think of it?"

"I called him once on his cell phone, but I couldn't reach him. But then Mr. Takeda called me, so I didn't worry any more."

"Mr. Takeda called you?" This was news to Suda.

"Yes. He told me my husband had just called from Atlanta, and everything was fine. I thought it was a little strange that Kentaro didn't call me himself, but often when he was really bogged down in his project, he didn't want to talk to me very much."

"Did Takeda know that you were worried about your husband?"

"I never told him that."

"Had he ever done this before?"

"What? Call me?"

"No, well, what I mean is when your husband was gone for a business trip, did Mr. Takeda ever call you?"

"I'm trying to remember…I don't recall his ever calling me when my husband wasn't with me."

The rest of Miho's account of what took place in the three days after Kentaro's departure to Atlanta contained nothing that attracted Suda's attention.

"Tell me, Mrs. Suzuki, how often did you speak with Mr. Takeda?"

"Very often. He was my husband's boss not only in the U.S. but in Japan, too."

"So how long have you known him?"

"About five years."

"What kind of a man is he? I know you told me he was a nice man. Do you know anything not nice about him?"

Miho had to ponder for some time before she could answer the question.

"He is one of those magnetic men who tend to attract a lot of people," she observed. "I think he knows it, too, and tries to use it to his advantage. My husband respected him, but to tell you the truth, I was not very comfortable in front of him…"

"Why?"

"I don't know, but, I felt he always looked at me as a woman. What I mean is when he looked at me, at least that's how I felt, he looked at me as a sexual object. I felt uneasy about that."

"Did he ever try to make a pass at you?"

"No, never. It was much more subtle. It was just the feelings I got when I was with him."

"Was he a womanizer?"

"I really don't know. My husband never told me anything like that, and I never saw him with a woman other than his wife."

"His wife lives in Japan with their children, I understand."

"Yes, they live in Aoyama."

"Do they live in a rental property, or is the house their own?"

"They own a three-bedroom condo, I was told once."

"Is their marriage stable?"

"As far as I know…"

"What kind of a woman is Mrs. Takeda?"

"To be honest, I don't care for her. She's a typical so-called 'Education Mother.' She would do anything to put her children through good schools. She's very unpopular among us wives of the company men."

"Seems like Mr. Takeda does not have a very happy marriage."

"I don't think Mr. Takeda cares about the family very much. He's a true company man. For him, the family comes second after the company."

"Did he marry into a wealthy family by any chance?"

"Not that I know of. If anything, Mr. Takeda came from a pretty wealthy family."

"How wealthy?"

"Not super rich, if that's what you mean. If he were super rich, he wouldn't be working for Zatech. Just well off."

A three-bedroom condo in Aoyama area could be worth as much as a few million dollars, depending on the grade. If Takeda actually owned the place, he would be a wealthy man. If, on the other hand, Takeda were still paying off the loan, his financial state would not necessarily be good.

"You've not heard anything about Takeda's financial health," Suda continued questioning. "I mean, with his wife being the kind of woman that you say she is, it seems she must be a big spender."

"Oh, yes…She's a big spender," Miho replied. "She always wears the latest fashion and expensive jewelry. But I think Mr. Takeda's getting paid well. My husband certainly never told me Mr. Takeda was in any sort of financial bind."

At least it appeared that money had not been the cause of this crime.

"I'd like to ask you one more time. Your husband never mentioned anything about Mr. Takeda's affair with Lisa Parkins?"

"I don't remember anything like that."

"Do you think it's possible that your husband was blackmailing Mr. Takeda?"

"I don't think so, but I really don't know," Miho sounded unsettled. "There're many things I didn't know about my husband. Do you think my husband was blackmailing Mr. Takeda?"

"I don't know, Mrs. Suzuki. Right now I'm only trying to find the reason why Takeda killed your husband."

"Sounds like you're sure Mr. Takeda is the murderer."

"No, I'm not sure yet," admitted Suda. "But everything seems to make sense if we assume he's the perpetrator."

"I can't believe it…I just can't."

Suda could picture Miho on the other side of the line, shaking her head in dismay.

"Mrs. Suzuki, I wanna thank you for answering all the questions. Please don't tell anyone about this conversation. We don't want Mr. Takeda to think he's suspected in any way."

"I understand."

"You don't mind if I call you again and ask you more questions, do you?"

"Of course not. Please let me know what's going on."

"One more thing. I need the names of your husband's closest friends, not just company friends but anyone close to him. He could have told them something very important. If you have their phone numbers, too, that'll be helpful."

Suda jotted down the names and phone numbers quickly and said good-bye to Miho. Some of the names belonged to people Suda had previously spoken to at the beginning of the investigation, but it would be worthwhile to speak to them again in light of new information. Suda had one more place to call in Japan—Kokusai Detective Agency in Tokyo where Hajime Kohmoto worked.

3

Takeda's residence in the city of Moeling was protected by an intricate security alarm system that directly connected the house to the police department. Any unlawful entry would sound the alarm in the neighborhood, and at the same time, alert the police. The police would make a phone call to the residence, and if no one answered the phone after eight rings or if anyone other than the legal resident answered the phone, the police unit would be dispatched to the house immediately. The system would be very effective unless, of course, the police itself was involved in the break-in. All Vicky had to do was to deactivate the alarm at the police department prior to the planned entry to the house.

Suda still had the neighbors' eyes to worry about. Fortunately, all the houses had been built far enough apart from each other that he could pretend to be a Zatech employee without anyone suspecting otherwise. Using the copy of the master key kept at the police department, Suda was able to enter Takeda's residence from the front door in broad daylight.

The inside of the house was very neatly cleaned and organized for a dwelling of a man without his wife. Suda had been told that Takeda had weekly maid and gardener services every Friday. The house was a single-story large three-bedroom house with a screened patio in the back. The backyard was covered with a lawn and was well secluded from surrounding houses by a wooden privacy fence and a row of trees. A small garden next to the patio was well groomed and maintained although the season was still too early for blossoming flowers.

Setting up microphones inside Takeda's telephone in the bedroom and in an electric outlet by his desk in the study took no time. With these devices, Suda could listen in on Takeda's conversations from as far as two miles away, depending on the weather. The problem was to look for any documents or objects that could possibly connect Takeda to the killing of Kentaro. Suda had to work quickly and yet very carefully. Vicky could not help him every day.

The search produced phone bills, credit card statements, car insurance bills, and bills from various magazine subscriptions. All of the bills were no older than six months. The phone bills contained only the calls to Japan. Suda jotted down all the phone numbers that were listed on the bill. The credit card statements didn't show any suspicious charges. Takeda's personal computer sat on his desk in the study ever so enticingly. Much to his chagrin, possessing no hacking skills, Suda could not get access to Takada's e-mail correspondence. Suda called Hajime Kohmoto and asked him to identify and check out the owners of the phone numbers listed on Takeda's phone bills.

The Zatech office was harder to break into. The alarm system had no connection to the police station, which meant Vicky could not cut off the alarm, and there was no master key. In addition, a private security firm patrolled the compound every two hours. Suda knew of surveillance devices that would allow him to listen in on the conversation within the walls of the Zatech office without his physically setting up a microphone inside. Such devices, unfortunately, were prohibitively expensive, and even if he could afford them, were not readily available to the public.

There were still ways, but these methods could possibly end up destroying Vicky's career ambitions, and Suda could not put her through it. Suda gave up the idea without much distress since Takeda was not likely to have left any incriminating evidence in his office, and furthermore, he would unlikely be talking to Lisa Parkins in his office or on the office telephone. Thus the trap was set. All Suda had to do was to wait for Takeda to step into it. The problem was Takeda might never step into it.

As Suda had expected, the death of Lansford W. Bartlet delivered a fatal blow to the political power of the Bartlet Corporation. Only a week after his death, the date of John Campbell's trial was announced in the newspaper. Rumor had it that the Bartlets received a large sum of money from Zatech and simply decided to back off. The only hope was the defense attorney handpicked by Lansford Bartlet himself. Teressa Bartlet called Suda and told him that Bartlet had stipulated in his will for the defense attorney to remain as Campbell's lawyer as long as necessary.

"I just couldn't convince the rest of the family to fight on. I'm sorry." Teressa was apologetic to Suda on the phone. "If there's anything else I can do, please let me know."

Suda received another phone call that night, and it was from Hajime Kohmoto in Japan.

"Boy, you put me on a difficult case, Suda. I think you're going to owe me one after this," said Kohmoto jokingly.

Suda could almost see Kohmoto's wry bony face on the other side of the wire. Kohmoto was like a hound dog when it came to investigation. If he hadn't drunk as much as he did, he would have been promoted in the company long before.

"What did you find out?"

"I'm afraid I have to disappoint you, Suda," said Kohmoto. Apparently Kohmoto was calling from inside a taxicab. Suda heard him say something to the cabdriver.

"Nobody's talking in the Zatech headquarters," Kohmoto continued. "They all clam up the minute I mention Kentaro Suzuki's name."

"What about his friends? I gave you the list of the names."

"I know. I'm talking about them, too. Clearly there's some sort of a gag order inside the company. What great friends they are, huh?"

"Shit. Is that all you have to tell me?"

"As a matter of fact, no. I've found something interesting about Takeda. This may have no relevance to your investigation, but according to a reliable source, Takeda has lost a lot of money in the stock market. Takeda's wife, man, this woman is a monster. Apparently she's the one who put her hand in the stock market first. It was like gambling for her. She was doing it out of her pocket money first, but that didn't satisfy this woman. She ended up borrowing a lot of money and practically blowing it off to the last cent."

"When did this happen?"

"Oh, it's been going on for sometime apparently, but a major crisis was between October 2002 and March 2003."

Suda remembered that there was another talk of a financial crisis in Japan around that time, and as a result, the Tokyo stock market suffered another major plunge.

"What about those phone numbers? Did you find out anything on those?"

"Wait a second, man. It's gonna get juicy from here. I checked all the places Takeda's wife borrowed the money from, and guess what? The money was returned on time in full. Now how the hell do you suppose that was possible, huh?"

"She probably didn't make the money in the stock market."

The haze was clearing. Suda remembered that Kentaro had been an expert in financial matters, and he had in fact been in charge of finances in the office. Kentaro's dissatisfaction with his work, and his apparent discord with his boss, Takeda. And Takeda killing Kentaro!

Everything seemed to fall into place quite naturally. Takeda must have been embezzling company money in order to cover his wife's loss in the stock market. Kentaro must have discovered it and probably confronted Takeda. Being a loyal company man and at the same time being a loyal follower of his boss, Kentaro must have spent many days debating with himself what to do. The gravity of Takeda's offense had prevented Kentaro from speaking to anyone, including his own wife, Miho.

Whether Kentaro had known about the affair between Takeda and Lisa was a question yet to be answered, but it was clear Lisa had known that Takeda had killed Kentaro. She could even have helped Takeda murder Kentaro. She had probably been receiving a good deal of money from Takeda before and especially after the crime to keep her mouth shut. Lisa could have been blackmailing Takeda. Did she also get murdered as a result?

"I wonder if there's any way of proving this," said Suda to Kohmoto.

"No such likelihood, Suda. Only way we can do that is to get full cooperation from Zatech, and it's not gonna happen. First of all, we don't know if the company ever found out about Takeda's wrongdoing. Even if they had, they wouldn't wanna talk to us. They would do their best to keep it secret. Their financial credibility and corporate governance are at stake."

"And the phone numbers that I gave you?"

"How do you think I came up with all this info? One of the numbers belongs to a stockbroker. The stockbroker Takeda's wife's been dealing with. Of course, it took some arm twisting to get him to talk."

"Do you think we can get him to talk about this in court?"

"Not likely there, either. Even if he did, what would that prove? Sure he can say Takeda lost a lot of money in the stock market, but so did most investors at the time. The broker doesn't care where Takeda gets the money as long as he gets paid."

"What about other numbers?"

"Nothing material. Like I said, as long as Zatech don't talk, there ain't much you can do, I'm afraid."

4

The story was now all too familiar. All speculation and no evidence. The conjecture made a plausible story, but there was no strong evidence, circumstantial or material. There was not a single document that could substantiate the fact that Takeda was siphoning money illegally out of Zatech's account. There was no paper that articulated the story of his wife's huge loss in the stock market. Even his affair with Lisa Parkins was based on flimsy eyewitness accounts.

Takeda had yet to step into the trap set up by Suda some two weeks earlier. His phone conversations were mostly with his family in Japan, and they did not contain even a hint of his embezzling the company money, much less killing Kentaro Suzuki. His everyday behavior showed no pattern of abnormality, and there was no sign that Takeda was in contact with Lisa Parkins, which seemed to indicate that probably she had been murdered and her body hidden somewhere.

Suda and Vicky came down to the cabin at the lake for the weekend. Rain did not cease all Friday night and Saturday, but it made no difference since they wanted to stay inside anyway. They didn't discuss the case much. Suda built a fire in the fireplace, and Vicky cooked. The rest of the time they made love, watched TV, and took a leisurely stroll on the shores of the lake, whose sandy bottom was still partly exposed like an old scar.

Suda had spent two weeks watching and listening in on Takeda. He was a good company man and a good boss in the office, and he was a good husband and a good father on the phone. The more Suda watched Takeda, the more hatred he felt toward the man. The more Suda listened to him, the more anger he felt toward Takeda. The construction of the factory was well on its way. Every day new pillars were added, and new foundations were built.

Vicky lay sprawled next to him, sated and relaxed, her face turned away and her naked back still glistening with sweat, her arms casually tossed to the side, and her long legs stretched out. She was silent, but Suda knew she was not asleep yet. Up until five minutes before, she was under the spell of Suda's relentless devotion to her carnal pleasure, with her back arching sensuously and her hips bucking wildly.

"What are you thinking?" Vicky raised her head suddenly and turned to Suda, keeping her hair from falling into her face. Her voice, slightly hoarse, and her gaze, somewhat unfocused, tenderly and surely sneaked into Suda's heart.

"Nothing much."

"You're thinking about Takeda again," she said admonishingly.

Vicky was the one who had suggested they come down to the lake. The idea was to forget about everything related to the case. It was impossible.

"You can't spend the rest of your life obsessed with this case, Koji." She slid her luscious body onto his and rested her chin on Suda's naked chest, looking up. "Sometimes you just have to let go," she said, gently stroking his face and hair with her hand.

Suda gazed into Vicky's face. A beautiful woman with expressive green eyes that harbored intelligence and sensuality at the same time. Maybe she was right. Maybe it was time to let go.

"We've done all we could," she whispered. "You can keep on tapping his phone, but what does it prove? It's not gonna be admissible in court whatever the bastard says. You have no legal right to tap his phone, Koji."

Vicky had spoken to Shugert about her suspicion on Takeda. He was sympathetic but still reluctant to move. The pressure from Zatech seemed so overwhelming that many state and city officials were determined to end this case the way it was. Monumental evidence would be needed to indict, let alone convict, Takeda.

"Campbell may get the death sentence," said Suda as if to himself.

"I don't think so. I think the deal was already cut between his lawyer and the prosecutor. He'll probably get something like ten years."

Still Suda found the situation unpalatable. His thoughts went to Miho, whose life had been marred forever. His thoughts went to John Campbell's children, who might have to live for the rest of their lives with the reputation that their father was a convicted killer. His thoughts went to Lansford Bartlet, whose dignity and determination unlike any he had ever seen.

"Let's go to sleep, Koji."

"You go to sleep, Vicky."

"What're you gonna do?"

"I'm gonna think for a while."

Vicky shrugged, moved off his body and turned her head away, and in no time, she fell asleep. Suda's thoughts flew to the funeral of Kentaro, and to his parents' faces distorted with sorrow. Then he thought about his own father's funeral. And his own mother's funeral. The relatives and friends all had gathered to pay their condolence, but it didn't mean much to Suda. Only he, and nobody else, had understood the sorrow he felt, and only he, and nobody else, could have helped himself overcome it.

Suda had wanted to attend Lansford Bartlet's funeral, but he didn't. He thought he was not sad enough to attend the funeral. He felt as though he had no right to be there.

Suda's thoughts jumped to Teressa Bartlet. She certainly looked like Lisa Parkins. She was studying to be an actress. Maybe she could even sound like Lisa Parkins. Then it struck him like a lightening bolt…Yes! She could sound like Lisa Parkins!

"Vicky, wake up!" Suda gave Vicky a violent shake.

"What is it? What's happened?" Vicky jumped.

"I've got an idea!"

Vicky rubbed her eyes and gave out a big yawn.

FIRST PHONE CALL TO TAKEDA

"Hello, Mr. Takeda?"

"Yes, speaking."

"My name is Teressa Parkins."

"(Silence)"

"Don't you know me? I'm Lisa's sister."

"(Silence)"

"You know Lisa, don't you? She talked a lot about you, Mr. Takeda."

"I'm not sure what you're talking about."

"Oh, come on, Mr. Takeda. Let's not play any games. I'm calling about my sister. I haven't heard from her for a while. Do you know where she is?"

"Lisa's no longer with us. She quit her job last October."

"It's funny she stopped calling me or writing to me."

"(Silence)"

"Mr. Takeda, I know you killed the Japanese man."

"(Silence)"

"I have e-mails from my sister. She told me everything. I think you've killed my sister, too."

175

"I...I don't know what you're talking about."

"Of course you do. Do you want me to read you Lisa's mails?"

"(Silence)"

"I know you were sleeping with my sister."

"You're crazy...I don't know who you are, but if this is your idea of a joke, I..."

"Mr. Takeda, I can go to the police."

"(Silence)"

"Would you like me to do that?"

"Look, I really don't understand...What do you want?"

"I'd like to see you."

"(Silence)"

"I'd like to talk to you about the e-mails and letters Lisa sent me."

"Are you trying to blackmail me?"

"Let's just say I'd like to discuss a few things."

"(Silence)"

"Well?"

"Where do I have to go?"

"I'll call you back and let you know."

"Wait..."

After she hung up the phone, Teressa Bartlet, with her cheeks slightly flushed from the tension of the phone call, turned to Suda and Vicky.

"How did I sound?"

"Perfect." Suda smiled approvingly, as he kept listening in on Takeda's residence.

"Is he calling anyone?" Vicky asked Suda.

"Not right now."

If Lisa had been alive somewhere, the first thing Takeda would have done after such a phone call was to call her and question her, but there was no indication of Takeda's calling anyone either on his cell phone or fixed-line telephone.

"Any movement in the house?" Suda asked Vicky.

"Nothing. As quiet as it can be," Vicky answered, standing by the window, looking through a pair of binoculars behind a see-through curtain.

The three were in the house across the street from Takeda's residence. The house was far enough that it was ideal for monitoring Takeda's movement as well as his phone conversations. The house belonged to one of the employees of the Bartlet Corporation. The owners of the house were very cooperative largely due to Teressa Bartlet's presence.

"Do you think he bought the story?" Vicky asked Suda.

"I think so. No one's supposed to know about his affair with Lisa, let alone the fact that he killed Suzuki. I think he's really rattled now."

Fifteen minutes passed after the phone call. Still there was no movement on Takeda's part.

"What do you think? Do you think he's just waiting for another call from Teressa?"

"I don't know, Vicky. Let's wait a little longer." Suda looked at his watch.

"Isn't the recording of the phone conversation enough to incriminate him?" Teressa asked Vicky.

"Not really. He hasn't admitted anything yet. I don't think he's about to do that right now. Besides, it won't stand up in court. We need something more solid."

"But Lisa Parkins didn't have any sisters, right?"

"That's right, but Takeda doesn't know that. Even if Lisa had told him she didn't, he knows he can't trust what she said."

The fact that Takeda had not called Lisa seemed only to strengthen the case, as Vicky and Suda had long suspected, that Lisa was no longer alive.

Thirty minutes passed, and Suda gave a go-ahead signal to Teressa.

SECOND PHONE CALL TO TAKEDA

"Hello?"

"Hello, Mr. Takeda."

"Look, I really don't know what you're talking about. I think you're mistaken…"

"I want you to meet me in the parking lot of the Westgate Mall in exactly thirty minutes. I'll be standing in front of a silver Jaguar outside the movie theater entrance."

"What do you look like?"

"I look like Lisa, of course."

Takeda's black Cadillac pulled in next to Teressa's silver Jaguar as Suda watched from behind the trunk of a pine tree some twenty yards away. Teressa was motionless, leaning her shapely body against the hood of her car. From that distance, her resemblance to Lisa Parkins was uncanny. In this morning hour, there was no other figure in front of the movie theater complex. Takeda came out of the car, looking wary. Suda could see his face tighten when he acknowledged Teressa. Suda approached him fast before Takeda could say a word to Teressa.

"Hello, Mr. Takeda. It's been a while," announced Suda with a wicked smile, loud and clear. Takeda's face turned to Suda and became as white as chalk.

"You…"

"Mr. Takeda, let me introduce you to Miss Teressa Parkins. She is Lisa Parkins' only sister." With a certain flare, Suda stretched his arm like a circus ring master introducing the next performer.

"I'm glad you decided to come see us today, Mr. Takeda." Teressa smiled graciously at Takeda, as he stood suspended like a poorly sculpted statue.

"I suppose you know why we asked you to come," Suda said to Takeda with a friendly tone of voice.

"No, I don't know what this is all about." Takeda's words stumbled out.

"Mr. Takeda, as Miss Parkins told you on the phone, we know all about the crime you committed. We have Lisa Parkins' e-mails and letters to prove it. Now you have two choices. Either you pay us money, or we go to the police."

Takeda's face showed an expression of disbelief. He was apparently in a state of shock from the sudden turn of events that had taken place on this day.

"You…You are blackmailing me," he stammered.

"Call it what you want, Mr. Takeda," said Suda derisively. "We have nothing to gain by going to the police. We need money."

"This is nonsense. Why do I have to pay money for something I didn't do?"

"You were fucking my sister, you bastard!" Teressa lashed out, her eyes glaring with hostility. "I can get you hanged if I want to, you little shit! Give me my sister back!"

The verbal outburst from Teressa's mouth seemed to totally undermine the last ditch effort by Takeda to regain his composure.

"Mr. Takeda, we want a million dollars in cash in return for the letters and our promise that we will erase all the e-mails and keep our mouths shut," Suda said coldly.

Suda's offer appeared to have taken a while before it finally sank into Takeda's brain.

"That's outrageous!" Takeda barked in protest. "Where would I get that kind of money?"

"We happen to know you've been swindling a substantial amount of money from Zatech's account, Mr. Takeda," said Suda, point-blank. "In fact, that's why you killed Mr. Suzuki. I'm sure you can accommodate us."

Takeda gasped.

"You're out of your mind, Suda. I know nothing of such a thing." His words came out shaky despite his best effort to control them.

"Well, it's your choice. You pay, or we'll talk."

Takeda's face had no blood left in it. His eyes looked unfocused. He was no doubt desperate.

"We'll give you three days to come up with the money. We'll tell you where to bring the money at that time."

"How do I know I can trust you not to talk?"

"You just have to take that gamble now, don't you?"

Suda and Teressa left Takeda standing in the parking lot like a defeated fighter. Suda wondered if Takeda would try to skip out of town and go back to Japan. The chances of that were remote, however, for Takeda knew if he were to get indicted in the U.S. for the murder of Kentaro Suzuki, he would either have to come back to the U.S. to face the trial, or at best, he would have to stand in a court of law in Japan. Either way, his life as he knew it would be over.

It was a chilly blustery night. Suda and Teressa Bartlet waited for Takeda's arrival on top of a grassy hill just east of Martin Dam. A cold northern wind shook the treetops and seemed to even cool the spirits. The pale rays from the full moon above, only occasionally interfered with by passing shadows of ominous clouds, enabled them to identify each other's faces several feet apart. Suda was trembling inside partly from the cold wind, partly from anticipation and fear.

Exactly at ten o'clock, Takeda showed his tall lean figure, walking up the hill slowly. He was carrying a compact suitcase in his hand. Suddenly the wind died down and an eerie sort of stillness settled in.

"Good evening, Mr. Takeda. You're on time." Suda forced the words out. He could see Takeda trying to identify the woman standing by next to him.

"Hello, Mr. Takeda. Glad you made it," Teressa said to Takeda calmly. Then, Takeda started to laugh.

"Suda, you almost had me fooled," Takeda growled, putting the suitcase on the ground. "I don't know where you found this woman. She does sound like her all right. She looks like her, too. But you know, Suda, Lisa had no sister. In fact I spoke to her brother today. It took me a while to find him."

Takeda pulled a revolver from the pocket of his trench coat. Almost instinctively, Suda moved his body in front of Teressa, shielding her from the gun.

"I did kill her, you know, and now both of you will be dead, too."

"Police! Drop the gun!" Vicky's voice came from somewhere behind Takeda. Suda couldn't see her.

Takeda froze. Suda saw Takeda's eyes move swiftly to the side. No sooner had Takeda's right arm showed a twinge of moving upward, than a gunshot broke apart the darkness. With an ugly thud, Takeda's body hit the ground and rolled over, and Vicky came into clear view, standing with her legs apart, with her gun still pointed at Takeda.

"I thought you wouldn't make it on time," Suda said to Vicky, letting out a huge breath of relief.

"Do you think I'm gonna miss a date with you?"

Vicky's voice quavered as she spoke. Suda had asked Vicky to follow Takeda all the way from his home so that he would not try to make some tricky move at the last moment. The last thing Suda needed was to get ambushed. This was the first time Vicky had actually shot a man. She knelt down to check Takeda's pulse.

"Is he dead?" Teressa asked Vicky. Before Vicky could answer, Takeda let out an almost inaudible grunt.

"I didn't wanna miss him," Vicky confessed. "I didn't want the bullet to hit you guys, either. I had to shoot him exactly where I wanted." Vicky rose to her feet, and Suda held her close.

"Thank you for your help, Teressa," he said, glancing over at her.

"I did it for my father," replied Teressa quietly, her eyes firmly fixed on the man on the ground.

The wind began to blow again, even harder than before, and the three shadows stood on the hill without moving for a long time.

5

The hideously decomposed body of Lisa Parkins was exhumed from the woods some five miles south of Birmingham. According to one of the workers, the red soil surrounding her body reminded him of a pool of blood. Following the identification of the body, Iwao Takeda was officially charged with the murder of Lisa Parkins, to which he had confessed along with his killing of Kentaro Suzuki. In less than twenty-four hours after Takeda's confession, Zatech Corporation announced its withdrawal from the state of Alabama. The bad publicity in effect delivered the blow to the mighty Zatech that Lansford Bartlet could not.

CONFESSION OF IWAO TAKEDA

Against my wish, my wife decided to put our money in the stock market sixteen years ago. It was like a hobby for her at first, so I thought I should just let her do what she wanted to do. At the beginning everything was going great. The problem was that the more profitable it became, the more greedy she became. Without consulting me, she had borrowed a lot of money from banks and friends to invest in the market. She even mortgaged our condo in Tokyo to play the game of speculation. The market crashed, and we lost a lot of money.

The final blow, however, began in October 2002, when the stock market suffered yet another monumental loss. The upshot was we once again ended up owing a lot of money. Declaring personal bankruptcy was out of the question. Can you imagine what that would have done to my job? I couldn't ask the company to lend me the money, either. Our debt was in the millions.

So I decided to move the money on my own. Since I was in charge of the entire project in Alabama, it was easy for me to overcharge the company for the cost of the construction, legal fees, and so on. All I needed to do was to prepare two separate documents—one for the contractors and associates in the U.S., and the other for the headquarters in Tokyo. I asked Lisa to help me with this scheme in return for a share of the money we made as a result.

It didn't take long until we got physically involved with each other. But that was a mistake. Mr. Suzuki grew suspicious of our relationship and decided to investigate the situation. He was a very able man. I think it was easy for him to spot the double accounts, which I kept. He confronted me. I tried to talk him into joining us in this scheme, but he refused. I felt I was left with no choice but to kill him. But before I did that, I had to make sure that no one else knew about the scheme. Mr. Suzuki foolishly gave me his word on that. You see, Mr. Suzuki was not interested in derailing my career. I'd been a good boss for him. He just wanted me to stop what I was doing because he loved his company so much.

I told Mr. Suzuki to come to the office before he went to Atlanta. I told him I decided to stop taking the money and wanted to discuss damage control with him. He trusted me completely. He was totally unsuspecting of me when he came into the office that day. The killing was amazingly easy. I hit him from behind with a hammer, and when he hit the floor, he was already dead.

Lisa was absolutely horrified when I told her that I killed Mr. Suzuki. I had to tell her because she knew Mr. Suzuki was aware of our scheme, and if he'd disappeared suddenly, she would have suspected me immediately. I told her if she went to the police, she would be thought of as an accomplice. Besides, I think she was still interested in the money she was receiving from me and didn't want that to stop.

The problem was what to do with the body. We weighed several options and decided to dump it in the lake. We decided to do it on Monday night. We couldn't take any chances of anybody looking for him, so I called the lawyers in Atlanta, pretending that I was Mr. Suzuki, to cancel the meeting. I also made up a lie that Mr. Suzuki called me on Monday from Atlanta. Now that I think about it, perhaps I was overly cautious.

But I thought that way the police would assume Mr. Suzuki disappeared in Atlanta and would not think of looking for him around here. In order to ensure this, I drove Mr. Suzuki's car to Atlanta and left it on the street. I ditched his laptop computer and cell phone there as well. Of course I asked Lisa to follow me so that she could give me a ride back. My miscalculation was that I thought his car would be discovered much sooner than it was. If his car had been recovered sooner, I think the focus of the investigation would have moved to Atlanta.

The police came to ask me many questions about Mr. Suzuki after his disappearance. When they told me about the gas station attendant, it almost stopped my heart. The man and woman he saw were Lisa and me, but fortunately he couldn't make a positive identification. In fact, he thought, as you know, the couple was Mr. Suzuki and some blonde woman. Well, I decided to use that to my advantage. I decided to make it look like Mr. Suzuki might have eloped with the woman. I made up a story that I saw the two together in Birmingham and gave a totally wrong description of the woman so that Lisa wouldn't be traced. It worked better than I thought it would, at least for a while.

Then Suda came to see me. I was very alarmed. He said he was a brother of Mr. Suzuki's wife, but I figured that he was a private investigator hired by Mrs. Suzuki. I tried to misdirect him as much as I could without making myself look suspicious. Obviously, I failed.

Suda's presence disturbed Lisa also, so much so that she wanted to tell everything to the police. I had to persuade her several times not to until finally I felt she was too dangerous. So I talked her into moving to an apartment in Birmingham, all expenses paid. She wanted me to pay her more money for keeping her mouth shut. I agreed. One day, we took a long drive to the countryside. I told her I wanted to have sex with her in the car. She was a nymphomaniac. She would have had sex practically anywhere if I'd asked. I stopped the car in the woods, and while she was undressing, I choked her to death.

I had a hell of a time dumping Mr. Suzuki's body in the lake even with Lisa's help before. So I decided to bury her right there on the spot. I dragged her into the woods and dug a hole about a foot deep. It took me several hours. Then I drove her car to Atlanta and left it on the street again. I came back by bus.

I was shocked when Mr. Suzuki's body turned up. I'd never been to the lake in the winter, so I didn't know the water level went down like that. Lisa didn't know it either apparently. We should have dumped his body farther away from the shore, now I realize, but at the time, all I could think about was not to be seen by anyone. We had to do it as quickly as possible.

I didn't know that Suda was attacked by those thugs until recently. But when I found out about their arrests, I jumped at the opportunity. I asked Tokyo to pressure the state officials and the police here as much as they could to solve this case. I believe they even told the local officials here that they were going to nix the whole factory deal if the case was not solved soon.

Exactly how my company approached the government officials here or who they contacted, I don't know. I know that the police are still looking for who paid them off and how, but I honestly don't know. I was surprised myself when those false witnesses kept on showing up, in fact. All I can say is that they must have pushed the right buttons, and well, the effect was great as you saw.

Of course, I had to be very cautious not to overdo it. When the FBI got involved in the case, I was a bit concerned. I was worried that if the FBI got too deeply involved in the investigation, they might be able to expose the true murderer, namely me. So I had to tell Tokyo not to go overboard on this thing. It was fine with them since they didn't want any more friction with Washington than they already had.

When I got the phone call from the woman claiming she was Lisa's sister, I couldn't believe my ears. I remembered Lisa telling me that she had a brother and she hardly spoke to him. As far as I knew at that time, Lisa had no close friends or relatives. That's what she had told me at least. So the phone call really caught me by surprise. You can imagine how I felt when she told me that she knew I was the killer. I felt as though all my blood got suddenly sucked out of my body.

And then there was Suda. I knew he stayed around in town for a while after the funeral of Mr. Suzuki, but I thought he had been long gone back to Japan. When I saw him with the woman who was supposed to be Lisa's sister, I knew I was finished. I knew that he knew everything. I was convinced that I had to kill Suda. The rest of the story I don't think I need to tell you. Suda won, and I lost. It's as simple as that.

Maybe this is the best way to end it. I feel a sense of relief in a way. I don't have to worry about anyone exposing me any longer. I just would like to apologize to everyone. To Mr. Suzuki's family. To my own family. To the company.

(Signed) Iwao Takeda

LETTER TO MIHO SUZUKI
Dear Mrs. Suzuki,

I think by now you must have read the whole story in the newspaper. I'm sorry the case had to end this way, but I hope you're feeling some vindication in the fact that your husband was trying to do the right thing. Takeda is recuperating in the hospital from the gunshot wound. I'm convinced he will be found guilty and receive a maximum sentence whatever that may be.

When I look back on this long and complicated case, it leaves me with the impression that this was a crazy incident that took place in a crazy world. This was one of the tragedies so often repeated when money becomes more important than life itself and when an organization called a corporation becomes a way of life. It seems our society encourages the proliferation of men like Takeda, who put their personal gain and promotion ahead of anything else. I don't wish to call him a victim. I think your husband was the victim. But I can certainly understand why Takeda fell into the hole so easily. When the only life he knew was the life of a company man, he could not think of himself as someone outside the company. For him, the end of his career meant the end of life. So he desperately tried to cling to it. He did not hesitate to kill in order to stay on the payroll of the company.

I've learned a great deal handling this case. I've met many intriguing people along with many despicable ones. I've learned what it means to be courageous and what it means to be strong. My only regret is the fact that your husband is not returning to you alive. My sympathy will always be with you, Mrs. Suzuki. I know it is difficult, but I hope now you will put everything behind you and lead a happy and productive life.

Best regards,
Koji Suda

REPLY FROM MIHO SUZUKI

Dear Mr. Suda,

Thank you very much for your letter and the kind words. When I first came to see you in your office in Tokyo, I never expected I was going to be involved in a nightmare of this magnitude. Now that everything is over, I still find myself helplessly standing in the midst of distress. Everything has changed so fast, so violently, that I am not even certain what to think. Of course, if I could do it all over again, I would do things a lot differently. But life cannot be repeated. That is the tragedy, isn't it?

Ever since the arrest of Mr. Takeda, Zatech people stopped calling me. I think they somehow hold my late husband partly responsible for the company's failure in Alabama. I really don't care what they think. As far as I'm concerned, I don't want to have anything to do with Zatech any longer anyway.

I am looking for a job now. I am hoping to find a position as a translator or an interpreter. A friend of mine is working for *The Japan Daily News*, and he might be able to help me get a job there. The winter season is over in Japan. Hopefully it will be over for me soon, too.

Again, I cannot thank you enough for all your help. Please take care of yourself.

Sincerely yours,
Miho Suzuki

As he read her letter, Suda reminisced about the day Miho had appeared at the door of his office. She was a beautiful woman filled with anguish. In many ways, her anguish was still there after all these months. Miho thanked him in her letter for helping her, but Suda wondered if he had really been a help to her. Kentaro Suzuki's body would have eventually turned up regardless of Suda's investigation into this case, but at least, if Suda had not been involved, Miho probably would not have had to come to terms with the troubled marriage with her late husband or the ugliness of Corporate Japan. It seemed not only had she lost her husband, but also she had lost a lot of friends as a result.

There was nothing more Suda could do for her at this point. In fact, he would probably never see her again. For a short while, their lives had crossed paths, and now they might never meet again. Another mysterious process of life at work. As she stated in her letter, Suda prayed that the winter season would soon come to an end for Miho Suzuki.

6

It was only March, but Alabama already was gearing up for the summer. Suda needed no jacket on a day like this. The warm rays of the sun filled the air, and the dense forests of Alabama sprouted young green leaves everywhere. Even the people at the airport appeared fresh, having cast away the heavy and cumbersome winter clothing. A team of high school cheerleaders was about to board a plane, laughing and carrying on, quite fitting to the day's atmosphere.

"Well, here we are again," declared Vicky, gazing around the airport, as they walked toward the security gate. "It's deja vu all over again, as Yogi Berra said."

Suda and Vicky did not discuss anything about the future again. Vicky had never brought it up. Suda had sensed Vicky was waiting for him to initiate the discussion, but he had never volunteered.

"You know there's one thing I don't understand," said Vicky, turning her eyes to Suda. "How did you know Takeda was gonna try to kill you?"

"I didn't," Suda admitted. "But here's the man who already killed two people, and he was in a dire predicament. What else could he have done?"

"He could have just paid you the money, too."

"Do you think he would have trusted me to take the money and shut up? Besides, as far as he was concerned, Teressa Bartlet knew too much already, too. He would have had to trust both of us, and I didn't think he was gonna take that kind of a risk."

"Did you think he was gonna pull a gun on you?"

"Of course, I didn't. But that's the gamble I took. He would have had to kill us sooner or later, so I thought he just might do it there. That's why I chose a deserted location like that to make it easier for him. I just had to count on your marksmanship."

"You know you're really Mr. Intrepid," Vicky said proudly.

"Don't forget that without your help, I'm a dead man today."

In fact, if Vicky had not suggested the resemblance between Kentaro and Takeda, Suda would never have even suspected Takeda. Suda felt this case was ninety percent solved by Vicky.

"What're you gonna do after this?" Suda asked, putting his gear down on the floor.

"I'm gonna go home and go to bed." Vicky yawned and stretched her body, smiling.

"Thanks for everything."

"Shoot. It's you who didn't give up. You're one stubborn bastard, you know that, Koji?" Vicky lightly pushed at Suda's chest with her hand, and they laughed.

The long line at the security gate was beginning to shorten.

"Well, looks like it's almost time." Vicky sighed deeply, peering toward the gate. "What're your plans in Japan?" Her eyes came back to Suda.

"Oh, I think I'll sell my condo in Tokyo. That'll give me some money to live on while I look for a job here," Suda announced nonchalantly.

"What?" Vicky's big eyes became even bigger. She stared at Suda's face as if she had never seen him before.

"Will you marry me, Vicky?" Suda said, extending his hand to Vicky. In his hand was a black jewelry box.

"Oh, Koji!" Her face lit up instantly.

"Open it."

Vicky's hands shook as she discovered in the box a diamond ring sparkling brilliantly, reflecting the bright sun of spring.

"I don't believe it," she exclaimed. "When did you think of this?"

"I haven't heard the answer yet."

"Yes! Of course, yes!"

Suda took the ring out of the box and gingerly placed it on her finger.

"I'll be," said Suda jokingly. "It's a perfect fit."

Vicky leaped into Suda's arms. The weight of her body directly translated into the weight of happiness. Suda didn't care if people were all staring at them with the same curious looks. The announcement for his flight number interrupted the long embrace.

"Damn you, Koji. Why didn't you tell me sooner?"

Vicky had tears in her eyes. Suda held her face between his hands and kissed her. She was trembling just as she had done the first time he put his lips against hers.

"I love you, Vicky."

"I love you, too."

The passengers began moving smoothly through the security gate, and Suda picked up his suitcase.

"Well, I've gotta go."

"Call me when you get there."

"Right."

"Hey, Koji!"

As Suda started to walk off, Vicky stopped him.

"Job well done!"

Vicky said and stuck up her thumb. She was beaming. This time there was no sadness in her face. Job well done! She was right. Suda returned a salute with a big smile.

As he walked through the boarding gate and onto the airplane, Suda was thinking about the red earth of Alabama. Someone told him a legend once that the soil in Alabama was red from the blood of the soldiers who died in the Civil War. Suda had encountered the deaths of three people on this land himself. But he didn't want to look back. For him, the red earth of Alabama stood for the passion of the woman he loved.

Many things had happened. Many days had passed. As he looked down at the land beneath him, Suda felt the red earth of Alabama was pulling at him ever so gently, awaiting his return.

The End

About the Author

Michiro Naito, a winner of the 2002 Columbine Award in the Moondance International Film Festival, was born in Tokyo, Japan, as a son of a private investigator. He holds a Ph.D. degree in nuclear physics and currently works for a major U.S. investment firm as an equity derivative strategist specializing in Japanese equities. His previous works include novels, *Project Kaisei* and *Mendiola*.

Printed in the United States
26549LVS00003B/205

9 781420 815603